TYLER'S ONLY FRIEND

TYLER'S ONLY FRIEND

BRIAN RADER

This is a work of fiction. Names, characters, places, and incidents either are the product of the author's imagination or are used fictitiously. Any references to public figures, agencies, institutions, violent crimes, rampage killings, rampage killers, mental disorders, adventurers, nomads, wars, atrocities, pet massacres, shady government programs, human anatomy, statistics, books, authors, firearms, journalists, presidents, or treasurers of Pennsylvania may or may not be true and serve as a backdrop to the characters and their actions, which are wholly imaginary. The statements, beliefs, and opinions expressed are those of the characters and should not be confused with the author's.

Cover Art by Jason Arias

ISBN 979-8-9884979-0-5 (paperback)
ISBN 979-8-9884979-1-2 (ebook)

Library of Congress Control Number: 2023944059

Cincinnati, Ohio

This book is dedicated to those who bullied me.

Contents

CHAPTER ONE

Chemistry 101

"Do I know you?"

Startled, Tyler looked at me. He shook his head in a fast, faint motion.

"Didn't I sit next to you in Chemistry 101? Yesterday morning? In the huge lecture hall?"

He didn't show any sign of recognition.

"You were left-handed. You had to reach over to write anything down because that fold-out desk is only on the right side of the seat."

"Uh, I am left-handed. I do take Chemistry 101. That was probably me. I'm sorry, but I don't know you."

Tyler hadn't spoken in Chem 101, so this was the first time I heard his voice. It was shaky and meek. It fit his body language. He seemed uncomfortable standing next to the snack table, a pretzel squeezed between his thumb and fingers.

"You definitely look familiar. Anyway, I'm Dylan." I offered my hand, using the greeting they had taught us at orientation: offer name and then offer hand.

"Tyler." Now I knew the name of the classmate I had sat next to in my very first class of college. But I didn't know I was shaking the hand of a young man who would become a close friend, and, two years later, during a raging blizzard, kill four students at random, then himself, in an act of senseless violence. An active shooting that came with no obvious warning, no threats, and no known motive, carried out by the student I was currently facing. He seemed all right when I met him for real that day. More than a little awkward. I didn't think of that as too unusual; the whole welcoming party was horrifically awkward and forced. Someone had written "Welcome to Harris Hall" in purple glitter paint that oozed shiny purple tears on a banner that sagged over the front desk. Tyler's hand reached out toward mine but stopped before it made contact. I shook it. His hand felt limp and sweaty. He swallowed with a wince.

"Yesterday, when Professor Chandra told us to look at the student on each side of us and said that one of us, statistically speaking, wasn't going to graduate, I saw you. You didn't look at me, though. You were still taking notes."

"I fell behind. It was hard for me to write on those desks. They're new to me." Tyler glanced down and made a bashful smile.

"Hey, you have braces."

Tyler opened his mouth to show me. They were bright blue. They gave his teeth the look of sapphires adorning bumpy ivory. "I got them late. They don't bother me—at least, not anymore."

"Never had any myself. My sisters had them."

Tyler didn't say anything. He kept looking down and then back up at me, like he was trying to make eye contact but couldn't figure out when or for how long.

I sighed. "So this is it. College. Midwestern University. Very creative name."

"I don't think it is."

"What do you think of Harris Hall? I didn't expect it to be so old. Look at the walls here, they're all concrete blocks. I thought this campus was modern."

Tyler said something but the racket from all of the students near us buried his words.

"What?"

He breathed in and spoke a little louder. "I just wish it had air conditioning. It's so hot I have trouble sleeping at night."

It was odd that he said this, since he was wearing a long-sleeve shirt that draped over him. The September heat had not relented, even though the sun had already set. Cold bottles of water had been provided for the welcoming party, and they were disappearing at an alarming rate. I had a half-empty one in my hand and, like all the other freshmen in the lobby, I was wearing a T-shirt.

I took a sip and bumped into someone behind me. "I'm glad I got the twelfth floor, that's the top one. It's one of the best views. No other tall buildings around. And with the windows open, it's nice and breezy. What floor are you?"

"Same as you."

"Really? Sweet. What a coincidence. We have the same chem class and we're on the same floor. That's why you looked so familiar. I'm sure I've seen you up there. There aren't that many people per floor. Are you closer to the north end or south end?"

"South."

"I'm north. Right next to one of the quads." Speaking about dorm rooms reminded me that I hadn't seen my roommate Henry at the welcoming party despite the mandate that everybody in Harris Hall had to attend. I scanned the lobby again for him and still didn't see him. He was the only person I knew in the dorm, and I only knew him because we were roommates. When the welcoming party started, I tried to find him but couldn't, and then I tried joining one of the tight, cloistered groups of students that the welcoming party had fractured into, but I couldn't do that either. Everyone already knew each other. It seemed like everybody had already made friends, or had carryover friends from high school, in the dorm. I wasn't so lucky. And it looked like Tyler had run into the same trouble. He had marooned himself next to the snack table after the rest of the dorm had picked the table almost clean. After I heard one of the groups making teasing comments about the lonely, silent boy munching on pretzels, I paid more attention to him. That's when I recognized him. Getting to meet Tyler was an unexpected victory in my book. I couldn't wait to make new friends in college. He seemed like a perfect candidate. The other students mocking him from near one of the couches only made me more eager to befriend him. I couldn't stand the joy they were having at his expense.

"So, do you know anybody here?"

Tyler shook his head rapidly.

"Are you an engineering major?"

"Yeah."

"I'm not, by the way, just undecided. Seems like most people in Chem 101 are in engineering."

"Oh."

The groups surrounding us grew louder the more we learned about each other. The welcoming party sounded closer and closer to an actual party. Girls' laughter pierced the rising chatter, and some guys had started playing pool in the corner. Sweat started to bead on Tyler's forehead.

"Okay!" a girl shouted. She strolled up to the snack table, followed by several others. "If everyone could quiet down." A wave of silence crept from her to the corners of the lobby. We all turned toward her.

She introduced herself and welcomed us to Harris Hall and Midwestern University. A senior, she was one of the Resident Advisors of the all-honors dorm. Each floor had a Resident Advisor, she explained, an older student who lived on the floor, enforced the rules, and helped us freshmen adjust to dorm life. And, if we hadn't yet noticed, each floor was gender-specific—odd floors for girls, even for boys. Now, each RA would call their floor together to meet up and get to know each other. She called hers, the first floor. Tyler and I looked at each other with smiles burning up our faces, shaking our heads. We knew we would be the last called. We had the highest floor.

As each floor was called and gathered, I watched different groups of guys and girls shuffle to different parts of the lobby. At around the seventh floor, I caught Tyler staring at me.

"Do you want to sit next to each other tomorrow in class?" he asked.

"Sure," I said, without thinking.

By the time the tenth floor retreated past the front desk like prisoners chosen for hard labor, it hit me that I would have trouble finding Tyler in the massive lecture hall. "Wait, how will I find you in Chem 101?"

"I'll sit where I sat last time. I like to sit in the same place."

"Okay."

The last RA stepped forward. I saw him on the twelfth floor during move-in week. He clapped his meaty hands together.

"I guess we're the twelfth floor," he said. Nearly two dozen guys were left, all pushed in toward the snack table to make room for the other floors. "Gather closer. I know, it's uncomfortable, but it's loud in here."

In the shuffle, Tyler and I got separated from each other while making room for the other guys. He was short and rail-thin, so I only glimpsed his face bobbing forward between taller shoulders and wider chests. He looked too young. Acne dotted his face and he had probably never shaved in his life. He had blond hair down to his eyebrows and blue eyes. Some news outlets would incorrectly label him an adolescent.

Our RA cleared his throat. "I'm Jeremy. I'm twenty-one years old, and no, I won't get you beer. Unless you pay me." A lot of the twelfth floor snickered and exchanged looks.

"Okay, so, there's some things I have to go over." Jeremy pulled out a wad of papers from his pocket and unfolded them. "I'm supposed to tell you that MU is the best rated public university in the Midwest, and one of the largest, but this is all bullshit."

More of the guys scoffed and laughed.

"As you can tell," Jeremy started, glancing around, "we got screwed with Harris Hall. It sucks. Some of your grandparents might have dormed here. There's no air conditioning at all, so I hope you brought fans." He yawned. "The other thing these papers tell me I should do is have everybody introduce themselves and say a little something about their lives. We won't be doing that, because that's gay. I'm sure everybody here knows how to make friends. And party. That's a requirement here. Now, we need to establish floor rules. These are any rules you guys want to create for the twelfth floor. Let's hear some ideas."

At first, nobody offered possible rules, until Jeremy gave some examples about behavior and keeping the floor clean. A short debate followed where a few guys made some suggestions. They got whittled down and simplified, and without giving any additional input, Jeremy passed two rules into twelfth floor law by slamming his hand down on the snack table.

"That's official. Rule one is don't be a douchebag. This includes not going into your room if your roommate has a sock on the door handle. He's getting lucky and he needs his privacy. Rule two: Don't shit in the shower. Let me write those down." He did so with gusto, scrawling them on the back of one of his papers in marker. I didn't participate at all in coming up with the rules and neither did Tyler. He watched in apprehension, even squirmed at times, unable to relax. I caught his gaze once and he grinned, as if it took great effort, and then looked away.

"With those absolutely perfect rules squared away, any questions?" Jeremy checked up and down each side of the table. "This is your final offer."

A shorter guy with a buzzcut raised his hand.

"You don't have to raise your hand, dude."

He lowered his hand. "Is it true if your roommate kills himself, you get free tuition?"

"Nope. Total blasphemy. It's not even a good rumor. I spent half my freshman year trying to convince my roommate life wasn't worth it. But then he got a girlfriend and I knew it was a waste of time.

Besides, there are suicide-prevention screens over the windows here. If someone does kill themselves in Harris, I'd be impressed."

There was more shocked laughter from the floor. I had expected a lot of wild things in college, but not this from an RA. It dawned on me that Harris Hall was going to have a lot of surprises under Jeremy's leadership.

Tyler had a face of disbelief. His hands, which had retreated into his sleeves, contorted into knots. Everything about the loud, disorganized welcoming party and Jeremy's crude words seemed to overwhelm him. Dorm life must've been something completely different from what he had anticipated, and, crucially, it bothered him more than excited him. I was sure the other guys around the snack table couldn't have expected what the welcoming party and our RA were going to be like, but their reaction was more excitement than worry. Big grins spread over their faces each time Jeremy mentioned the possibilities of partying, alcohol, and sex, and their uneasiness faded each time he said something ridiculous. It was going to be a free-for-all.

"So if any of you guys wanna come work out with me at the Rec Center, or learn how to use the machines, I'll make it happen. And if any of you can bench more than me, I'll buy you a beer. Oops, I mean non-alcoholic beverage. You guys aren't quite old enough yet." Jeremy clapped his hands together again. "All in all, the point here at MU is to have fun. Maybe, if you get bored, go to some classes. Now, you guys stay here, chitchat. I'm heading back up to my room—I have a hangover to sleep off. If you're wondering why I have a hangover on the second day of classes, then don't worry, you'll learn—give it some time."

Jeremy turned and weaved his way through the other floors still coming up with their rules, headed toward the dingy elevators. The rest of the twelfth floor stood around at first and made a few offhand remarks about him. Conversations slowly grew around what Jeremy had brought up. All I did was listen. The twelfth floor had no shortage of views on how to make the most out of the college experience. The outspoken guys dominated the discussion, quickly getting to know each other. Judging by their progress, I was already falling behind. I checked to see if Tyler had done anything, but he was gone. I did a lap around the snack table to make sure bigger guys hadn't blocked him from view—nothing. He had vanished. It didn't bug me. It intrigued me. I wanted to know more about him. He came across as somebody who followed the rules, but he had ignored Jeremy's order to stay put.

Within minutes, the other floors broke from their meetings and the groups dissolved into more chaotic clusters, boys' and girls' floors intermingling. Talk turned to the upcoming weekend and the first real parties of the school year. I stuck around to do one final check for Henry and to see if Tyler had returned—he could've gone to the bathroom—but he never did. I wondered if he had heard the other students teasing him. Maybe he figured he had fulfilled his duty to attend the meeting and didn't need to be there anymore.

I never did find out why he left. It didn't occur to me to ask him the next day in Chem 101, where I found him in the same seat, the seat he said he'd be in. I had a whole set of classes and an unfamiliar campus and college life to sort out.

I had discovered him by chance. Randomizing computer programs had placed us in the same Chemistry 101 lecture and on the same floor of the same backwater dorm. I didn't dwell on him. Nothing about him hinted at danger or hostility. If anything, he gave the impression of a boy unable to even stand up for himself.

———

Tyler and I sat next to each other in every lecture for Chem 101 and didn't talk about much outside of basic chemistry. He had a different lab section for the course, but the lab sections all did the same thing every week, so we would compare notes for the lab reports before Professor Chandra began his lectures. We were not friends at this point, as some reports claimed. I only saw him a few times on the twelfth floor of Harris Hall and barely anywhere else. Our rooms sat on opposite ends of the floor, and we spent a lot of the time tucked away behind our steel doors, studying and, at least for me, feeling homesick. When Chandra suggested we all find study partners, I asked Tyler at the end of the lecture if he wanted to work with me. A great chorus of desk-folding and backpack-gathering from students filled the auditorium in a kind of flat commotion. The echo-dampening panels on the wall did that, stealing all the depth and texture from the noise. Tyler said yes. The panels made everybody in the auditorium feel distant, out of reach, including him. He asked if meeting up to tackle chemistry would be a regular thing. I said sure. We called it a study session because we couldn't think of anything else to call it. I arranged the first one at his room. Henry liked to take long absences from my room and I hadn't yet figured out any pattern to them. I didn't want to risk Henry interrupting us in the middle of balancing equations.

The day of our first study session had gorgeous weather. A Monday evening in the breezy calm of early fall. Returning from math class, I took a slower route back to the dorm, winding around buildings for the fresh air instead of going through them. Harris Hall clung to the western edge of campus—a tall brick rectangle right alongside Lyndon Avenue. I had spent the day in classrooms, so I took in the sights of MU's buildings, a mishmash of age, size, and architecture. The new ones, all steel and glass, looked like summaries of buildings. The sun peeked over their roofs. Plenty of students strolled or hurried along the paths. To me, it was weird to see thousands of people my age all living in one small place. Campus sometimes felt like a miniature dystopia. As long as the weather stayed pleasant, the walkways at the center of campus boasted as much foot traffic as Lyndon Avenue did vehicle traffic. Small sections of flat, well-maintained grass filled in the space between the concrete walkways. Larger green sections in more open areas had been raised into tall hills or mounds. The university did this on purpose to increase its greenspace surface area, which increased its government funding.

The calming background track of distant cars whistled through the maze of nearby streets, creating a comfortable mood—like crickets chirping outside a tent on a camping trip far from home. It was an experience I couldn't find anywhere else in the city. The time I spent on those paths, sometimes with Tyler, became some of the best moments of my college life. I got to see all kinds of clubs, activities, protests, promotional giveaways, and other sights and sounds I'd never seen before. Outdoor meditation classes. Cosplay battles. Public marathon-Bible-reading sessions. I once saw a group standing in a circle holding onto a parachute, waving it up and down to bounce a ball like my gym class in grade school. Students used the green space to sunbathe and toss football or Frisbee. Not a lot of fraternizing happened on the walkways, though—everybody had earbuds in, wires draping their faces, blasting music.

I stood at Tyler's door. The colorless beige paint coating the door had chips and marks on it, scars from years of freshmen and whatever the hell they had been up to. Dubstep music blared from a room further down the floor, closer to my room, echoing dull and flat along the stone block walls, which had been painted a sickly off-white. Tyler's side of the floor looked just like my side. The low, dirty ceiling made it feel like an insane asylum. Even the windowless doors all lined up and looked identical. The weathered tile floor reminded me of tectonic plates, as each tile piece had shifted on its own over the decades, creating gaps or smashing into neighboring tile pieces or pushing under it. Many were cracking or had corners missing. Three empty energy drinks rested on the tiles at the end of the hall. As the dubstep thumped, I knocked again on Tyler's door, wondering how productive our studying would be.

The door unlocked and he let me in. The room key on my lanyard clanged against the doorframe as I entered. He didn't smile, only looked at me and went back to his bed where books and papers lay scattered in various piles.

"You like dubstep?" I asked.

"No."

I shut the door behind me. The music still oozed in. His dorm room nearly reflected mine, except the beds weren't lofted and the whole room looked cramped. Two tiny desks: one near Tyler's bed covered in books and papers, the other one holding nothing but a mouse and USB drives. Clothing littered the floor. The one window was right over Tyler's bed. It faced east, toward the center of campus. No setting sun from this view, only shadows and stoic buildings.

His roommate wasn't there. The room had a messy stillness—the clothes on the floor, the dubstep thudding off the walls. It felt like an upstairs bedroom during a house party where all the secret things happen.

"Dylan, you can use my desk," he said.

I took the black plastic chair. A calculator and an array of pens and loose-leaf sheets were stacked and lined up on the wood laminate. I pulled a notebook out of my backpack.

"Yeah, too bad there aren't any spare chairs in here," Tyler said, squeezing his bare feet on the bed.

"What's your roommate's name?"

"Jake."

"Why not use the chair by his bed? Unless he's a total dick he won't mind."

"Oh, okay." He got up and hurried over to move the chair closer to me.

He set the chair down and slid into it. His thin, bony shoulders drooped. He had the body of a boy at the dawn of its teenage years. Even his voice cracked and wasn't that deep. Somebody who saw him on campus might've assumed he was a high-schooler getting a tour. I had broadening shoulders and a jaw starting to square up. And we were both eighteen. He hadn't cut his hair since I had first seen him and it was starting to look messy and get into his eyes. He didn't keep it short until closer to the shooting.

"Did the fish die?" I pointed to a fish bowl on the dresser. It was full of water and nothing else. No pebbles on the bottom and some kind of plastic top screwed on. I didn't see any fish food around.

"No, my roommate, Jake—oh that's right, you already know his name—he hasn't bought anything yet. Says he's picky about what species he wants." We both stared at the fish bowl.

"Oh, really? Is he weird or super into animals?"

"He's a business major. I don't know."

"Ehh. He probably wants it for the novelty. A conversation-starter. It would be a good way to get girls interested." I looked back at Tyler. He had his hands jammed in his pockets. "And plus, I've heard of way worse quirks from my friends about their roommates. If goldfish is all, you got a lucky deal."

"Yeah." Tyler freed his hands and grabbed his chemistry homework from the bed.

I took it as a sign to get down to business and that's what we did. I wasn't mad about him short-circuiting a little small talk. I was kind of glad he wanted to hit the books. We could've talked more about roommates, and we did in later sessions, but to see a hint of initiative came as a great relief to me. In my first weeks at MU I had seen a lot of the same apathy about academics that I had seen in high school.

The dubstep beyond the door cut off as we worked over some concepts and practice problems. The pointed shadows outside the window consumed the campus below. When we tackled a difficult problem and tried reworking it, my mind filled with nothing but letters and numbers. I became so focused I forgot where I was, forgot I was twelve stories up in a stifling dorm with no air conditioning. Even that nagging feeling of getting a slow start to jumping into college life faded. Tyler wiping his forehead of sweat was my one distraction. We plowed through the lesson and finished a lot more than I expected.

After studying, we did a few housekeeping chores for that first meeting. We traded cell phone numbers. I'm not sure why it took us that long. I was the one who asked. He almost never asked me questions as we got to know each other. I hadn't yet figured out how deep his shyness ran. I thought he was having freshman butterflies, still getting used to a new environment. At least that's what his behavior was relaying to me.

"What's your last name?"

"Eberle," he said.

"Like ebb and flow of a river. Pretty unique name." The news mispronounced his name a lot. They could never get the *lee* at the end of his name. "Mine's Evans. I think my family changed it from a German name to fit in. That's why some last names are so common. Immigrants wanted the most generic American last names to fit in."

"Yeah." He looked at his feet. "I don't know many people with my last name."

"Where're you from?"

"Peach Grove."

"So you're from around here?"

"Yeah. Out-of-state tuition is too expensive. This is as much student debt as I'm willing to take."

"Don't worry, I get that. I'm just south of you. I'm from Little Turtle. That means we're both from suburbia-land. I guess that's one thing we have in common."

"Yeah great," Tyler said, "I bet my lawn looks better than your lawn."

He smiled. Though many accounts described him as a dry, unexpressive young man, he smiled plenty around me. Not goofy, wide smiles that showcased his braces, more like meek signs of appreciation, like he was happy that I talked to him in a casual, pleasant way. Although telling exactly what his smiles meant could be hard at times, I grew used to them, even expected them. He had plenty of small, honest expressions that students and professors around him missed.

"How do you like it here? Living on your own, away from parents?"

Tyler made a big shrug and fiddled with his pencil. "Well, it's okay. It's always loud here. I feel like I'm always on edge."

"At least here things happen. Before MU, school was always so boring."

"I know. Classes were too easy for me. I didn't understand why other students had trouble learning the lessons."

"I'm starting to think classes here are going to be easy too. This homework is mostly reviewing what I had in high school. But here, like Jeremy said, classes are secondary. It's what else MU has—the experiences. But that's not just Jeremy, the other guys say that."

There was a brief silence. A humid breeze flowed through the open window, ruffling and crinkling papers.

"Can I tell you something?" Tyler asked.

"Sure." I didn't expect anything too personal, but it did surprise me to hear a question like that during a simple study session. I steeled myself for what it might be.

"When you first came up to me, at the welcoming party, and asked if I knew you from class, I did recognize you. I just said I didn't."

"Why?"

"I was kind of frozen when you asked me. It was a split-second decision, but I was afraid. I thought you were going to ask me a bunch of questions like 'Why are you alone by the snack table?' or 'Why were you so quiet in Chem 101?' I've been asked questions like those before. Or worse, that you were just there to make fun of me on some kind of dare by other guys. I'm usually...I don't know. Defensive. So I played dumb at first, but then you seemed to ask innocent questions. It took me a while to realize what you were really doing." Tyler glanced up from his pencil to me, a wince seeping out of him.

"Alright." I kept my tone neutral. He was so sincere I didn't know what to make of his small confession. "I guess that's fair enough. Here it can still be as brutal as high school, maybe even more so."

"If I had known you better, I wouldn't have done that to you."

"Look at it this way: At least you're honest."

CHAPTER TWO

Dorm Meeting

My closest friends from high school also went to MU but lived in different dorms. Out of concern for their privacy, I have created fake names for them—Mark, Derek, and Charlie. We had known each other for four years, and when we graduated high school, we had expected to remain buddies throughout college and all the way into real life. And really, a good portion of my graduating class fed straight into MU, which wasn't too far away; everyone wanted to keep the costs of traveling and tuition down. I had already seen several of my high school classmates around campus within the first few weeks.

I met up with my high school friends a few days after my first study session with Tyler. We all grabbed supper and ate together at a circular table in the student union. Tyler was there at the table too. This came from another random coincidence. As I was heading to the elevator in Harris, I saw Tyler entering it, reaching for the main lobby button. He saw me coming and held the door. He was going to get a bite to eat by himself, so I asked him to join me and meet my friends. Maybe I pitied him or wanted to befriend him or something else, but I offered, and he accepted. During the meal we talked about high school in Little Turtle and Tyler spoke very little. Not until after we had finished eating did we change the subject.

———————

"Four. I think that's a fair number to have when you graduate. A satisfactory number."

"Four is definitely respectable. That could be a good goal for all of us."

"I have two already, so I'm halfway there."

"Bullshit. No you don't."

"Why? Where are you at?"

"Only one. Tracy. Remember my date at prom?"

"Yeah, yeah. Well it looks like you've got some catching up to do."

"I think all of us do if you're at two. Charlie, you and Miranda have been dating for how long?"

"Two years. She's my only one. But this is college now. Things could change."

"I doubt it. But I was thinking, if we get, say, one per year at college, and we all start at one, then that's five total."

"Okay, that's assuming we all have one to start with."

"We better. You have to get one before you turn eighteen."

"If you're still at zero and you're entering college, you're doing something seriously wrong."

"And if you get through a year in college without seeing a vagina: Kill yourself. At that stage you've already lost."

"Okay, Mark says he has two, Charlie has one and is still with Miranda, I've got one from my prom date, and Dylan? You've been quiet during this."

"Dylan, don't tell me you're stuck at zero," Mark said.

"No, I'm not stuck at zero."

Mark's phone buzzed and stole his attention. We had chatted for too long. All of the tables around us were empty. I thought Tyler would've been bored at this point, but aside from a few glances at his phone, he was listening.

"Then who was it with? Your prom date like Derek?" Charlie asked me.

"I kissed my prom date at the after-party and that was it. Don't you remember?"

"I don't know what happened afterwards. I was busy with Miranda."

"I'll take Dylan's word for it," Mark said. "None of us are that far behind and we've established five as the final number. But I'm shooting for higher. I'm not settling for the minimum here like you losers. My brother said he had seven when he graduated, and he joined a frat and my dad joined one too—that's where you can find success. I've got some work to do. Might join a frat."

"I don't think achieving a number is good enough," Charlie said.

"Like what?" Derek asked.

"Like you've got to do something wild and crazy. This is college, we finally get to start living, and I can't wait to start doing that, but we could do something that's above what we should do."

"Like drinking till we puke every weekend?"

"No, that's expected. I'm talking something special, something more."

"I know what he means," Mark said. "Venturing into new places. Opening up different doors."

"Like some weird stuff you see on Urban Dictionary? I gotcha," Derek said.

"Absolutely, but no gay stuff. Didn't we look up what a donkey punch was once? Remember that?" Charlie asked. "That would be worth a lot. If you could pull it off."

"Wait, remind me what donkey punch is again," Mark said.

Charlie reminded him that a donkey punch happened during sex, when the guy punches the girl in the back to make her bray like a donkey. Derek disagreed and said the punch was to make her tighten up for more pleasure. A big debate broke out over which effect best suited the meaning. I didn't add to the debate. Next to me Tyler had his shoulders bunched up, slouched over his food wrappers, watching my friends argue over sex acts and their values. He looked back at me. It was all that I needed to know. He was only listening to be polite. He was sick of conversations like these. He had heard them too many times at his high school and probably before then, like I had. We both wanted the conversation to end. Dejected, and a little angry, he looked like he had nothing to talk about, or at least nothing he wanted to bring up in front of my friends. I couldn't think of anything either, and so our unspoken exchange went nowhere.

That image of Tyler looking back at me made a big impression. He had the potential to become a close friend. He had patience and could think beyond being clever. He had reached a maturity I hoped my friends would soon reach.

Charlie and Derek agreed to disagree on the nature of the donkey punch's meaning. They concluded that bizarre sex acts had gray areas, and something out of the ordinary should be part of our college experience. Missionary sex alone wouldn't make the next four years worthwhile.

"If any of you pull that off, I want to hear about it," Derek said.

"Dylan? You've been quiet. Got something on your mind?" Mark asked.

"Like big dicks?" Charlie added.

I pulled myself out of the reverie and looked at them. "Your voices only make me think of small dicks. It's getting late. Tyler and I gotta do some studying."

"So that's what they call it these days," Charlie said.

"You two just happened to sit next to each other in chemistry then find out you're on the same floor in Harris?" Derek asked.

"Yeah," I said. "Out of the thousands of kids dorming here, we end up next to each other at two different places."

"That's weird," Mark said, checking his phone. "Nobody in my dorm has the same classes as me."

Derek looked at Tyler. "What number are you at?"

Tyler looked back at him, a little confused. He had barely spoken since I had introduced him earlier.

Derek raised his eyebrows for emphasis. "What we were talking about before. How many have you had?"

"Oh." His eyes darted to the tile floor. It took him a second. "Just one."

"When?"

"Huh?"

"How old were you?"

Tyler's eyes still scanned the ground. He fumbled for words. After a painful amount of time had passed, he muttered, "Eighteen."

"So this year?"

"Yeah."

"Yeah. Sure." Derek turned to the rest of us. "I know I've said this before: I think eighteen's still too late. You should know what sex is like by then."

———————

The rest of the talk meandered down the path of scheduling another get-together and possibly going to a party—a real college-level one. We broke for our dorms. By then the student union had emptied. It felt abandoned—giant and hollow. The outdoor campus lights had flick-ered on, warding off the dark. The chatter of our chairs on the tile and the rustle of our backpacks and wrappers echoed off the walls and huge curved windows. We dispersed. Mark, my closest friend of the bunch, walked with me and Tyler past the deserted tables and shuttered fast-food counters. At over six feet, Mark towered above both of us.

"What are you going to do when you get back to your dorm?" I asked.

"Jerk off." He itched his nose. "I really am trying to get into a frat. A lot of us are. I think I can get us into some parties soon. And you know, good ones, like the ones that are jam-packed and fucking crazy."

I scoffed. "I doubt it. Not us fresh meat. That's a recruiting scheme. They won't really happen for us. Like all those big scholarships we heard about when we were looking at colleges. Turned out to be nothing."

We rounded a corner into a thin hallway that tapered to an exit. White block walls on both sides. Our voices thundered down it. Tyler silently strode behind us.

"You're gonna miss out, man. I got a lot of dumb things I want to do and frats are really gonna help me out with that."

"Don't worry. I'll get my fair share."

Mark smiled. "I hope so. Like Charlie said, it's time to start living."

We pushed through a set of glass doors. A second set stood guard between us and the outside. Mark stopped to put his phone back in his pocket after checking it again.

"I always thought your first time was that girl you took to prom," he said to me.

"What?"

"You never said who your first was. If it wasn't your prom date, then who was it?"

"Remember the girl I dated junior year? Her."

"Really? You didn't date that long."

"Yeah, it was her. Seriously."

"Huh. Maybe you did. Still, I'm worried about you, Dylan. I got to say this: You've been single for a while." Mark was no longer smiling. He had a curious, prying look. "College is that time where a lot of people experiment, find themselves. Have you had any worrying signs lately? Are girls not that attractive anymore? When you walk past all those dudes lifting weights in the Rec Center, does your butthole start to quiver?"

"Only when they're shirtless."

"I'm serious, Dylan. Dead serious. Charlie's been worrying about you too. You have to step up your game, or you might wake up one morning with a dude in your bed and a sore, throbbing asshole and a big smile on your face."

"Sure. In your wet dreams."

"Hey, if you start to swing the other way, remember to practice safe sex."

"Speaking of buttholes, I need the bathroom."

"Well don't get too excited."

"I thought you had calculus to study for."

"Trying to change the subject?"

"Yes. You texted me about homework you had earlier."

"Ehh. I learned differentiation last year in Ratburn's class. I should still remember it. Good 'ol Ratburn. Too bad he lives in a wreck of a house. Enjoy the shit. And nice meeting you, Tyler."

"Thanks."

"Later."

"See ya."

Mark pushed the door open and paced away under the tall pole lights.

I turned to head back inside and saw Tyler standing still inside the doors.

"I have to go to the bathroom," I told him. "You can go on ahead. I'll meet back up with you."

"I can wait for you. I don't mind."

"Okay." I didn't have time to urge him to go ahead or tell him that staying for me seemed a bit weird. Nature was calling.

I went further back into the union and entered its massive, empty restroom. I laughed to myself about Ratburn. Mark had come up with that nickname. The four of us had made so many dumb jokes in high school. We had gone over a ton of them when we ate. Tyler must've been lost on all of them. We used to look up our teachers' houses on the county auditor's website in study hall. That led to some interesting discoveries, like Ratburn's worn-down house.

A little while after the shooting, Ratburn died of a heart attack. I thought of going to his funeral but decided against it. We weren't close, but he did a good job teaching us. I really regret not going now.

When I returned, Tyler was standing where I had left him. His arms were crossed. He wouldn't look up at me until I looked at him. Neither of us said anything. I pushed open the doors and Tyler followed me out into the night. I breathed in the fresh air from MU's green space, full of concrete paths and those banked islands of grass. I noted the few stars in the smoggy night sky and we headed back to Harris.

A college campus on a weeknight made for a frightening, yet somehow peaceful, scene. The new buildings, contorted from their warped designs, lit by floodlights tucked into the landscaping, stretched high and ugly into the murky air. The old buildings, looming behemoths, stalked the campus like ghost ships trailing you at sea. The security cameras anchored to the walls and roofs watched every path below. A few students walked the paths back to the dorms and off-campus houses. The ones who did moved in small, fast-moving groups. The part that I liked but nobody else seemed to, except Tyler, was the quiet. He enjoyed it as much as I did. The patches of grass and trimmed trees prevented our footsteps from echoing. The other groups of students coming out of buildings and disappearing behind them made no noise. The campus had decayed from the furious activity of the day to a dead zone at night. The whole experience scared a lot of students. I knew some who wouldn't walk the campus at night—not because of possible crime, but from the creepy desolation of it all.

With Tyler beside me, my mind wandered off. I had a brief revelation: I was in college. This was it. The best time of most people's lives was happening for me right now. I had the whole college experience in front of me. This was an opportunity I had to seize. I imagined all the exciting and memorable times I would have here at MU. There'd be no second chance. I only had one life. I couldn't waste it.

A random array of lit windows glowed from the brick face of Harris Hall as we approached. I scanned my student ID to unlock the door and we headed for the elevator behind the lobby desk. A student work-er behind the desk sat hunched over a laptop. As we walked around the desk they didn't move, didn't even blink, until the elevator door closed.

I checked my phone and it was almost ten.

"Tyler, it's getting late. I think we might have to put off studying."

"Yeah I guess. We're already ahead."

The elevator creaked open and I heard Jeremy announcing the floor meeting would start shortly. I had forgotten all about it. The first floor meeting since the welcoming party.

"Meeting starts in two!" *Bang! Bang!* "Let's go, get your asses out here!" *Bang! Bang!*

Jeremy trotted from door to door, pounding on each one. I had learned more about him since the welcoming party. A fourth-year ju-nior, he acted like a tough guy but didn't take his own act too seriously. He had played tight end in high school and claimed he had been Prom King. He was fond of T-shirts with the sleeves ripped off. He exagger-ated his voice and his expressions, the opposite of the jock upper-class I was used to in high school, who had mixed arrogance with stoicism. He cussed a lot by my standards but had a PG-mouth compared to some of the other guys on the floor. He also didn't tease or taunt the two guys on our floor who were obviously gay—another opposite of the upper-class I knew in high school. Hell, they had called me a fag-got for playing soccer—until they needed help with homework.

"Alright, it's ten. Circle up!" He clapped his meaty hands in short bursts. "Can't get your shit together for a floor meeting, you won't make it to Christmas break."

The floor was a simple straight hallway with a small, open lobby in the middle. The elevators came up to one side of the lobby and the hallway ran along the opposite side. The lobby had no windows. Guys seeped out of their rooms and into the tiny space. Flip-flops slapped the tile. Weary and bored faces appeared. Though the floor wouldn't show it, we approved of Jeremy. The only thing we didn't like about him was his girlfriend, and that was only because she was hot. My high school friends couldn't stop complaining about their RAs—even though none of them enforced any of MU's rules, they were boring. But my floor's approval of Jeremy came from more than his leniency. He was aware of his zealous-athlete gimmick, and the cheeky self-mocking he put into it paid off. The floor despised sincerity, and he knew it.

"Alright, it's our second meeting," he said, rubbing his hands together and looking around at the circle of freshman guys. Tyler followed my lead and leaned against the wall next to the elevators. Thick, soiled light coated the room. The panels diffusing the fluorescents had an oily sheen and needed to be replaced. The ceiling itself hung low, giving a cramped, submarine-feel to the place.

In a motherly voice, he asked, "How's everybody liking college so far?" That got some chuckles. "Uh, hopefully you saw the fliers on the corkboard for this little get-together. Next time I'll post them earlier. Or I'll shout the date in your face when I see you. I figured we should have our meetings late at night on weekdays when most of us will be free. And it looks like most of us are here and made the effort to show up. So, you guys want to keep doing ten?"

Small signs of agreement travelled through the lobby. I didn't see Henry.

"From now on we'll have these once a month. Every time I'll pick a theme and we'll talk about it and about how our girlfriends feel about the theme. Nah I'm just kidding. We're going to kick the other floors' asses and show them who's the best floor in Harris!" He clenched his fists and pumped them into the air, his muscles bulging from his arms. The whole floor already knew he spent too much time at the Rec Center. Half of us shook our heads, smiling.

Jeremy's eyebrows rose up to his gelled black hair and his eyes pointed down at the floor. "I know it's a total sausage-fest in here, but have a little spirit, a little pep in your step. You're at MU, motherfuckers. Show it. Or the girls on the other floors are going to notice. Just don't over-correct. If you show school spirit for longer than four hours, you should call your doctor." He clapped his hands and rubbed them together again.

"Alright men—well, maybe you'll be men one day. I want to remind you boys of the rules we created at the welcoming party." He turned around and grabbed the rules paper taped to the wall and read from it. "Rule number one: Don't be a douchebag. Not too difficult. And I don't think there's been any douchebaggery here. Rule number two: Don't shit in the shower. So far, mission accomplished. The showers are shit-free. And there haven't been any problems I've noticed. All in all, you guys are doing a fine job. I'd pat you all on the back but freshmen are disgusting. Don't take it personally—just make sure to wear lots of deodorant." He clapped his hands once more with the paper sandwiched in the middle, crinkling the whole thing. He looked down at it and tried to smooth it out.

Jeremy stuck the paper back on the wall. All over the lobby and hallway, fliers for events and clubs and dorm ice-breakers hung with their wild fonts and exclamation marks. They always listed a URL or phone number on the bottom of the page. I guessed it was the RA's responsibility to tear down old ones and put up new ones.

"One thing I do want to talk to you guys about that does matter. It's the one complaint or reminder or whatever you want to call it. See these garbage cans and these recycling cans?" He pointed out two gray garbage cans, the big kind on wheels about four feet tall, and two blue recycling cans, same size as their garbage counterparts. They stood in pairs on opposite sides of the lobby. The garbage cans were completely full of empty beer cans and beer bottles of all types. Plastic, aluminum, glass, and a hefty variety of brands, skewed toward the cheaper end, heaped up in a mound rising above the lip of the cans. I had noticed the tremendous amount of trash our floor produced when I went to throw crap away but never paid attention to the labels. I thought they were energy drinks and pop cans. Somehow they didn't reek of alcohol. Either my floor consumed every last drop or the janitor did one hell of a job. "Okay, see them?" Jeremy kept pointing.

"One thing: Please recycle." Next to the beer-landfill of garbage cans, the recycling ones were half-full. "See, the recycling cans are blue and have that triangle on them and say 'recycling' on them. The garbage cans are gray and have black bags. The recycle ones have white bags. Come on. Think about the environment, people." He snatched one beer bottle from the garbage pile and dropped it in the recycling can. Tyler and a couple other guys snickered.

"I'm not your babysitter and I'm not your mother. I won't clean up after you and I won't nag you to clean up. You're just going to piss off everybody else here if you make a mess and that garbage overflows. Okay? Before you can go back to hitting the books we have to do one last thing because I am required to. We each have to say what we've been up to. I know it's the gayest thing in the world, but, hey, it's not a bad thing to see how you are adapting to MU. And introduce your-selves, cause we didn't do that at the welcoming party."

Everybody had at least something to say about the first couple of weeks. Partying was the most common topic. Jeremy listened and asked some questions. I talked about staying in touch with my high school friends on campus. Tyler, clutching his arm and stumbling over his words, mentioned a study partner he had made in Chemistry 101 with-out ever saying it was me. I thought it was clever. It would avoid any potential teasing from the rest of the floor. We had enough understand-ing that I didn't have to say anything about it to him after the meeting.

"If your study partner's reliable, try to sign up for the same classes next semester," Jeremy added. "A study partner is huge. You can cover each other's ass if you miss class or if you need notes or homework."

The meeting wrapped up quarter after eleven. Nobody seemed that bothered by it. No one ever went to bed before midnight. Jeremy kept shouting even as we scattered, like a coach getting in last-minute reminders.

"If you guys need any advice on where to eat, what to eat, or good places to study, just ask, you know. Or not. Remember the rules. All two of them."

Tyler and I arranged the next study session as everyone shuffled back to their rooms. We parted ways, heading to opposite ends of the lobby. I trailed a group chatting about Jeremy's girlfriend: *Have you seen her? Hell yeah, she's short, great body, blond hair. Got boobs and a Kardashian ass. Hotter than my girlfriend. Don't know her name yet. She took the elevator with me one time and got out on this floor. Wearing yoga pants. How did Jeremy snag her? He just flexed his muscles. I heard she takes showers here in the mornings. I won't believe that until I see it. My cousin said it happens all the time in the dorms. Girls like to take showers on the boys' floors. It's like a sign of conquest or pride or something. But don't shower on girls' floors, you'll get arrested. Oops, too late. Shut up you don't know any girls here. If I see her next time I'll play dumb and ask her what floor she's on and see what she says.*

The group disintegrated into the rooms down the long and narrow hallway. I unlocked my door and saw a foot sticking out from the covers draping over Henry's bed. Henry stirred when I shut the metal door behind me. Because of the loft beds I couldn't see him other than the one hairy foot protruding off the edge.

"You missed the meeting."

"Shit. It's that late already?"

"Yeah, just ended. Jeremy banged on the doors."

"Heh, banged. I came back here and went to bed at two. Didn't think I would sleep that long. Oh well. Shit happens."

"It's Wednesday, what've you been doing?"

"I went to morning classes, for once. I didn't feel like going to afternoon classes so I came back here. Usually I stay awake thirty-six hours and sleep eighteen. This'll count as a nap. I won't sleep again till Friday. Shit, I can't. I've got two parties to go to. Oh yeah, reminds me, there's some beer in the fridge. Corona and I forget what else. Michelob? Maybe not. I know I drank all the Miller. Help yourself."

I opened the fridge to make sure. Henry sometimes inflated his claims. They were there alright. Twelve bottles. "You know it's against policy to keep alcohol in here? It's a freshman dorm and we're all underage."

"This is college, Dylan. Nobody ever checks. And Jeremy hasn't said a fucking word about the cans in the garbage. They're full as shit. And I barely contributed."

"Jeremy just told us to recycle the cans."

"That's what the fuck I'm talking about. That's college life. And if they ever crack down, we'll hide them in the ceiling tiles. Other dorms do that."

"I know. Wanted to make sure you're aware. I'm the one who's here most of the time."

"All Jeremy cares about is calling his girlfriend up here and stuffing her. Shit, I can't blame him. You seen her?"

"Nope." I had. Not at the dorm but at one of the food courts. She was with Jeremy.

"God, if I could have sex with one girl as hot as her, my life would be complete." Henry took a deep, loud breath. "But like I said, those beers are communal. Share them with your friends." He shifted his weight on the bed. The metal joints squeaked like old springs. "Want to watch some TV?"

"No, I was thinking of finding a movie online." I had classes at eight the next morning. Normally I stayed up past one, endured the sleepiness during classes and caught back up with an afternoon power nap. I did homework on weeknights, sometimes with Tyler, or between classes.

Still only a foot sticking out from his bed, Henry mumbled, "*Call of Duty?*"

"That'll work."

CHAPTER THREE

Midterm Eve

Absolutely nothing struck me as abnormal about Tyler in those first few months. Some people did see his very quiet nature as abnormal, but I didn't think there was anything wrong with any of that...even his aversion to too much eye contact. He was shy, plain and simple. He did become a little more talkative in our private study sessions—a crowd or larger group scared him into silence every time. He needed more intimate settings to open up. I couldn't tell if he wished to join the partying and drinking on campus and his shyness prevented him, or if he really had no desire to join the weekend festivities. When we weren't together, I had no idea what he was doing. I didn't keep tabs on him. I didn't know if he had friends from his high school at MU. We only texted to arrange dates and times to meet up and study. Reports on what Tyler did or didn't do on campus conflict to this day. His old roommate Jake never spoke publicly for fear of reprisal.

The study sessions with Tyler continued on a regular basis throughout the semester. After the first one almost every session took place in my dorm room. Henry showed up less and less—we basically had the whole room to ourselves. Having that space helped us get schoolwork done. The window in my room overlooked Lyndon

Avenue and the urban sprawl of off-campus houses and apartments. High up on the twelfth floor, the steady flow of cars offered a soothing tempo to our work.

The attendance rate of the Chem 101 lecture had fallen rapidly after the first week of classes and remained below fifty percent as the weeks progressed. The class took on an eerily empty feeling. We sat next to each other in the same spot as we had in the very first class. If someone occupied our seats, the first one who showed up, which was usually Tyler, picked a new spot and the other sat next to him. Even deep into the semester we didn't talk much. We paid attention to the professor and took notes and shared them if we missed a PowerPoint slide or a definition. When we did talk in those brief periods before and after class, subjects never ventured far from classes and majors. Tyler liked engineering-in-action and understanding complex systems that took into account a long list of variables. He once explained to me how internal combustion engines worked in clear and concise terms. They were explosions focused in a direction, the same principle as a gun. I was mostly interested in earning A's and impressing my parents, taking strong steps toward a degree with a high GPA. I suggested we could sign up for the same classes next semester and keep studying together, but it became clear that would be a challenge. We had different AP credits from high school, and Tyler said he had mandatory engineering classes to take. He seemed close to distraught over the possibility of not sharing any classes.

When we bumped the studying up to twice a week before midterms, Jeremy had gotten used to seeing us together on the floor. He always waved to us and asked how it was going if he caught us walking down the hallway with our backpacks. Sometimes I let my door open and he popped in to talk or offer some protein bars. Jeremy put some effort into connecting with the guys on the floor, targeting the ones who spent a good deal of time at Harris—the ones who had trouble making friends and joining student groups and finding things to do. At that point, I still hadn't gone to any real parties and could've been classified as one of that group. My studies remained my priority, though I did try some other things MU had to offer.

In September I went to an intramural soccer league try-out. I had seen something about it at the welcome week fair and wanted to see what it was like. The try-out—which wasn't really a try-out, since nobody would be cut—took place at the outdoor fields for one night under the lights. The problem was that every player came with a group of people they already knew and teams were formed based on those groups. Except me. All of my friends declined to come. Even Tyler said no. I had to join a team of juniors who had been in the league for two years. They played sloppily and slow enough to hold a chat about the last season. I had no cleats and wore my gym shoes on the soft AstroTurf. We didn't keep score.

At the conclusion of the try-outs everyone was invited to a nearby bar for drinks and socializing. The team captain approached me and complimented my ability to pass accurately, a crucial skill in a league where a girl on the team had to touch the ball on a drive for a goal to count. She handed me the team's contact sheet and admitted that the competition was much fiercer in the league's social events than in the games—the social events were where the guys would really compete for the girls' attention. She asked if I wanted to join them at the bar, which admitted anyone 18 and over. I declined.

When I got back to my floor at Harris, I lobbed the crumpled contact sheet in the recycling can, where it perched on top of a mountain of beer cans that had risen to an unstable height. Jeremy's plea for the environment had worked.

———

I got to know Tyler through the study sessions slowly but surely. The more I learned about him, the more I liked him. First was his intelligence. I had partnered or grouped up with students in other classes. Most of those morphed into me tutoring them for free. Not with him.

Not only could he keep up with the equations for the rote calculations, he grasped the concepts easily and could show me a new angle on an old idea. I had never felt challenged in school, not even at MU. I had spent way too many hours in classrooms spacing out because the material was too redundant or the pace too slow. Tyler had the same problems. We shared stories of recurring daydreams we had in classes. Neither of us were geniuses, but it was clear we had similar abilities and cared about our grades. I started to enjoy studying with him.

Our growing camaraderie led to what happened on the night before the Chem 101 midterm. It marked a turning point for us. For the first time we switched from studying together to hanging out. If I had to pick a time for when we became friends, it would be that night in late October, and it wasn't something we had planned.

Professor Chandra chose to have the midterm on a Friday. The whole class was pissed. Professors never scheduled a midterm on a Friday, but Chandra had fallen behind in the curriculum. That meant when the rest of the student body celebrated the end of midterms on Thursday night, our class would be stuck studying. During Wednesday's lecture, I asked Tyler if we could study in his room on Thursday night to prepare for the exam. Henry had mentioned that he might come up to my room that night to grab some beer. I didn't want him barging in on us.

On Thursday I finished the last few greasy fries of my supper at one of the food courts and made my way back to Harris. The concrete path took me past the Rec Center. Guys in ripped muscle shirts worked out in front of the floor-to-ceiling windows that wrapped around half the building. One of the beefier guys had sweated so much his earbud wire clung like a dried-out worm to his sopping, salt-ringed shirt. If Mark had seen me then, hurrying to another dude's room, staring at the sweating, grimacing guys pumping iron, I would've never heard the end of it. I could hear him and Charlie and Derek making jokes in my head until I reached the twelfth floor of Harris.

Tyler and I left our doors unlocked for each other by that point. We had grown comfortable enough to head right in without knocking so we could hit the books running. Daylight was fading when I made it to his room. He sat on his bed with his laptop open, the harsh white light throwing shadows on the wall behind him. Jake, who spent more time at Harris than Henry, but was more predictable, had left as he usually did on party nights.

"Hey Tyler."

"Hey."

"How's it going?"

"It's fine, fine. Mind if I keep this on?"

"Sure. Go ahead." I could tell he was reading something, but not which website he was visiting or even if he was online. I didn't try to peek over his shoulder. I didn't ask either. I didn't want to make him feel like he had to answer out of politeness, which he would've done. So far we had maintained a certain distance between us by not asking too many personal questions.

We spent that evening predicting what types of questions Chandra would ask on the midterm the next day. Our combined experience helped us assemble a list of problems he would have to ask and the strategies to solve them. We worked practice problems over and over. The boiler kicked on and off and on again. Hours passed without notice.

I looked over our notes on Tyler's bed. "Still mostly a review of stuff I learned in high school."

"Yeah, it's like acing a test before we take it."

"Hey that's like what Sun Tzu said. Battles are won before they are fought."

Tyler moved to check on his laptop. He could've been downloading something.

The doorknob rattled. The person outside tried to turn it and then tapped the door. We kept the door locked while studying to keep lost students from interrupting and asking where the beer pong tournament was. The quad at the end of the hall held one every Friday.

"Open sesame, Tyler. You know who it is." Jake the roommate. He sounded tipsy. That meant the night was still young. Whispers and giggles shadowed Jake's voice. I looked over at Tyler and he looked right back at me.

"I hope you're not making out with your boyfriend. Not that there's anything wrong with that. I've just got—got some girls with me and they don't want to see that. Also some dudes too."

"Hold on," Tyler said, and then whispered to me, "What about the midterm tomorrow? Or do you think we're ready?" His hands gripped his bed comforter.

"Yeah. Definitely. I bet we've spent more time on this than anyone in the class."

Tyler hopped off his bed and went for the door. I grabbed my things together and stuffed them in my backpack. At the door he turned the lock with a heavy metallic snap, a sound similar to a bullet being chambered. Jake and his posse piled in. They wore coats and jeans and backpacks, with duffel bags hanging from their shoulders. The rustling from all of their things filled the room.

"It is fucking balls-cold outside. Like nut-sack solid cold," Jake announced as he and his friends unloaded their belongings. Tyler returned to the bed and helped me pack, moving frantically as if the Chem 101 notes held some incriminating evidence.

Jake saw us. A small guy with a wide grin and even teeth. He reminded me of a sleazy salesman. A business major. "Studying today? Midterms are over."

"Not for us," I replied. "Chandra's got us for tomorrow."

"That's pretty much rape," one of the girls said. "I heard he's done that before. It's his fault he falls behind then he screws us over to catch up. I'm never registering for a class with him."

"Sorry, these are my friends," Jake said while hanging up coats, facing away from us. "They're all commuters."

Some of them waved and some of them smiled. We did the same back to them. Nothing was said, no greetings or anything. They took out their phones. Jake and his four friends and all their stuff cramped the whole room. The temperature instantly rose and I saw no clear path to the door. Tyler sat on the edge of his bed and I did the same beside him. Our weight sank the mattress and our thighs touched. I could sense Tyler shifting his body away. I felt rude sitting there, but Tyler kept looking at me and I couldn't figure out why.

Jake pulled shot glasses from his backpack and lined them up on his desk. He muttered "shots, shots, shots, shots," during his meticulous placing of the glasses.

The girl who complained about Chandra opened the mini-fridge door and then the freezer door. She had a squeaky voice. "Did you forget it? I told you like last week. There's only orange juice and ice and Monster in here."

"One second." Jake turned from his neat row of shot glasses. "Don't go accusing me before you have the answers. When it comes to contraband storage, I don't take chances. Look at Grant Hall. Whoever's in charge ordered all the RAs to sweep for alcohol because of an incident on the second floor. Amateurs who can't control themselves. They shit their pants when they got caught. There's a chance my RA might actually crack down on alcohol if he's ordered to. So let me say this: I think outside the fridge." He looked out the window next to Tyler and me. The dark view towered above the bed. We had kept the curtains open and the dim campus lights seeped into the room. The ceiling fluorescents glared down at Jake's head and lit his glazed eyes. He grinned. "I got a little magic trick. I'll make vodka appear in the room from totally nowhere. And I better get some fuckin' fanfare for this. It'll blow your fuckin' mind. Kyle, could you grab that fish bowl off the dresser? It's real glass, so watch it."

His tall friend reached up and slowly lowered the fish bowl to the desk. "It's full of water—that also has alcohol in it." And Jake took a bow. "Clever."

"Wow."

"Thinking outside the fridge?"

"You gotta be fucking kidding me."

"I'm impressed." The girls clapped and bounced on their feet. The guys pressed Jake for more info.

Jake unscrewed the cap. "I had to go out and buy this thing just to store liquor in. You're welcome." He took one shot glass and submerged it in the clear liquid, holding it there. The glass, the bowl, and the vodka bent and refracted the light into bizarre distortions. "Came up with the idea when I read the dorm agreement part about pets. They're all banned except things like fish. So I wanted a fish, but you know, there are so many species of them I can't decide."

Jake lifted the glass out of the bowl and held it there for the excess vodka to drip back in.

"Alcohol kills all the bacteria," he tilted back and emptied the glass, letting the liquid vanish into his mouth. He winced hard then licked his fingers. "You don't have to worry about double-dipping. The only thing you have to remember is that this does not leave the dorm room. You can't even suggest the idea to anybody else."

"Why?"

"Nobody gives a shit. They'll copy me without thinking twice and they'll get caught, and then I'll get caught."

One by one his four friends filled their glasses and downed them. They broke out the orange juice, ice and bigger plastic cups for the screwdrivers. Small talk picked up about parties and mixed drinks.

From their side of the room, Jake called to us. "Tyler. Dylan. Want some? There's dick-loads. And I don't do any retarded 'owe me' plans either. Have some then have some fun. Kill brain cells. Let loose. This is why you go into student debt."

It wasn't the oddity of the situation or the tension of sitting awkwardly on the sidelines that kept me from leaving after I had packed. I had to lay out a plan in my head first. I couldn't leave Tyler there, trapped in his own room. It felt cruel. He looked uncomfortable and too indecisive to speak up. And plus, he had the midterm the next day like I did, and he didn't have a chance at sleep with a miniature party feet from his bed. If I asked him to come to my room while he sat next to me, he would probably decline. He had trouble accepting help face-to-face. I couldn't explain why, he didn't seem to trust an act of kindness when it was right there in front of him. Over the past weeks I had learned to offer him favors via text, like bringing snacks for a study session, when I could've walked to his room and asked. If I did do something for him, he thanked me and insisted I didn't have to do it again. So I planned to head to the door and then ask him back to my room. With some distance between us I had a better chance of convincing him to leave with me. I slung my backpack on and crossed the room, excusing myself through the crowd to the door. Jake's friends were polite and parted for me. I spotted Jake looking my way. He raised his screwdriver in an offer.

"Midterms, remember?" I smiled and gestured at Tyler even though he was already watching me. I mouthed the words "my room?" at him. The picture in my head of Tyler sitting on his bed, his skinny legs draped over the edge, all alone on his side of the cluttered room, framed by the shoulders and heads of Jake's friends seared into my memory. It looked like a staged photograph.

He rose cautiously in the frame of my photograph and ducked through the chatter to follow me out the door. He closed it behind him, shutting out the noise inside only to isolate the rap music on the outside. A simple bass-heavy beat pounded the walls and our ears, repeating itself over and over like a broken record, playing from all directions with no distinct origin.

Tyler had left his backpack, laptop, and everything required to study back on his bed and desk. He had only remembered his coat. His bare feet smacked the tile with each step. I didn't say anything. We looked at each other and set out for my room. The picture of Tyler perched on his bed bothered me as we took the long walk down the hallway, blank steel doors shut firm on both sides.

I can recall that picture now but Tyler is missing from it. I can see the shoulders and heads bordering the rippled blue bed sheet where he sat, his notes scattered and his laptop on the desk in sleep mode. The vodka fish bowl on the desk.

———

I checked my phone. Midnight. The partying had begun to hit its stride. Faint shouting bubbled up from the belly of Harris Hall. Thumping music sounded like monsters stalking the floors below. Any non-midterm classes tomorrow would have attendance rates closing in on abysmal.

Halfway to my room, while we passed the lobby and the garbage cans, Tyler spoke.

"Thanks for, you know, thanks for this."

"It's nothing. If something like this happens again, and it probably will, just come right over."

"Thanks. So, uh, you ever heard of Budd Dwyer?"

"Please?"

"You ever heard of Budd Dwyer?"

"Who's he?"

"He was the Treasurer of Pennsylvania in the eighties. He was convicted of accepting a bribe. He called a press conference the day before he was going to be sentenced. All the TV stations showed up with cameras and reporters everywhere. They all thought he was going to resign publicly before he went to jail. You know, it happens all the time now. So at the press conference, he said he was innocent of the charges and that, basically, the criminal justice system is broken in America. Then he pulled out a revolver and put it in his mouth and killed himself."

"Okay."

"And the cameras got every moment of it. The full video is online. You can hear the reporters trying to talk him out of it."

"You have to show me this. I'm surprised I haven't heard of this guy."

"And that's not even the full story. Most people know Dwyer as that guy who killed himself on TV. The news stations who recorded it had to decide how much to show for their broadcast. Most censored it, but a couple played the whole thing on the news. Can you imagine a news channel playing something like that today? I don't think they would."

"Hold on. Did he accept the bribe?"

"I don't think he did. Somebody lied at the trial to shorten their own sentence for offering the bribe in the first place."

A scream of fright followed by laughter trickled in from somewhere in Harris.

"He does nothing wrong, has his life ruined, and decides to end it. That sucks."

"Yeah, but I got all this from the internet, so—"

"True. But it sounds like they caused a man to go to the brink—guess things were crazy even back then."

Tyler shivered. He put on his coat despite the toasty air from the boiler.

I had to chime in some more. My high school friends never talked about something like this. I could see them mentioning it, but not bringing up the whole story. "The news today would show as much of the video as they could without the FCC fining them, and then that's it, not go into the issues behind it or question if he was guilty. Then everyone would go online and watch the video."

"And that was the eighties and he's still known as the guy-who-killed-himself-on-television. That's all anybody knows about him."

The elevator in the lobby opened. No one was inside. I waited for Tyler to finish zipping up his coat. It draped over his shoulders. I had never expected him to bring up something like Budd Dwyer. I was glad he did though. He had me interested. This was our turning point—I no longer saw him as my study partner; maybe he saw it that way too.

CHAPTER FOUR

Midterm Day

Tyler and I walked down the hallway, side-by-side, headed to my room. We passed by a wide-open door and panicked whispers stopped us.

"Dylan, come here come here."

"Quick. Quick."

"Bring your friend."

"Shh. Shh."

About a dozen guys from the floor were in the room. Some of them sat, some stood, and some leaned against one wall, ears pressed up to it. One sat upright in his lofted bed, looking down at us. None of them moved; they all stayed in their exact spots. It looked like a moment in a play where all the characters froze for dramatic effect. We stepped in and closed the door behind us.

"Listen."

"Carefully."

"Jeremy's room."

One guy who enjoyed running up and down the hall in his bathrobe screaming for "party time" pointed to the wall that some of the guys were resting their heads against. Jeremy's room. At first, I couldn't hear anything and Tyler showed no signs of recognition. Fortunately, the ancient boiler stopped running. The window was shut. Only muffled music crept into the room. Before I heard anything else I noticed the heat in the room. Though it was chilly outside, Harris had a monster of a boiler in the basement. The biggest guy on our floor, about 6'6", hugged the wall with no shirt on. Most of the room wore only T-shirts and shorts, and everyone held beer bottles or cans. Condensation coated the glass and aluminum containers. The water droplets gave them a bumpy, diseased look. Someone else sported a bandana wrapped around his head, drooping wet over his thick prescription glasses and freckled cheeks.

Tyler and I stared at the floor to concentrate. It took some time for our ears to adjust. Faint sounds surfaced and sharpened in clarity. Covers and sheets scratching each other and maybe something sliding against the floor. Tyler was still searching.

"He moved the mattress to the floor."

"Shut the fuck up."

The rustling grew in intensity and picked up a rhythm, an irregular rhythm. Slapping noises began. The movement in our room went from subtle breathing and swaying to statuesque as we all tightened. Meaty, forceful slapping noises eclipsed the rustling.

"Oh my god," someone in our room mumbled.

"Fuck yes."

The meaty slaps picked up in speed with a wet, lip-smacking touch of ferocity.

"Lucky bastard."

That's when the heavy, feminine breathing caught our ears and the room leaned closer. The breathing synced up with the slapping and became more like panting through the thick block walls. Panting of an exasperated strain that took up a vocal, low-intensity moan. The slapping produced brief gasps that punctuated the moan. The escalation plateaued at a high level and persisted for seconds. Agonizing seconds. I looked up from a section of the block wall bordered by two guys and recoiled when Tyler's head crossed right in front of me, his blond hair almost touching my cheeks.

"Sorry," he whispered.

The guys with their ears to the wall had plugged their other ears. The guy on the dorm bunk leaned precariously over the front of his bed to get closer to the sounds. Many hands clenched into fists or grabbed their shirts and squeezed. The freckled boy had closed his eyes to focus better and maybe imagine what was beyond that wall. If the door was open and someone passed by, they would have a tough time telling if they were in a dream—a dozen or so of us young men frozen, close together, all of our attention directed at a wall.

The activity in Jeremy's room didn't have a peak from what I could hear. The plateau trailed off in a steady decline, the moaning ended and the panting returned to heavy breathing. The slaps lingered at longer intervals. The tension in our room broke. Fists unclenched, breathing reverted to normal and legs stretched and feet shifted. Neither Tyler nor I spoke.

"Shit on my dick, Jeremy is an animal."

"God damn that's a pounding right there."

"And I bet he's got a big one the way she enjoyed it."

"No wonder why he can keep a girl that hot. Shit."

"That's doggystyle. I mean that's got to be doggystyle, right?"

"No, pile driver. That's how he got their hips to slap."

"Bullshit. Even porn stars have to practice pile driver to get it right. It takes skill and practice. But they did sound like champs."

"Have you seen how small she is? He couldn't go that hard on her doggystyle—he'd push her right over. Pile driver's easy when the girl is small."

"What the fuck you talking about? You don't get laid. Get laid first, then get laid some more, then you can talk about positions."

"I'm no rookie. I've proven myself on the battlefield."

"Really we should go ask him. After she leaves. I don't think he'll care."

"Guys, guys, you're missing the point: Our RA gets it done. He's a beast."

"Twelfth floor, that's what I'm talking about. The best floor."

"The floor that gets it done."

"I don't think they came."

"I'm pretty sure they did."

"They didn't. It didn't sound that way. He never peaked."

"I'm sure he came. She didn't. If she did we would've heard it. She'd let the whole dorm know. Jeremy can't win everything. He's good, but he's not a god."

Everybody laughed. Tyler watched with amusement.

"There's no way you'd do that without someone popping."

"You guys are a bunch of losers. Is your only experience watching porn? You can have an orgasm without screaming."

"We should all give him a round of applause. I'd tell him congrats and shake his hand, if he washed it first."

"I want his autograph and some advice."

"Yeah call up the local news and get him interviewed. Reporter and all that shit."

"Breaking news out of MU: Harris Hall claims best railroader in the Midwest."

"Come on over and try him out."

The giggles and laughter rose and fell from their jokes and bickering. I wondered if Jeremy and his girlfriend could hear us. Jeremy did wear earbuds all the time, though. I never saw him without them on or at least draped around his neck. He and his girlfriend could've been listening to some song to drown out the background noise and heighten the sensations.

"Come on, let's go," I told Tyler. We crept out of the dorm and closed the door behind us. Nobody noticed.

Down the hall, we passed more closed doors under the grimy lights and low ceiling. We fast-walked to my room, checking behind us to see if Jeremy's door was still closed. The air rushed past my face and

Tyler's braces flashed every time his head turned. It seemed like I had reverted to childhood, momentarily, with Tyler. The whole journey of that night from his room to mine felt like we were kids navigating a party of adults where they talked about things we didn't fully understand. I used the key dangling from the lanyard around my neck to get us in and we locked the door behind us.

"Henry's not here again?" Tyler asked.

I rushed to my desk, opened my laptop and turned it on. "Guess not." Tyler still had not met Henry yet. I thought the colder weather would keep Henry in the dorm more, but so far he went missing at the same rate. Tyler wanted to meet him. I couldn't see why.

"That was crazy back there, wasn't it?" My laptop slowly booted up.

"Yeah, that was," Tyler said. He stood still in the middle of the room. Henry's crumpled and creased sheets hung off the bed behind him. The cool breeze from the open window caressed them away from Tyler's head.

"Ever listen in on anybody doing it?" I asked, glancing back.

"No." He paused, then smiled. "Uh, well, not before tonight. Has anybody heard Jeremy doing this before?"

"No. His girlfriend usually comes around—yeah, *comes*—when the rest of the floor's gone like weekday mornings or party nights, and tonight is basically a Friday. Since most of the guys are gone from Friday afternoon till Saturday afternoon, Jeremy and his girlfriend probably thought the floor would be empty. The cold snap must've kept everyone inside—except Henry."

An outburst of fast footsteps outside, twelve stories below, rushed toward the dorm. An impromptu race. Flip-flops struck against the concrete and stopped with a flurry of laughter and slurred accusations above the rushing cars of Lyndon Avenue. I considered shutting the window, but turning my room into a sweatbox seemed worse than some outside chatter.

"Here we go." I opened Firefox and searched. "You think MU monitors what we look up?"

Tyler stepped closer and leaned over my shoulder. "Probably. I don't think they'd care about this. I've looked up all sorts of stuff like this in my room."

I found a result for R. Budd Dwyer, loaded the page, and let the video buffer a second. "I guess as long as we're not looking up how to make a bomb, they don't give a shit."

"Here's the video." I unplugged my earbuds from the laptop and raised the volume.

The video was from the view of one camera aimed at Dwyer, who stood behind a podium. An older white guy with thinning gray hair in a suit and tie. The podium was covered in a mass of microphones jutting up at him like a mesh mountain range. He handed out papers to some staff members, a crowd of press around him. He grabbed one of those big yellow envelopes from a shelf in the podium and pulled out a massive revolver. It took the reporters a second or two to realize what he had pulled out and they called out to him and begged him not to do it. He told them to leave if this will affect them and motioned for the crowd to stay back. The camera zoomed expertly up to the gun and his face—a fast zoom, but not so fast that it was jarring—and then he opened his mouth, moved the barrel into it and the gun fired and he dropped to the floor. The crowd's chorus of attempts to convince him to put the gun down turned into screams, panic, and curse words of surprise and anguish. After zooming out when Dwyer's body collapsed, the camera made another rapid zoom right up to Dwyer's head, or what was left of it, and captured the blood pouring out of his nose in a heavy stream like a running faucet. The large exit wound at the top of his head also streamed blood down his now serene face. The mayhem of the crowd died down and requests were made for a doctor and the police.

"Can we watch it again?" Tyler asked.

"Okay." I didn't know why he asked to see it again—he had seen the video before, I hadn't. The second time through, I focused on Dwyer more instead of waiting for the gun and the carnage. He seemed in control for knowing full well what he was going to do in front of an audience and cameras.

"It's eerie how calm his face is," Tyler said. "He looks so peaceful even with blood pouring out of his nose."

"I wouldn't think so much blood would come out of his nose. The bullet went up through his head and out the top." I replayed the video again, this time starting from when he pulled out the revolver. "In the movies it looks so much cleaner, just a spurt of blood and that's it. His nose is practically a waterfall of blood the whole time the camera shows it."

"Yeah the first time I saw this it shocked me too," Tyler said. "It looks so unnatural, the whole thing."

I paused on the close-up of Dwyer's bloodstained face. The image took up the whole laptop screen. "What kind of revolver did he use?"

".357 Magnum."

"God, that's huge."

"Yeah, it's a bit of overkill. Probably gave the people around him hearing damage."

"And PTSD. Shit. I'm sure people had nightmares and mental scars for years."

"Yeah."

"Somebody lies in court and that leads to this. What a shame."

"Go to the Wikipedia page on it."

"This has a Wikipedia page?"

"A big one. It gives all sorts of background info."

A black-and-white picture on Wikipedia captured Dwyer from his left, whereas the video got his right side. His empty hand, out-stretched toward the camera to keep it at bay, his right hand wielding the revolver, and his face all fit well within the edges of the frame. His eyes stared in worried fear.

We browsed over the article, repeating any important info we picked up to each other. His speech before he pulled out the gun fo-cused on the American justice system and fixing its flaws. He wanted people to focus not on his suicide but on the injustices carried out by a broken system. He hoped that people would care and do something about it.

"Look, look, it says here he might've done it so his family could receive benefits from his job because he never resigned," Tyler said, pointing to that part on the screen. Another breeze snuck into the room, frigid from the night air.

"I'm sure he thought about what would happen after he, you know, took his own life. And Tyler, you were right. The only reason it got on the internet was from one local news station that played the whole tape on air. The rest of the channels all cut it short or didn't even play it."

"That's awesome," he said. "Wish we had more news that showed what's going on."

"Oh yeah. I agree."

We scrolled up and down the page for more interesting info.

"What about Christine Chubbuck, heard of her?" Tyler asked.

"No." When I looked up to him, I saw the reflection of my laptop screen in the blue of his irises.

"Christine Chubbuck. She was a news reporter and the first person to kill herself on live television. She was like thirty years old. Pulled out a gun in the middle of giving news then said something and killed herself."

"You know all the terrible stories. Let me bring that up." I didn't have to ask Tyler to spell her last name because the auto-complete suggested it. "Is there a video?"

"No. The only copy was destroyed."

"Bummer." The page loaded right up. Chubbuck was a promising young reporter for a local news station in Florida in the early seventies.

"She dealt with depression," I noted. "Complained about still being a virgin."

"She attempted suicide once before, a couple years earlier. Not on TV though."

"She made jokes about it. Even about buying the gun. See right there, nobody took it seriously."

"Yeah, and then she—" Tyler leaned forward, his hand on the back of my chair. "She did a story on suicide. Even after she shot herself on air, everybody still thought it was a prank. After the jokes, after the attempt, after it actually happened, they still couldn't believe her." He looked toward me, waiting for something. I raised my eyebrows, giving him the best non-answer I could think of. "I never got why she did it near the back of her head," he added.

"That's easy. You're not the only one who knows some sick things."

"Oh really?" I couldn't tell if Tyler was joking, challenging me, or curious. The question came in his soft voice and did not inflect at all. Either way, I felt I had to show him I knew something beyond chemistry.

"Really. There are gaps between lobes of the brain. And there's a gap between two at the temple. It's possible for a bullet to hit that gap. It'll only give you permanent blindness cause it severs your optic nerve. Further back are the older parts of the brain, which control the basic stuff. If that's damaged, you're dead no matter what."

"Wow. So she did her homework?"

"That's what it sounds like." I opened a new tab on the browser to find more about her. Some images popped up, showing a young, attractive, and determined woman.

"She was the inspiration for *Network*." Tyler said this with his cheek resting on the palm of his hand. He was leaning so far forward now his elbow rested on my desk.

"What about *Network*?"

"The movie. Have you ever seen it?"

"Nope. What about you, have you watched it?"

"No. Now I want to."

"Okay." I swallowed. "Did you hear about Bethel, Alaska?"

Tyler shook his head and his hair swept across his forehead.

I didn't look this one up on my laptop. I didn't need to. And I wanted to tell him this story face-to-face. "It's a small town in Alaska, and in the nineties, before Columbine, there was a school shooting there. Some kid who was bullied and abused brought a shotgun to school, shot some people, the usual deal. But the interesting thing was a bunch of the students knew his plans and came to school that day with cameras and staked out the areas to get the best view of the bloodshed. They didn't tell teachers, or parents, or police. They came to watch. And to record. That part sounds like something that would happen today."

"Yeah, everybody brings out their phones. Take a ton of selfies, put them online, and hope to go viral."

"It's like—don't even record the event. Record yourself at the event." I imagined a line of kids all holding phones, all aimed at their faces with injured students behind them.

"They focus on themselves when the focus should be on what's happening."

"I think it's more about getting credit for the experience. Whether it's a selfie or not. They have to make other people aware of what they went through. Like whenever somebody tells about a scary situation they were in, it always seems more about what they went through and what they felt, not about the scary thing itself."

Tyler stood up straight again. "They should've told teachers or parents before it happened. Using a crime to watch it or say 'I was there' is extra disturbing."

"Definitely."

———

We wandered around the web some more, drifting in and out of the morbid. The midterms, long jettisoned from my mind, were replaced with these devastating acts of public violence. As we talked about other infamous crimes, I couldn't stop Dwyer's tape from looping in fractured segments in my mind, like some kind of video error. And my imagination built the other stories, the ones without video, filling in the gaps in gruesome ways. Once I had talked my way to a dry mouth, I offered Tyler a drink.

"I'm thirsty. Do you want something?"

"What do you have?"

"Let's see." I got up and checked the fridge. There were two cases of Henry's beer, some orange juice, and nothing else. "Just a small amount of alcohol. It comes standard with the dorm. Orange juice too."

"No fish bowl?"

"Sorry, no fish bowl. This is all Henry's, but he only said I could share the beer, not the orange juice."

"Really?"

"I'm kidding. I have cups if you want orange juice."

Tyler took his time deciding. I waited patiently. He didn't give a sign either way. I didn't know if he was straight-edge or a secret alcoholic or what. I had never heard him talking about drinking. At MU, refusing an alcoholic drink was social blasphemy. It was an insult, like refusing an important gift. Personally, I didn't care what he chose.

"Listen, if you don't want any beer that's fine. I'm not gonna make fun of you for it."

"Yeah, Jake's given me crap over it already. He's always offering drinks, even on weekdays." Tyler mulled it over, his lips tightening, standing next to me, arms crossed.

"I'm gonna grab one myself." I reached down.

"Yeah. I'll have one."

The bottles clanked together. I handed one to him.

"I've never actually had one before. Wine, lots of wine from years of going to church."

"I won't tell anybody this is your first. I had my first in high school. Not until junior year though."

"Cool. Do you know where Henry got these?"

"I don't know where he bought them. I don't know if he bought them. He's got a brother lives off campus."

"He won't mind?" Tyler tried to twist the cap off, his hands straining on the cap and glass. I slid my hand under my shirt and twisted the cap off my beer and then he did the same.

"I think Henry really wants me to drink them. Get rid of them, I guess. I think he gets enough at the parties he goes to."

"Really?"

"Yeah. Like these." I went over to the window and opened it further. Below were the Greek houses and apartments where some major partying was going on. Tyler finished taking a sip and followed me around my bed's supports to see the fun below.

"I don't know if Henry's down there, but—" Whatever point I wanted to make slipped away. Tyler held his beer in front of his heart, ducking his head to get a better view through the screen and to avoid the reflections of the window glass. He stood mesmerized at the window, watching, staring with an awed intensity at the movement below.

"What're you thinking?" I asked.

"It's a great view. Makes me jealous. I don't have a view like this."

The window reached to the ceiling. The wood frame looked sickly yellow where the white paint had peeled off, which was almost the entire frame. Below, a car or two zoomed along Lyndon Avenue and we heard the rushing wind from its wake. On the far side a sidewalk clung to the road, cracked by roots that sprouted from dying trees, trees older than the campus, that, like ripped umbrellas, did a terrible job of protecting the yards they towered over. Students swarmed the yards in a mellow frenzy, someone always spilling out of a house or disappearing into one, a red plastic cup in every right hand. Their collective chatter reached us, twelve stories up, a muted white noise. Down all of Lyndon Avenue, students filled the yards, standing, moving, milling about, all in coats and jeans and enjoying the last outdoor get-togethers of the year. And this went beyond the one row of houses to the streets behind it, where small apartment buildings looked like active insect hives, every window lit.

We alternated taking swigs of beer while we studied the view. Despite living in that room pretty much alone for two months, I hadn't appreciated what the window could offer at night. The off-campus area shined into the dorm and lit up our faces. I wanted to open the window all the way to see even better, but MU had screwed metal slats to the upper window track, probably to secure the suicide-prevention screen.

"Those house parties are packed," I said, leaning toward the window, my breath fogging up the glass. The night air kept the pane cold. Our breath began to condensate in circles near our mouths.

"I've never seen that many of us at one place."

"I haven't since welcome week."

"Definitely not at any classes."

"No."

We watched some more. Groups passed by on the sidewalks headed home or to another party. The chatting circles on the yards morphed and melted into one another like droplets of water on stained wood. They looked random to me but I still felt their flow could be predicted.

"A car could take out half that crowd," I said.

"A drunk driver speeding could do it. It could go right up that little hill." Tyler wiped the fog from the window.

"They'd die partying. Living life."

"I wonder if they're all thinking the same things."

"Like what?"

"I don't know." Tyler squirmed a little. He twisted his knees and bent down some. "Like if they all had thought-bubbles and we could read them, would they all sound the same?"

"That would be cool, but I'm not sure. They all might be about if they want to bang the person they're talking to or not. Or, um, how much more they can drink."

"That could read like AI in a video game. Just different ways of saying the same thing."

"Those would get boring fast." I checked my phone. It was well after one. "It's later than I thought."

Tyler checked his phone too. "Yeah, I need sleep for the midterm."

"Me too. Are you okay with taking Henry's bed? I'm sure he won't come back tonight."

"You don't mind?"

"I wouldn't expect Jake's fish-bowl celebration to be over by now. And Jake's friends are probably screwing on your bed anyway."

"Gross. I don't know. I guess I should stay here. Thanks. I don't want you to feel like I'm intruding too much."

"Nope. You're great company. Much better than Henry."

We watched for a few more minutes. I compared the partiers to an unproductive ant colony. Tyler didn't bring up the thought-reading experiment again. Later I regretted not engaging him more on the philosophical stuff. I could've learned so much more about him.

We left the beers in the fridge, not even finished. Tyler climbed on top of Henry's bed and slept on top of the sheets in his clothes and coat. I turned off the laptop and set my alarm and didn't lower the window, so the room stayed chilly even with the blasting heat.

We didn't say goodnight or see you tomorrow, we didn't say good luck on the midterms or anything else; something between us said we could go without them, and we would be alright. It did feel awkward at times, like some special sleepover. Our beds were raised to the same level, where we could look at each other from across the room and watch each other's nighttime habits. The din outside did not subside until the small hours deep in the night. The partying on Lyndon always went close to dawn. I couldn't tell when Tyler fell asleep—he laid still and the darkness shrouded his face.

The Chem 101 midterms went well for us. We breezed through the exam and finished an hour early. We sat next to each other, Tyler still in the clothes he had slept in, though he did return to his room before the exam to grab his socks, shoes, and backpack. We were almost late because of the twelfth floor's restroom, where someone had passed out in the stalls, his body spread underneath three of them on the stained floor, like he had crawled under them. The whole restroom reeked of alcohol. There were no urinals, so I had to wait for Tyler to use the one stall the body wasn't able to reach.

We didn't cheat on the midterm. Neither of us had any need to. I got an eighty-four and Tyler earned an eighty-two. The class average was a sixty-one. The curve pushed us both up to an A. That's all we had to do in the large lectures—beat the average. Grades were really based on competition, not mastering the material, something that Tyler and I picked up on.

CHAPTER FIVE

Party

Not long after midterms, my high school friends finally arranged to attend a true party. Up until that point we had texted nonstop about going to a decent one and having a good time, even anticipating something memorable, something worthy of college, right in the vein of reckless abandonment, but for all that talk we made no specific plans and didn't do anything about it until after midterms.

We worked out a Friday night for us to go. We invited others but they had plans or didn't respond, except Tyler. I texted him when we couldn't find anybody else and he said he was free that night. A healthy debate followed on how we should meet up, but we figured it suited us best to meet up on campus before the party to set a few ground rules. For privacy, we gathered at a classroom. The university kept all classroom buildings unlocked all night, and since not even graduate students haunted those halls on weekend evenings, the classroom proved far more private than any dorm room.

The third floor of the History/English building maintained a hum of fluorescents in the halls and nothing else. All of the doors stood shut to the classrooms. It reminded me of the insane-asylum look of the dorms. But all of these doors were left unlocked. The four of us filed into one classroom and did not flip the lights on. Tyler joined us not long after. We were still skittish and scared of attracting attention. We didn't know if campus police roamed the grounds to bust kids misusing facilities. Mark and Derek had wrapped their six-packs in hoodies and Midwestern University spirit shirts and stuffed them in their backpacks. They bought them from liquor stores in the dense streets enclosing the campus. The foreign owners didn't ask for IDs. They made fantastic business. Charlie and I packed our backpacks with textbooks, notebooks, and tons of school supplies in case we needed to give the appearance of a late-night study session. But we never used them. We had no need to, and it was one of those overly-cautious freshman moves. Clever, but useless. Nobody even asked what we were doing or why our backpacks were bloated. Not that night or any other. Not long after we adopted a more casual and confident attitude toward moving our contraband. By the winter we would stride with utter impunity under the soft glow of the street lights, proud of our journey and practically showing off our alcohol.

"It's a non-frat party, what is there to be worried about?"

"Cause we're going there with no chicks."

"I told you and Derek this already. We've got the beer. That's our admission ticket." Mark's gestures cut across the glow of our phones in the dim classroom. "Girls are the prime choice, but since we don't have any, that's why I asked to pool our money. To buy the beer."

"I am tired of all this drinking-in-dorms shit," Derek said. He went back to his phone.

"That's right. And remember: Charlie doesn't have a girlfriend."

"No more Miranda?" I asked.

"Not for tonight. I've got to get my number up to two, and fast."

Mark set his phone on the desk. We all sat at the corner furthest from the door. A rectangle of light from the door window peered into the classroom, like some sterile chunk of purity reaching out for us. I expected an angel to glide by in the hall.

"I just want to get drunk. Black-out. Party so good I can't remember. I'll have a blast. I need to live a little."

"I thought the plan was to work together. We can't go straight for the liquor. Unless we're giving it to girls. Teamwork here, right Dylan? One of us can be a dick every so often so the other guy seems really nice."

"And some of us can be assholes without even trying."

"Hey, sometimes they go for the assholes."

"That sounds so gross."

"Now we're strategizing."

"Charlie, when Miranda checks your phone and finds pictures of you with your tongue down some girl's throat, it won't matter cause she'll stab in you in the dick. With a rusty knife."

"You can get tetanus from that," I said.

"Yeah, probably," Charlie said. "Worth it."

"You could die from that."

Charlie's eyes broke from his phone. "Eh, there are worse ways to go. Accidentally hanging yourself while jerking off would be the most pathetic."

"That's how Mark wants to go."

"You know it. A dignified death. You gotta respect a guy for something like that."

Now Derek put his phone down. "Why do they do that? Why choke yourself and beat your meat at the same time?"

I jumped in here. "More pleasure. It's supposed to give you super-powerful orgasms. It's autoerotic asphyxiation." With that they wouldn't bug me for keeping too quiet until we got to the party. I really wanted to talk to Tyler about R. Budd Dwyer and Christine Chubbuck, but I didn't want to bring it up in front of them. They would cannibalize those subjects, marvel at their spectacle, crank out a few jokes, and then move on. So I didn't say anything else, like Tyler beside me.

"No, auto-erotic is when you have sex with cars."

"Shut up."

"If it's in the pursuit of pleasure, I can't blame them for it," Charlie added.

"Well, yeah, Charlie sticks dildos up his butt and I don't fault him for that."

"Hey, nothing goes up my butt. That needs to be clear."

"That auto-erotic stuff sounds like way too much effort."

"Everything is too much effort for you. Regular jerking it is too much for you."

"No, I said jerking without porn is too much effort because you have to fantasize."

The conversation died off there as our phones absorbed us. The other three were texting at a blitzkrieg pace. I scrolled through old pictures that I had forgotten—forgotten even taking them. We didn't want to arrive at the party too early and made no rush to leave the still classroom. Tyler pulled out his phone too.

We heaved ourselves up the steep, flaky concrete steps to the front door. A massive brick house squatted in front of us, scarred from years of abuse. It predated World War II. The cracked front door looked like it was scowling at us. Light escaped the shades guarding the windows and chunks of brick had scratched ugly patches under our feet. The whole house had shed bits of mortar and brick like a tree in autumn. A ring of debris had collected around its base. The things this house must have seen. Older than my grandparents, within sight of the campus, and surrounded by more party houses, I was sure it offered good times. A sound system hummed behind the door. A whole ensemble of sound systems hummed behind the doors of every house buried in the darkness of the street.

"Fuck I'm outta breath," Derek let out, unshouldering his back-pack. "Mark, you know the girl who runs this place, ring the doorbell."

"It doesn't work. Here." Mark knocked on the dry-rotted wood and splinters shed off and showered the stoop. The porch light anchored to the wall flickered.

Within a minute a girl answered the door. The hinges screeched in their rust. She looked confused until she recognized Mark.

"We got beer," he told her.

"Yeah." She cocked her head down and swung the door open more, jamming it against the wall. Music flooded the front porch. The girl took two sips from her bottle. "There's coolers in the main room, you can put it in there. Thanks for coming." She burped and paced back down the hallway without waiting for us.

"Sweet," Mark said. "Party time."

"This music is ancient. Do you guys remember this?"

"They must be playing some old school stuff. Must be a decade old."

"That's almost Pre-Columbian."

We hauled in our backpacks and filled the coolers and got a good look around. Tyler entered last. These older houses had far less indoor space than the exteriors suggested. Small circles of students crowded the place, but not too badly. Nobody was wild or rowdy and everybody carried some kind of drink. We could hear beer pong downstairs. We stashed the backpacks, minus the booze, in a hallway closet and struggled to adjust at first. It looked like everyone here had their group of friends that they knew and showed no interest in anybody else. They packed tightly into their circles, making sure not to stay quiet in their group for too long. The rooms were abuzz with voices, butting in and cutting off, vying to tell the juiciest rumors and the harshest judgments of classmates. I had already run into this on campus. It reminded me of those terrorist cells you hear about. Getting into one did not give you any more access to the others because they were so cloistered. I said we should all head downstairs for some beer pong.

The speakers switched from blasting the old music to trap music. The chatter downstairs was louder. Everyone had to shout to overpower the pounding bass beats. Ping-pong tables and foldout tables supported several beer pong games.

Deeper in the basement near a makeshift kitchen was a large card table covered in orderly rows of plastic cups and beer cans. It looked like an assembly line to me—mass-produced fun. The students there eventually noticed us, a group of fresh and jumpy players, and we got paired up for matches. My first game I played some athletic guy who towered above everyone, even Mark. He wore a shirt one size too small and had a tanned face, clean-shaven to expose a square jaw. He seemed alright but he didn't talk to me, except to comment once on the game, if you could call that talking. His girlfriend leaned on him, her long curly hair trailing over her shoulders. She cheered when he scored. I could sense my friends looking at her. I lost three games in a row and admitted total defeat. Tyler watched the games, standing near me, arms at his sides, silent. He would look around every so often. At first it looked like he was watching other students out of curiosity, like this was his first chance to observe them in their natural habitat. Then his eyes would dart back to the game if someone else met his gaze. Close to the end of the second game, as the party grew louder and more students crowded into the basement, he changed a little. When he turned to look at the rest of the party, his eyes glazed over, and instead of watching he seemed to be staring around, not focusing on anything. I made a mental note of it. I had never seen anyone sink into deep reveries in the middle of a party, at least without the help of drugs. His eyes would wander, sometimes boring into a far wall and then drifting over partygoers. When others caught him staring, his eyes didn't dart away like they had before. A few people gave him odd looks. I saw one even tap his friend on the shoulder to point it out. Tyler, who was at first acutely aware of anybody looking at him, now seemed oblivious to some of the reactions he was getting. I didn't understand it, but the couple I was playing never even noticed him throughout our three games, and no one ever said anything to us.

Mark and Derek won their games and drew a small audience. They had practiced obsessively on dry games of beer pong in their dorms when they had spare time. Charlie spoke to a girl watching the games. He rambled and flicked his hands in a sweeping motion. He was the palest of us four but not bad-looking. The other guys had a tough time concealing their jealousy when Miranda was brought up. She was cute and had a sense of humor. Charlie had been trying to cheat on her, or at least said he had been trying. He claimed it was a challenge to cheat on her. He didn't care if she found out. Either she would forgive him or leave him, and he didn't seem to mind either possibility. I wasn't so sure that he thought of it as a challenge. He spoke about the goal as if he wanted to make a memory, like he wanted to cheat on her, have the arguments, and deal with the emotional carnage in order to have the experience.

A girl who recognized me from our Chem 101 lab challenged me to a game. I said alright. Her girlfriends watched from her side as we played, criticizing her performance. Tyler continued to stand nearby. This time he did say something and gave me a nugget of advice barely loud enough for me to hear. The girl didn't learn from her mistakes and failed to correct her left-leaning aim from her right hand, while I spread my shots to avoid repeating the same tosses. Shouts and close-call gasps came from Derek and Mark's table. They battled some tough challengers. The girl from my Chem 101 lab lost to me and suffered a torrent of her friends' good-natured, profanity-laden insults for losing the game. She shook them off and smiled at me. I thanked her for playing and we talked—no, shouted—at each other about Chem 101.

"What'd you get on the midterm?" she asked. She had black eyeliner and blinked a lot.

"Ninety-seven after the curve."

"I got a seventy-two after the curve. Did you cheat? I heard like a third of the class cheated. And no one got caught."

"No, I was a loser and studied." I nodded toward Tyler. "Me and him worked together. But we didn't cheat." Tyler glanced down at his shoes.

"Yeah, I didn't either. But I don't regret not studying. It's almost not worth it, you know? I can spend the time better and still pass."

"I'm not sure. Maybe you're right."

"And that's chem. I'm an education major, what does it matter?" She downed some beer and mouthed something to her friends. "You know where I was the night before midterms?"

"Where?"

"Right here. Except then it was actually wild and awesome here. Jammed with people and fucking vodka everywhere. Weed too. Not like this letdown."

"Wish I was there."

She was right. The music made the party feel much livelier than it was. It seemed like plenty of people were here, but it lacked that electricity. Only a few couples danced in the middle of the basement. Nobody was wasted—at least not yet.

"Oh, me and my friends are thinking of going to another party tonight. We hear that one's doing a little better."

"You go between parties on the same night?"

"Oh yeah, usually we make three or four every Friday night. Have to try them out. We're always looking for that great party, you know? Sometimes we find it. And cause we're three girls, we get invited to every place we want," she yelled over the music.

Across the room Derek held a full cup of beer in one hand and tossed a ping-pong ball with the other. He drank out of two cups at the same time when his opponent scored on him. A few girls squealed with laughter when he did this.

Some of the partygoers in the crowd shuttled in new sets of cups on trays for a fresh round of beer pong. A group prepared cups at the back table in a line. Each member had a specific job: unstacking and lining the cups, pouring the beer, opening the cans, and counting them out in batches of ten.

"Are you with them?" She looked toward Derek and Mark.

"Yep. We're freshmen. Anxious to get a taste of this."

"Don't worry, you'll get it," she said.

"Upperclassmen?"

"Juniors. I've seen it all when it comes to these. But the really bizarre things will happen at parties like these half-dead ones. Saw a girl resting her head on her boyfriend's shoulder and she threw up on his chest and his lap. He was so drunk he didn't freak out, just got up and left, and she laughed out the rest of her puke and then passed out. Funniest thing I've ever seen in real life."

"How many parties you think I need to go to? Like how many for a real taste?"

She untucked her hand from her crossed arms and checked her phone. "Hmm, good question. Half-a-dozen per semester. And that's decent ones. The boring ones don't count. The point is to have a great time."

"Alright six, I'll make that my goal," I said.

"How tall is your friend over there?" She pointed to Mark.

"About six-three."

She consulted one of her friends. I couldn't hear them, but it appeared to turn a little combative.

"What is it?" I asked.

"Oh, arguing about height."

"What're you looking for?"

"The tallest guys."

"Is this sort of a competition?"

"It's a little game. Anyway, he's not tall enough. Hey, listen, I like, need to get another drink from the back."

"Okay. Do you know where the bathrooms are?"

"The one down here doesn't work. Your best shot is upstairs at the end of the hallway."

"Cool, thanks."

I weaved between students crowding the base of the stairs and made it up to the much darker first floor, where the music rose from the basement, stripped of its intensity, like a downpour when you're inside. More secluded groups in corners or on couches talking in casual voices. Most of them still wore their coats and were huddled together. My ears started ringing as I moved past the kitchen and down the hallway.

The yellowed plaster of the walls had cracks and dents. The hardwood creaked with each step. I did like these kinds of houses. They had character and a bit of warmth that made my dorm feel even more like a prison. But this house's bathroom lacked that warmth. The one tiny stained window emitted darkness and the one bare incandescent bulb needed some company. I checked my phone. No texts. Nothing new. The light from my phone hurt my eyes and I turned it off.

When I left the bathroom Tyler was waiting right outside of it.

"It's pretty dark in there," I said.

He hesitated, shifting his weight, his eyes lost, unfocused. I waited, watching him for a few seconds.

"I don't feel comfortable. I mean, I don't feel well."

"Are you gonna get sick?"

"No, well kind of. Yeah. I'm shaking."

He didn't appear to be shaking to me. He did look extremely worried. His breathing was rapid and shallow, and his face, pale and twisted, told me something had gone wrong.

"The bathroom's right here. If you don't feel better text me and I can walk you back to Harris."

"Somebody else might come. I need—need a break."

"Okay. Let's go up to the top floor. Should be more private up there." I didn't get why I suggested that plan. I kind of wanted to brush him off, leave him upstairs so I could rejoin the party and not miss out. I already had such a late start on parties for the semester. But I couldn't leave him.

Tyler agreed with a nod and we found the split staircase up to the second floor. The thin hall was empty. Nothing but closed doors. The music struggled to reach us.

We walked down the hall on the dusty hardwood, searching for anything: an open door, a bedroom. Somewhere we could rest or talk. But about half of the doorknobs had socks on them. I scoffed.

"I thought that rule was only for the dorms," I whispered.

I tried to open some of the sock-less doors but they were all locked tight.

"I'm sorry Tyler, there's nothing."

He scratched his head. "Alright, that's okay. Uh, I'll walk back to Harris by myself. I feel a little better now, but I can't go back down there. You can go ahead. Have fun."

"That's what you want?"

"Yes."

"Well, let me walk you to the front porch." I figured he would need help to at least escape the party. Maybe he hadn't been to something like this before and he felt overwhelmed. A long walk in the chilly fall night would help. The nice thing would be to walk with him, but the nice thing didn't seem like the right thing to do. He said he could do it alone. I didn't see a need to get pushy. He was an adult who could make decisions for himself, just like the students in those bedrooms.

We went downstairs and out the front door. No one noticed us. On the porch, Tyler's breath puffed out twice as fast as mine in the cold air.

"Thanks," he said.

"It's fine. I'll say you were sick. The sight of Charlie flirting upset your stomach."

"Heh. That works. I'll see ya." Tyler turned and eased his way down the steps.

I waved goodbye but he didn't see it.

I stayed on the porch for a few minutes, watching his figure shrink to a small point back toward campus. I hoped Jake hadn't started another party in their dorm room. He wouldn't be able to take refuge in mine this time. Did Tyler have any other friends to hang out with? I started to wonder. Everyone had friends; being alone was more against the rules than academic dishonesty. He had one, me, but who else? I guessed his friends could've started going to parties like these and Tyler didn't tag along. Or his friends had found other cliques more suited to their interests and he couldn't find his own.

In my head I could hear my high school friends and everybody else at that party laughing at Tyler for leaving. For getting scared. For quitting. I could hear those jeers and those jokes so clearly. I knew exactly what they sounded like. I had heard so many other scared kids get bombarded by them. My hands balled up into fists. It came as a surprise to me—the rage and how much I felt for Tyler. Screw those cackling pricks for not even trying to understand. They didn't give a shit. Yes, he might have been too timid, especially for a guy, to thrive at a huge college. He might have been socially disabled, as some later put it, but he didn't deserve ridicule for leaving a party. Of course, I was already planning a lie to save him from the worst of the humiliation, but I'm sure those same taunting and cruel words were playing in Tyler's head as he walked back to campus in the dark.

Back in the basement the girl I had talked with and her friends had now struck up a conversation with Mark and Derek. I had to move through a tight group of students to get to them. A dull pulse thudded against my skull.

I overheard Derek speaking as I approached. "You've heard of that, right? A lock that can be opened by many keys is a shitty lock."

"Yeah, and a key that can open a lot of locks is a great key," Mark added.

"I've heard of that one before," the girl said. "It looks like you guys aren't having any success here."

Mark frowned and shook his head. "Nope."

"So your keys aren't unlocking anything. Must be shitty keys." Her friends laughed along with her.

"Did the girls get tired of beating you in pong?" I asked.

"You missed it. Missed the intensity man," Derek said. "Some real close games."

"We're gonna go," the girl said. "We're late to our next party. Nice talking to you guys." They left without ceremony, vanishing into the group near the stairs I had passed through.

"What'd you do with your friend?" Mark asked me. "Play soggy biscuit?"

"Share dick pics?" Derek added.

"No, the screen's too small."

"So what really?"

"He felt sick. Stomach upset or something."

"He looked pale. His loss."

"Look at Charlie over there. Far side of the room, by the table full of cups, hitting on that chick. I feel so sorry for her."

"Miranda would feel sorry for her."

"Charlie's lost it. He's a wreck. Should we rescue him?" Mark held out his hand toward Charlie in a weak offer of assistance.

"He needs a few more beers. That'll knock sense into him."

"I doubt it," I said.

"Here, have a beer." Derek handed me one. "Should knock some sense into you."

"Thanks." I raised the cup to my mouth and pretended to drink.

Nothing big happened at that first party. None of us got laid. Nobody even made out with a girl. Charlie had no success cheating on Miranda, and no other girls showed genuine interest in any of us. The only person who made the most out of the night was Derek, slurring his words and stumbling in a half-dazed stupor before gracefully clocking out on a couch near a pile of discarded cups. His drool darkened a corner of the seat cushion.

Charlie, Mark, and I travelled back upstairs and talked quietly late into the night until we dozed off on couches. In the morning we heard vomiting in the bathroom. We collected Derek and looked to thank the girl who invited us, but we couldn't find her, so we went to Chipotle.

We sat around a table, weary and sluggish. I was exhausted from carrying my jammed-full backpack across campus. The meal worked to fatten ourselves up before we hibernated for the rest of the weekend. Conversation topics for our brunch included: dicks, Jesus, AIDS, Alexander the Great, if Jesus had a big dick, Catholic school girls, the P-to-V ratio of the party, how Alexander the Great was gay, and male sex slaves.

———

I never texted Tyler after he left the party. It didn't cross my mind. Maybe the raging trap music clogged my head or the alcohol obscured any clear line of thought. I wished I had texted him something that night, to check up. I imagined him on his bed with the light off, alone in his room, staring at the campus out the window. To this day I still hope he didn't feel that lonely so early on.

CHAPTER SIX

Life Points

I'm going to take a break here to say something. It's this theory I have. It's been on my mind for a long time, since before Tyler, but only after Tyler did it fully develop. I used to think that people valued their lives based on what they owned and how much money they made. Simple materialism, a system everyone in America learns at a young age. But for years, doubts grew in my mind about if people really lived their lives that way. My teenage years and my time at MU gave me strong reasons to think that this was an outdated view. Maybe my generation, and even my parents' generation, had come up with a new value system. I call it Life Points.

It's based on experiences. Everybody earns life points for experiences that they have and those points are constantly tallied up into an overall score. The goal is to earn as many points as you can and score more than the competition. The competition is everybody else. Think of a giant leaderboard ranking each person by their life points, with your name and the names of the people you know highlighted. It's a simple system, I know, but it explains so much.

So how are the experiences quantified? I think they're based on a combination of quantity and quality, with an emphasis on diversity and intensity of experiences. For example, if you spend a fun night hanging out with your friends and lose yourself in hilarious conversations and goofy antics, you earn a decent amount of life points. If you spend five hours of a night watching random YouTube videos you'll earn fewer life points, but you always receive a few every hour for being alive. So even if you spend a half an hour procrasturbating (masturbating to pass the time because you don't want to do something else) or reading through old texts or tweets, you'll still earn life points, but not as many as if you were going to a party and getting wasted or going on a first date with a very attractive person. Big life events will net you a large sum of life points and even more if it occurs in a dangerous or unique way. Say you lost your virginity when you were fourteen. That's worth far more life points than if you lost it at twenty. Sex is probably the largest point-earning experience for most people. It's an intimate experience that society highly values. All sorts of factors can influence life points from sex, like position, pleasure, the orgasm, and whether or not you've tried it before. Doing it the same way with the same partner over and over again will decrease the life points each time, but changing the methods or partner will increase them. More rare or taboo experiences can definitely make your life points skyrocket. If your partner goes down on you, that'll be like, 5,000 points. Then there's bonus points for a long session, or if you hold their head. Group sex or fulfilling some kind of perverse fantasy you're into yields plenty of points for you.

This isn't hedonism, though. Hedonism involves avoiding painful and negative experiences, but life points reward you for them. Terror and suffering are important life experiences. They are tests of your will and your character and they teach you a lot about life. If you come out the other side intact, then you have another experience under your belt and further proof that you have lived. Sayings like "better to have loved and lost than not to have loved at all" describe this philosophy well. We take risks and sometimes even engineer hardships for ourselves, sabotaging our own success to pile on life points. Sometimes we're afraid of succeeding because that will make us complacent, and complacency drains life points.

We all live by some version of this competition in life. Our values vary and life points will change based on who you ask. A devout Catholic will calculate a much lower life point score for a hard-partying frat boy than a fellow frat boy would. We compare and contrast our lives with everyone we meet, gauging their quality of life, secretly judging. How many awesome life experiences have they had? Not many. Definitely a lot less than I've had. They're weird. Nobody will get close to them. At least I've got my life experiences in. They've missed out, and they can't get it back. It reminds me of being called a loser. Whether it was to my face or behind my back, more often behind my back, what exactly were they accusing me of losing? What had I lost? It was a game. The game of life. A loser is somebody who is way behind on life points. A socially unacceptable amount below the average. Someone who succeeds in life is a winner, well on their way to earning a high score and ascending the ranks of the life leaderboard.

A popular theory on Tyler's motive for the shooting stems from something like this system. The best way that I can explain it is to use an analogy. Imagine you're playing a game with several people, a game where there are no teams and it's everybody for themselves. You start falling way behind—so far behind that you have no hope of winning or competing. So now, because playing the game the way it's supposed to be played has become futile, you change your strategy to sabotaging other players, paying no attention to how this affects your position. In fact, you probably have to do things that are harmful to your own standing in order to hurt other players' chances of doing well. You spread the pain and misery that you've been experiencing. This strategy also gives you new goals and allows you to accomplish something, even if it's out of a sense of bitterness and revenge toward the game as a whole. And you can bring the spirit of competition along, competing against others who have adopted this strategy before you did. So this was why Tyler decided to kill students at random. He changed his strategy in the game of life because he knew he was too far behind, and then killed himself to avoid a lifetime in prison, where he would only fall further behind. At least that's the theory. I'm not sold on it even though what he did works with this system. It makes Tyler a sore loser. And calling him a sore loser is only going to make life seem more like a giant competition, unless it is one. Either way, I don't know if I have enough distance to make any level-headed conclusions. Memories of Tyler still cloud my mind.

CHAPTER SEVEN

Spring Semester

The rest of the fall semester was fairly smooth for me. A few more parties, most of them similar to the first, except Tyler didn't come. To my knowledge, that first party was the only real one he went to during our freshman year. And we never discussed it until much later. On the other hand, we did have plenty of study sessions. Bud Dwyer and Christine Chubbuck and similar stories came up routinely, but not like the night before the midterm. We scored C's on most of our final exams, which put us at the top of our classes. The professors curved ours up to A's.

We both went home for Christmas break and did not contact each other until spring semester began. Even though we had each other's cell numbers and texted each other when classes were ongoing, we put that on hold when we went home for breaks or weekends. It was like our friendship only existed on campus our freshman year.

Christmas break went fine for me and I assumed it did for Tyler—we never spoke about it. I didn't tell my parents or sisters about him at this point, and wouldn't until the summer. My parents asked me about what parties I had been to. They wanted to make sure I was having a good time there, making jokes that my party attendance should beat my class attendance. They didn't ask me too much about classes. Instead they told me about their wild college adventures back in the day and some of the reckless things my sisters had done. They wanted me to have those good times too.

———————

The mass migration back to campus in January had students and parents hauling their belongings back to the dorms in the crunchy snow. The twelfth floor of Harris Hall grew busier than it was during moving-in week. Everyone brought in fresh supplies and new televisions and game consoles. Jeremy helped carry things up to the twelfth floor the whole day. The garbage cans and recycling cans had been emptied and replaced over the break and the scent of alcohol barely lingered. That didn't matter to the parents. I saw some carrying packs of beer up to the dorms. Some parents openly encouraged their kids to drink and live it up. After my parents helped me move back in, we ate supper at the student union. They asked me when I was going to start dating a cute girl. I said soon and told them that I was considering information technology for my major, but I still hadn't made up my mind.

The snow fell in bundles that January, dotting the air and rounding out the sharp edges of the campus. Students shuffled over the salted walkways and courtyards. Shoes tracked snow indoors, which melted, and linoleum and tile hallways turned slippery and squeaky. Everyone picked up the trick of walking through buildings to stay warm when moving through campus. Some of the older buildings had tunnels running between them. Even if they weren't the best paths, I'd take detours between classes just to walk through them. They had an ancient, cave-like feeling I found refreshing on a campus trying so hard to be ultramodern. MU dealt with snow every winter, and my freshman winter happened to be above average. Two years later the blizzard struck and broke records. But Tyler would overshadow those snowfall totals.

Tyler and I managed to sign up for one class together in the new se-mester—an intermediate English composition course. We both had earned the intro-level credit in high school and we both needed to fill language arts requirements, and the course worked with our schedules. Professor Melody taught English 2044. You may remember Professor Melody from the TV and radio interviews she has done, under her married name Carly Whitlock. We knew her as Carly Melody, a hyper thirty-something engaged to a man she had fallen head-over-heels for. She liked to use their upcoming wedding as an example for rhetorical devices in papers.

The class was in a typical room with about thirty desks, and every seat was full on the first day. After that, about fifteen students showed up on any given day. Tyler and I always arrived early and sat next to the windows, where heat vents dating to the seventies hummed like diesel engines. The rest of the class would stream into the room right before it began in a squeaky storm. We waited through Professor Melody's ramblings on wedding details to get to the lessons. She actually had some good points and could articulate her ideas well. She kept the lec-tures casual and did not talk down to us like so many other professors did. I learned more about composition from that course than in four years of high school. Tyler and I knew we had gotten lucky with this professor and paid close attention. We even sometimes participated in class, even though it wasn't required. When Tyler spoke up I could tell he limited how much his mouth and lips moved in order to hide his braces. It affected his speech. I'd always look at Professor Melody when he answered so he'd have one less pair of eyes on him. It was easy to tell that he became very nervous when he participated. I never brought up the answers or opinions he volunteered to Melody outside of the class. And he did the same for me. They were somehow off-limits to us. What we did talk about were the six-page papers we had to write on some issue. I felt a little dread over that; they were double the length of my high school papers. Tyler worried over it too. He wanted to start doing research in January. I told him to wait. The full papers wouldn't be due until later in the semester.

———————

The time between when Tyler and I arrived at English 2044 and when the rest of the class arrived was the most interesting part. The period before classes began carried an awkward boredom. Some rule or law banned professors from starting early, so everyone waited in near silence. Professor Melody was always there first, which meant the three of us sat in the room for about fifteen minutes, three days a week. You'd think Tyler and I would use this empty time to talk, but Melody's presence warded off conversation between us. We sat content, watching the courtyard or looking at our phones and notes. Melody would lean forward on the lectern, eyes searching her laptop screen and not blinking for painful amounts of time. She had brunette hair to her neck, a sharp nose, and preferred skirts with leggings. Maybe it was boredom, but sometimes she interrupted the quiet rumble of the projector and heat vents to get to know us.

"What did you guys do on the weekend?"

"Nothing much," I said. "Do you have your wedding cake picked out?"

"Not quite." She kept her eyes on the laptop. "Either of you going to the freshman dance on Friday?"

"Nope. I didn't like dances when I went to them in high school."

"I didn't go to dances in high school," Tyler said.

"Well, if you have girlfriends, I'm sure they'd love to go."

"Oh, we don't."

"You can go stag. I'll be there helping to run it."

"Like a chaperone?" I asked.

"It's more like an event coordinator. There are raffles and contests. My fiancé will be there with me."

"Do you like the slow dancing or fast dancing?"

"Oh, I like the fast dancing. It's great to just let loose." She went back to her desk and rummaged through her bag. "You don't have to know how to dance to go. I'm terrible at it. I think it's something everybody should try. You never know what you might like."

In another pre-class discussion, she encouraged us to join student clubs or to try some of the bars right off-campus that admitted students under twenty-one. I'd usually respond for the both of us, hinting that we might try some of her suggestions. Sometimes Melody asked plain, stock questions. Questions for getting to know somebody you just met. It was odd to us for a professor to show any personal interest in students. In both the large lectures and high-school-sized classes the professors rarely bothered to learn anyone's name. Melody's questions even revealed some things about Tyler that I didn't know. He wasn't hostile to the questions, more like resigned, like he had no choice but to answer them. I made sure to ask questions back. I didn't like to feel interrogated.

"Where are you guys from?"

"North of here. From the suburbs," I said. "Are you from around here?"

"No, Maryland. Grew up there. Then undergraduate at Minnesota and graduate at Boston. They're very different places, but lots of snow. Here there's not as much. I like it."

"I've only ever lived around here," I added.

"Me too," Tyler said. "Same house my whole life."

"Are you dorming this year?"

"Yeah, we're in Harris."

"And you're both freshmen?"

"Yeah."

"Did you go to the same high school?"

"No. We didn't know each other until we started here."

"That's good, making new friends right away. I see some students really struggle with that." She twisted her shoulders forward and backward to stretch. When she read from her laptop she tended to hold perfectly still and then every so often go into stretching fits. Tyler watched students outside the window.

"So do you like MU so far?"

"Yeah."

"You'd say it's been a good experience?"

"Sure. How do you like the atmosphere compared to the other colleges you've gone to?"

"It's been a few years but I remember them as, well, more wild and a little too crazy. Here it's quieter and calmer. That could be because I'm a professor now. It's a different perspective."

———————

The winter marked a low point for the twelfth floor of Harris Hall. The cold weather and snow cut the number of parties the guys could go to, so the drinking inside the dorms ramped up. Salt and slush accumulated in the lobby, the elevator, and the halls. The freezing air from the open windows alternated with the scalding boiler air. It caused a lot of colds and even cases of pneumonia. Empty beer cans started to show up on the bathroom floor along with more unconscious students, even on weekdays. Jeremy had to get hold of extra garbage bags to change out the overloaded recycling bags in between the janitors' visits. His constant reminders to recycle at the floor meetings continued to work. On weekends half the floor jammed into the quads, setting up sound systems and sometimes managing to invite girls, but most of the celebrations were what Derek called "sausage fests." Everyone commented on the pathetic P-to-V ratios. Jeremy would leave the dorm with his girlfriend on the weekends. And somehow Henry spent even less time in our room. He was nocturnal now, from what I could tell. I caught him a couple of times sleeping in his bed on weekday afternoons when I came back from class. His class attendance must've been atrocious.

I invited Tyler over to my room during the first week of the semester. We had nothing to study for, but I felt a little bad for not texting him during Christmas break. He still came over with his backpack, wearing jeans and a hoodie and gym shoes. It was six and already dark out. He looked worn down at first but perked up once we moved past the niceties.

"This English comp course looks easy. We won't have to do much studying," I said.

"I'm taking less credits this semester. I've just got my general engineering, math, physics, and this English one." Tyler sat on the carpet Indian-style. I didn't offer him Henry's chair. He looked pretty comfortable.

I sat down next to him. "I was thinking we could try to hang out more this semester."

"What do you mean?"

"Not parties, but like hang out in our rooms. Play some video games, talk about stuff like we did the night before the midterm."

"Sure. Sounds good." Tyler shifted his weight a little. "You know one time last semester I hung out with Jake when he used his vodka fish bowl again. But Jake just wanted to get me drunk. I did one screwdriver to make him happy. Like a week later I came back from studying at the library and there was a sock on the doorknob. So I went back to the library. I've done that a couple of times at night. I can't believe they leave all those buildings unlocked that late."

"Yep. They're creepy." I scanned the white block walls of the dorm. "If you want you can come over here if Jake has more parties, or socks. And Henry's moved out. Half his stuff is gone. Don't worry about spending the night here. Bring your pillow and some extra clothes."

"Really?"

"I'm totally fine with it."

"Cool."

―――――――

This was the golden age of our friendship. Tyler and I hung out about twice a week for the entire spring semester. Usually it was at my room, but we did meet at campus food courts to put dents into our meal plans, or Tyler's room, or in sound-proofed study rooms if we wanted real peace and quiet. The time we spent together was sort of an innocent kind, like kids playing: completely cut off from the world. The campus was a place to meet up at and we paid little attention to what was happening around us. The parties and shenanigans became annoyances to us. Didn't matter what day of the week, we settled into doing our thing and we did it. And mostly that was playing video games. Henry had his widescreen TV but had taken his Xbox somewhere else, and I had brought up my aging PS3 over winter break. That first weekend in January, Tyler texted me as Jake and his posse invaded his room again, and he came over and we started playing. He had games and so did I. We started with some popular ones and got sucked right in. Ignoring the outside world was so much fun. We played late into the night until a shouting match between guys on the floor ended the music coming from the earthquake-level sound system. Then we went to bed, and Tyler left in the morning. On some weekends we left Harris in the morning to get breakfast specials from the basement cafeteria in McKinley Hall. A couple of times we roamed the campus and off-campus areas for fresh air and exercise. We showed each other campus offices or labs that we had been to on our own. Tyler brought me to a few smaller, specialized libraries that were dead on weeknights. They had high shelves and tight spaces, tucked away on third or fourth floors where grad students researched. I used them to write papers and study in silence.

It was a slow process of becoming closer and closer friends. We exchanged normal bits of information—I found out he had a younger sister in high school, and I told him about my two older sisters and other family and situational stuff. He talked about his mom some—about how she pushed him to achieve good grades and wished he would go out with friends more and start dating. We didn't pressure each other for personal information. We both felt relieved at such a relaxed friendship. We weren't constantly asking each other about our past, or our plans for the future. We didn't pry. We could ask questions, but it was fine if they went unanswered. We volunteered stories and thoughts when we felt comfortable.

Another big topic that came up followed from the night before our Chem 101 midterm—tidbits of facts or stories that were morbid, disturbing, or tragic. We both used the internet to find and research these horrible revelations and then tell them as stories to each other. I'm not sure if Tyler had a habit of doing this before MU, but his stories about Christine Chubbuck and R. Budd Dwyer spurred me to find more like them, and he did the same. This wasn't a rivalry of knowledge, more like our own version of education, one that interested us more than our classes. We did sometimes bring up mass killings and school shootings. I mentioned the first one with Bethel, Alaska back before the midterm, but Tyler brought up several on his own. We tended to discuss shootings and mass murders that happened before Columbine because we hadn't heard of them before. They might have been decades old, but they were new to us.

Not that far into the spring semester, Tyler came over on a weeknight. This time he came with no backpack or books, only a coat dotted with snow and his loose jeans—loose because his legs didn't fill them. I kept my door all the way open along with the rest of the twelfth floor to circulate the air from the boiler. The window's suicide-prevention screen filtered out the snow. Tyler stood over it, gazing at the cars crawling on a powder-white Lyndon Avenue.

"How're classes?" he asked.

"Fine. Nothing challenging." I connected Henry's speakers to the TV and got the PS3 running. "And yours?"

"I've got a group engineering project coming up. In high school I had to do all the work for group stuff. I hope that's not true for this."

"I know what you mean. I hope there aren't many group projects in info tech."

Tyler didn't say anything.

"You like Melody so far?"

"Yeah." He shrugged. "She's pretty good."

"Which game?"

"You pick."

We sat on the carpet side-by-side. I wore shorts and a coat and tucked my bare feet under my butt. Tyler sat Indian-style, hunched forward. We looked like kids on the floor. The TV was perched low on a tiny, busted file cabinet I had found in the room when I moved in. The cabinet was no more than two feet tall. Decades of abuse had scraped off chunks of beige paint. It looked like bare metal sprouting out of a cocoon.

We went silent playing co-op. From somewhere below, a Taylor Swift song seeped into our room. Guys passed the open door heading down the hallway. Some were returning from showers and wore only bath towels, flip-flops slapping.

"Heard of John Kennedy Toole?" I asked. Tyler shook his head. "Reminded me of that Chubbuck reporter you told me about. Toole wrote a novel and nobody would publish it. So he thought of himself as a failure and killed himself when he was like thirty. His mom got the book published later and it was a huge success. Toole won the Pulitzer Prize eleven years after he died."

"Terrible. That's awful," he said. "Think of how much more he could've written. You know Taylor Swift's dad bought shares in a record label before they signed her? Her dad works at Merrill Lynch."

"What's Merrill Lynch?"

"Some investment company. They were part of the mortgage crisis back in '08. My mom almost lost the house because of it. That hit us hard."

"Huh. You know eighty percent of the music industry is owned by three corporations? That's it."

"I wish that one surprised me."

"The rest are independent labels."

We kept playing. Wild yells echoed down the hall. Then laughter.

Somebody from our floor stepped into the doorway. I recognized him from the floor meetings but I couldn't remember his name.

"Hey guys! What's going on in here?" He looked perplexed. "What, hold on, are you guys doing stuff in here? Like gay stuff? Are you? Kinda suspicious, two guys in a room—wouldn't want anything sexual happening."

I stared back at him and said nothing.

He paused for a moment, tapping on the doorframe, and then left.

We played for a little while longer in silence.

"Have you heard of a guy named Gilbert Twigg?" Tyler asked.

"No. What'd he do?"

"He wrote some letters about Winfield, the town where he lived, somewhere in Kansas. They were very clear and written well. He said people there had spread rumors about him and treated him poorly. Then he shot and killed eight people at random at a town concert and injured a bunch more. And then he killed himself. The letters were meant to be found after he did it. You know that was in 1903?"

"Crazy." I smiled. "That's way back in the day."

"Think about that, right? Before World War I started."

"Yeah, then they would use mustard gas knowing it would kill civilians and yet they kept doing it."

We delved into both of the world wars from there, listing their atrocities like we were studying for an exam. The whole time we had our controllers in hand, watching the screen.

—————

The video games we played tended to vary as the weeks marched on. To start I chose first-person shooters, the default game to play because every guy knows how to play them. They were my safe choice for Tyler—he refused to pick a game at first. We wore out our interest in them soon after that curious interruption by the guy whose name I couldn't remember—although it was not the last curious interruption we had. That's when our interests started to shine through. At first, we were reluctant to pick our favorite games. I thought we both feared admitting what we liked because it opened us up to ridicule. I'd sometimes suggest playing my favorites—not the most well-known games—to my high school friends, and then they'd use my odd choices against me. It taught me to conceal my interests. I got the sense that Tyler felt the same way.

I preferred slower, more analytical games along with some exploratory, objective-less ones. I learned Tyler enjoyed role-playing and horror games. We went through phases, rarely beating an entire game so we could move on to the next one. We never chided each other for making mistakes, and if we failed, we tried again. We avoided playing against each other. We worked on co-op campaigns or took turns on single-player games. Weekends we saved for horror titles. We would stay up late in my room with the lights out, door usually shut. The distant music, drunken screaming, and chanting that made its way into the room from near and far chilled us more than the games. Our only visual cue of what went on outside my room on those sinister nights was the thin strip of light under the door, sometimes broken by staggered footsteps. One horror game we enjoyed was *Silent Hill 2*. I remember it clearly, not only because of the fun we had playing it, but due to the infamous glue incident, which struck the twelfth floor not long after we started the game.

———————

The elevator dinged on a Friday night in March during the last frigid spell before spring broke winter's back. Tyler had met me for supper after I took an afternoon exam and we were returning to Harris for another night of gaming. The shiny doors parted. Harris Hall's twelfth floor had stumbled and lurched to a new low point. No music was playing. It was quiet. Both of the recycling cans stood upright and empty. The lobby floor was covered in a layer of empty beer cans and bottles. Tyler and I waded through the empty containers like autumn leaves, scattering them with our steps, bottles rolling at random, filling in the path behind us. A pitiful metallic and glass chorus that anyone on the floor could've heard.

"There is nothing else to fucking do! I'm bored!" somebody shouted from down the hall.

"This is what it's all about!" somebody else shouted back, and then howled like a wolf. A plastic clatter of cups being knocked over.

Across the lobby I stopped at the view down the long, straight hall. Tyler stopped behind me. White paste was strewn all over the block walls, ceiling tiles, doors, and floor. I looked back down the other end of the hallway and white paste decorated that end like cobwebs on Halloween. Some glue had dried in spatter patterns, while other strains had slid down the walls, and pools collected in sticky messes in gaps between the tiles. I estimated it had to have come from at least a dozen bottles of glue.

We looked at each other.

"Is this some prank?" I asked.

"Maybe someone is really drunk."

"I've heard of girls going into their RA's room and peeing on the carpet after drinking."

"I guess it's not too much of a stretch."

A door opened and one of the guys surveyed the mess. "Holy fuck! Who jizzed all over the place? That's a lot of cum!" He maneuvered over the puddles on his toes. "I hope the bathroom doesn't look like this. Jesus fuck." And he disappeared into the bathroom.

My first guess was that the all-girl eleventh floor had done this as a prank. They had a pseudo-rivalry with us that Jeremy encouraged. But nothing had happened between the floors before this. The floors had no real interaction with each other except in the elevators. The rivalry was empty rhetoric. And a glue-dousing seemed too destructive and risky. I could hear the sounds of the quad's weekly party. They probably knew who did this.

"Into the abyss?" I asked Tyler.

"Definitely." He grinned.

We had to take our time with each step, checking the walls before putting our hands on them for extra balance. Tyler giggled at our efforts. I made a leap and cleared a large series of puddles. I turned to watch Tyler. He stuck one foot out, reaching over the puddles, and landed it on a dry tile, his legs now split over the danger. He checked the walls, which looked like someone with white blood had been axed to death where Tyler was standing, and then he glanced up at me. Some of the coagulated glue bubbled under him.

"Having issues?"

He nodded.

I grabbed his arm and he pulled it away.

"This is just to help you over."

Tyler inched his arm toward me, offering it to me like I was a dangerous animal. I grabbed it and he was tense, but I heaved him over.

"Safe for now," I said.

"Thanks. It's like the glue is lava."

The rest of the hall had only trace amounts of glue oozing over the floor. We made our way toward my room, close to the open quad. I pulled my lanyard over my head to unlock the door. I didn't bother knocking to see if Henry was in there. I had quit that habit in the fall.

"Hey it's the boys who are always in their room."

The quad party had noticed us. Several guys crowded into the hallway, some shirtless. Thankfully it was still early in the night, and they had yet to drink themselves into oblivion.

"Do you know who did this?" one guy wearing sunglasses asked.

"No, we just got back. There's cans all over the floor by the elevators too," I said.

"We know. We didn't do that. We had the door closed for some pong. When we opened it back up the place was trashed. Our speakers must've blocked out the sound. We turned them off to hear if anybody came back."

It was an odd scene, us two standing next to my door, the quad guys appearing from the end of the hall, ten feet or so from us. They were muscular, flabby, tall, short—body types of all sizes. Staring us down, we turned our heads to face them, not our bodies.

Someone back in the quad said, "Those are the two that are always gaming. I've never seen them with any chicks."

"Yeah, so, are you guys like gay?" another one asked. "I mean I think it's cool and all. But you kinda act like fags."

"No," I said in as flat a tone as I could make. I couldn't see Tyler during any of this; he stood behind me.

"It's weird that you two are always together. You spend nights together and we never see you with any girls."

An awkward pause followed. I wouldn't look down from their bloodshot gazes. My fists clenched. The quad guys swayed in the still hall, prying with their eyes. Another door opened and broke the standoff.

"What the hell? Are you shitting me?" It was Jeremy.

We turned our attention back up the hallway, where Jeremy swiftly and skillfully stepped toward us, avoiding the glue.

"Who sprayed their load all over the goddamn place? Either somebody had the biggest orgasm of all time or a huge porn video was shot here during our nap and nobody even told us."

The "us" in his statement was answered when his girlfriend entered the hallway, her heels clapping on the floor. She had on a blue miniskirt. All attention was re-directed at her.

"Sorry about this," Jeremy said to her.

Holding her purse against her side, she made her way next to him. What the guys said about her was true. Even I hated to admit it. A soft face, slight dimples at the ends of her lips. Wavy blond hair and long legs.

"Did anybody here do this?" Jeremy asked.

We all shook our heads.

"Does anyone here know who did this?"

We all shook our heads.

His girlfriend giggled.

Jeremy gave a smiling glance to his girlfriend and then looked back at us. "Okay, tonight, I'm going to take my girlfriend to a nice party, and we're going to have a good time. This problem, here—" He signaled with rapid hand swirls. "—this jizz-galore issue, I am going to have an inquisition. Medieval, with torture devices. Whole shebang. But I am going to have that inquisition tomorrow. For now—fuck it. Drink and be merry."

The quad guys raised their cups and cans in honorable salute.

"Best RA on the whole goddamn campus."

"Turn the music back on, boys!"

They hollered and cheered as they retreated into the quad.

"You might want to take the stairs to the eleventh floor then get on the elevator," I told Jeremy.

"It's that bad?"

"Yeah. Less glue to navigate. The stairs are closer." We had to take the stairs during fire drills—they were on both ends of the hall. I turned back to my door.

"Hey." Jeremy's giant hand tapped my shoulder. "Not partying?"

I didn't know if he meant partying with the quad guys or in general. "We've got our own plans. It doesn't involve alcohol so it kind of doesn't work with any partying."

"Oh." Jeremy looked dumbfounded. "I hope you're not studying."

"No, it's a waste of time. Classes are too easy."

"Well, sure, take it easy. Just remember two things: We're here for a good time, not a long time, and whenever you get pussy, terrorize it!"

His girlfriend, looking down at her phone, burst out laughing.

CHAPTER EIGHT

A Spring Walk

We played a good chunk of *Silent Hill 2* that night and went to bed early, around two in the morning. Tyler and I slept fine in spite of the noise and woke up before ten. Fresh, lapping breezes from Lyndon Avenue fought the stagnant air of our floor. The sun lit up the Greek houses and apartment buildings I could see from my bed. A purifying light, even the cups and party detritus and passed-out students looked vivid on the green lawns. The trees that had stood there over so many years and thousands of parties swayed gently, budding in the early spring.

Tyler raised his head from Henry's bed. I caught his eyes in the morning glare. He lifted up a little further and hit his head on the soft ceiling tile. A small amount of dust sprinkled his hair.

"Hungry?" I asked.

Tyler had an unstoppable appetite. He didn't like to admit it. He could make meals disappear and not gain a pound. His metabolism had to have been off the charts. The real question I had asked him was if he wanted to sleep in a little more.

"McKinley sounds good."

We clambered down the sides of our beds. Tyler had on gym shorts. His chest was pale and grooved from the skin rising and falling over his ribs. A thin, faint patchwork of blond hair dotted his chest. Thin waist and shoulders almost as thin—a body riding the line between skinny and malnourished. I had black body hair, and my ribs were harder to see unless I sucked in. Tyler's body didn't change much in the two and a half years I knew him, while my shoulders grew broader and my chest muscles developed. We put on our clothes in silence.

Out in the hallway the glue had all dried to a smooth marble look. Like an experimental art project gone completely wrong. Neither of us took care to avoid the glue this time, reaching out and feeling the rock-hard trails on the walls. White stalactites hung from the ceiling tiles. Nobody else was around. All of the doors were shut tight, locking away the sleeping twelfth floor.

We brushed our teeth at the old-fashioned sinks in the bathroom, side-by-side. It had become our Saturday routine. The mirrors above them had spider-web cracks in the corners and smears and streaks so permanent they had become part of the glass. No glue had found its way into the bathroom, but someone had vomited in the shower a few days before, and despite eternally-open windows, the place still reeked. We checked out the dried mess behind the torn shower curtain.

"Do they know who did it?" Tyler asked.

"Nope. Several guys admitted that they blacked out and could've done it, but they don't remember."

"That's not a good situation to be in."

"No. Jeremy said to wait for the janitors to come. And if anyone's memory does come back, they should own up to it, then apologize."

"That gum is so gross. I shower here every day and I can't get used to it."

A layer of solidified gum coated the shower stall walls in a multi-colored mural. "Yeah. Years' worth of that crap. It's hard too, like concrete. I guess the janitors won't get rid of it, or can't."

"You'd think that'd be some kind of health code violation."

"Beats me." I closed the curtain to hide the vomit. We didn't take showers that morning, even with two puke-free stalls available.

We hit the campus paths leading to McKinley. Saturday mornings on campus were tough to digest. They were serene. I found them even more calming than weeknights on campus. On Saturday mornings everything was calm. The off-campus soundscape had been turned off. The student body slept in, and the commuters stayed home. I could look around and see almost no one. The campus squirrels would wait until we got within feet of them before fleeing. We preferred this niche of campus time and exploited it. Our walks during this gap in activity felt like actual friendship, worthy of the time we spent together. For too long hanging out with friends had felt like a means of wasting time with others.

"My high school had these gas-chamber-style showers," I said. "All the dudes would pile in naked and gross. It was really scary if you were a freshman. A lot of towel-whipping. Occasional dry-humping. I put an elbow into the stomach of any guy who tried that on me. And that worked. After a while they left me alone."

"So you went to Little Turtle High?"

"Yeah, but it's not little. Graduated top ten in my class. Not to brag, or anything."

"Saint Anne's had more privacy but I showered there only a couple times. I didn't like it. Really, I couldn't stand it."

A lone student splayed out on the campus grass to catch some sun. Dark sunglasses blocked their eyes and their mouth hung open.

"Anything special about going to a Catholic school?" I asked.

"Have to wear uniforms, with shirts tucked in. And the girls wear skirts. Religion classes are mandatory. To me the whole thing was a scary place. Everyone wanted to move up the social ladder and push everyone else down."

"I get that." I sighed. "We called our school Little Turtle Daycare. Free daycare for overgrown children. Teachers were babysitters. That was, like, our big joke we all told each other."

"St. Anne's was expensive daycare. My tuition there was almost as much as MU's is now. Least had a scholarship for St. Anne's."

"My parents are helping me out with tuition here, but not much. After my two sisters went through college, my parents were almost wiped clean helping them. And now I'm starting and they didn't have much time to recover."

We continued talking about our high schools, touching on classes, teachers, and discipline. Tyler had by now grown much more comfortable talking to me. He had less trouble initiating eye contact or even leading our conversations—two things he had struggled to do back in the fall semester. That hadn't bothered me too much. The true extent of Tyler's shyness was only slowly dawning on me. In the months since he had left that party, I had started to think of him as a late bloomer, someone who needed time to come out of his shell. He was emerging from his shell around me, and that confidence would translate when he met other students he didn't know as well.

Looking back, it's easy to point out how wrong I was and how he never did grow comfortable around anyone else on campus. He never came out of his shell. That's who he was. In fact, I think the "shell" metaphor is sometimes used as a euphemism for conforming. Maybe, for a time, I wished he would become more like everybody else on campus, even though I despised how a lot of students treated those who were different. Either way, I didn't realize how special of an exception I had become to Tyler. I was the only one on campus who had somehow disarmed his crippling shyness. To him, our friendship must have been his one bright spot at MU, the one thing he looked forward to besides going home on holiday breaks. I can't fathom how lonely he must've felt when I wasn't around—in his classes, in his room, or eating alone at the student union. It makes me think of what else I could've done.

———

We made our way into the cafeteria for breakfast. The huge, old-fashioned cafeteria had unpainted concrete pillars running down its middle, and though it was noisy, that was more from all of the hard, bare surfaces than from tons of students. It was less than a quarter full on Saturday mornings. We avoided this cafeteria any other time of the week.

We shuffled down the line, telling the lunch ladies what to put on our trays. Our breakfast orders barely changed throughout the semester. A slow group of guys in front of us had trouble deciding and we had to wait. They looked like holdovers from a full night of partying, preparing to fill up their stomachs before Saturday hibernation.

"So you called the showers at your high school gas chambers?" Tyler asked with a laugh.

"They were completely open with shower heads popping out of the walls. Looked like those Holocaust gas chambers you see pictures of just smaller. No bagels, thanks."

"You ever heard of Wernher von Braun?"

"Who was he?"

"He was a Nazi rocket scientist. He designed the V-2 rocket."

"I've heard of that. More people died building those rockets than were killed by them. They used slave labor."

"I'll take one, please, thanks," Tyler said, pointing to the bagels. "When the war ended, we took him and a bunch of other Nazi scientists back here to work for us. He created Saturn V, the rocket that got us to the moon."

I shuffled over to the sausages and cinnamon toast.

"I'll take two of each. That makes sense. If there's one thing I learned looking up stuff online, it's that war has its benefits. Just ask Richard Nixon."

"What'd he do?"

"When he was running for president, there were peace talks going on to end the Vietnam war, which were bad for his campaign, so he got those peace talks to end and he won the election and the war continued. Horrible, but it worked."

The lunch workers did not react to our statements. They seemed numb to anything students said except what they wanted on their tray. The boys ahead lazily threw packs of jelly at each other, gossiping about guys from their dorm, calling some faggots and some virgins. The workers ignored every word.

Tyler hesitated to move down the line to close the gap between us and the group. "That reminds me of this kid who picked on me years ago. When he was about fourteen, I think, he wanted to impress this girl on our street, so he ramped up how much he tormented me whenever she was around. And it totally worked. That was how he got his first girlfriend."

"I wish stuff like that didn't work. Two eggs."

"I guess I'll take two also. No three, three. That's what I usually get," Tyler said, scratching the top of his head. "You know babies sometimes die from circumcision?"

"No. Here's something freakier. Ever heard of the pet holocaust?"

He looked surprised. "Another horrible thing the Nazis did?"

"Nope. The British did this. Before World War II started, they knew they would have to deal with food shortages and encouraged everyone to have their pets put down. Close to a million pets were killed to save food."

"Wow. Hadn't heard of that."

We piled on bacon to top off our trays and went for drinks—orange juice for me and grape juice for Tyler. The war facts continued to spew out. Wars hijacked a lot of our conversations during the spring semester. It didn't help that we played video games set during wars, especially World War II.

I set my tray down at the end of a long, gray-speckled table and started on my pancakes, which were dissolving in syrup. Tyler took longer because he liked to load up on butter and grab some hot tea. We had already established the pattern of not waiting for each other when we got food.

The only other students at our table lounged at the opposite end, halfway through a plodding meal. A few guys and girls, weary-eyed and mumbling. I sat as far away from them as I could. I had the urge to go over and ask what they were doing, and why, after a night out together, they still insisted on eating a depressing breakfast together. I had stopped going to after-party breakfasts with my high school friends. I wanted to be alone after a party.

Tyler focused on balancing his overcrowded tray, walking past the row of pillars toward me. He looked awkward and out of place. His hair was still long, down to his eyebrows. I wondered if he liked it that way or wanted to make up for his lack of facial hair. Fortunately, his acne had cleared up somewhat. If not for his braces he could've passed for a college-aged student.

His tray clattered on the table. "I couldn't find you."

"I hope you're hungry. God."

Tyler had a small-scale mountain range of food. He had to take plates off of the tray to get to more food beneath. And he could finish the meal, too. Sometimes he could manage to eat a cookie after breakfast that the lunch workers mass-produced and brought out on trays every half an hour or so. A few times I tried eating as much as him, and I could never get close.

The facts slowed to a halt as we chowed down. The echoes of the cafeteria took over, and the light breaking over the pillars from the high windows mellowed as the sun rose. Our feast was interrupted when a girl from the other end of the table approached Tyler.

"Excuse me, sorry, could I have a couple of packs of butter? They're all out in the back."

"Sure. Yeah." He reached out to pick the butter but changed his mind and let her take what she wanted.

"Thanks." She smiled and angled her head because he wasn't looking directly at her. "Are you a freshman?"

"Uh yeah. But I know the campus pretty well by now," Tyler said, shoulders hunched. He withdrew his hands and put them under the table.

"Freshman year you're getting used to it. It gets better with the later years, like high school."

"I'm just waiting for the school year to end."

"You can still enjoy it. And I think your braces are cute."

I glanced down to the other end to check if her friends were paying attention. They weren't. I'd seen too many instances of bullies messing with awkward boys at dances and parties by making them more uncomfortable for their friends' amusement, but she sounded genuine.

Tyler said nothing and stared at his food. His face was redder than I had ever seen it.

"Seriously, braces here are something different," she said. "And better than a mouthful of crooked teeth."

Tyler continued to stare at his food. She kept watching him, expecting him to comment on the braces but he didn't. The girl never looked at me. Neither did Tyler. She waited some more, then she turned around and went back to her seat. We dug back into our food and I picked up listing senseless war tragedies. I tried not to listen to the other end of the table. But ignoring words of judgment was hard. The girl explained what had happened to her friends. They gave their reactions to the little story, and I caught words like "creep" and "loser" a couple times in worried tones. They talked about avoiding this cafeteria for the next few weeks. I didn't know how much Tyler heard or how much he cared. They gathered their trays and left, and I changed the subject.

"Ever had your braces described as cute?"

"No, don't think I have."

"How much longer do you have them?"

"Right after exams they get taken off. My mom can't wait. She's had to pay for them for years, but she's more glad that I'll have straight teeth so I'll look better. Says when I smile, I'll actually look happy."

"You could use a beard," I said, stroking my own trimmed jawline. "Look more thoughtful. Show how mature you are."

"My nose is too small for that. I'd look weird with a beard and a button-sized nose."

"Doubt it."

"No, I still want facial hair. I'd rather look weird than be mistaken for a boy touring the campus."

"I want to grow a great beard and dye it gray then roam the campus like the classic philosophers. People will laugh, but I'll be showing them how it's done."

Tyler scoffed and laughed. "How to really think. Brain power from the beard."

After breakfast we headed off campus through the neighborhood on the far side of Lyndon Avenue—the crowded land our dorm overlooked. Full of older houses and apartments packed tightly together on thin streets, many MU students called this place home. Out here no students used the overgrown sidewalks on Saturday mornings. A few older walkers or joggers popped in and faded out of view, surfacing like fish in a dark pond before melting into deeper rows of houses and apartments. It was peaceful. We strolled through the tangle of streets at random. It wasn't the first time we had walked off campus, but it felt like an exploration. The wind disturbed the massive, ancient oak trees that shaded many of the side streets. There were no large or old trees on campus. They had re-built and re-altered it so much that nothing could stand for too long there. At one point I think we might have passed by the house where Tyler would commit the murders.

Tyler sneezed. And sneezed again. He pulled out a crumpled tissue and wiped his nose.

"Bless you."

"Thanks. That's what I'm writing my paper on."

"On what?"

"On allergies—well, really auto-immune diseases and how grow-ing up where we have all this anti-bacterial stuff can cause things like allergies and asthma. Like, when I was a kid, I never had allergies, and now I get them every year. Our immune systems get bored and then attack our own cells. So yeah, that's what I'm writing my final paper on. For Melody."

"You already picked your topic? And you're already doing re-search?" I expected he would've told me when he started, or brought it up when Melody prodded us for updates on our work. We still had a week to decide on our topic.

"I'd been doing research on my own, you know, to tell you about it. There're studies that link clean childhoods with auto-immune dis-eases developing later on."

"They should take kids to Harris. They'll never get allergies."

"Yeah, they'll just get all the other diseases."

We passed by a yard littered with red plastic cups. The lawn was more red than green.

"Do you have citations for the paper?"

"Working on them." He scratched his head and an old, dead leaf twirled from his hair.

"Forgot to tell you but that leaf's been in your hair since last fall."

Tyler grinned and watched it float down to the sidewalk.

Our wandering had led us into unfamiliar territory. The hous-es were smaller, and in poorer shape. Some had uneven foundations and leaned like they were tired of standing. Cars lined both sides of the streets. Pollen coated some of the windshields. MU pennants and flags galore. Signs of partying were still everywhere. Cans spilled over porches and stairs, dinky front yards littered with more cans and lost scarves and hoodies. We both took out our phones to see how much time had passed.

"Should we start heading back?" Tyler asked.

"I don't see why we need to. Unless you got something to do today."

"No. I'm all caught up on homework. I've got nothing tonight except to work ahead on Melody's paper."

"Well, we can take a long way back."

"Okay."

We walked for several minutes in silence. This wasn't anything new to us. I enjoyed the peace and quiet, and Tyler seemed to drift off. I could imagine him reviewing his classes and anything that he might need to study in the future. He loved to plan out his academic work. Sneezing fits broke his concentration. At one point, when we had made it deep into some side street with woods behind it, Tyler spoke up.

"Hey, Dylan?"

"Yeah?"

"Did your friend Charlie ever, did he ever cheat on his girlfriend?"

"No. At least not that I know of. We haven't been hanging out as much. But I'm sure he'd let me know if he did."

"Why? Why does he want to? Isn't that something you don't plan for?"

"Charlie's a dude who—he likes to prove himself. He likes to show off even if it hurts him. I thought he would grow out of it, but now, in college, it's like he's doubling down. What do you think of him?"

"I don't know if I'd get along with him. He's not like you. He does things like they're missions to be accomplished."

"You could say that. In high school he usually failed at what he tried, and it was hilarious. Mark and Derek made jokes about it non-stop, so did I. We're all pretty clever. That's how we met and formed our little group—quick wit and honors classes."

"Are you in any classes with them? I don't hear you talking about studying with them."

"No. We all have different majors, and really they're more interest-ed in other things. Mark's on a crusade to join a frat, but the rest of us aren't. Charlie's getting a little too caught up in himself. Like, I can't approve of what he's doing. He's trying to make mistakes; maybe he wants to make them before we're all grown-up. I guess college is a time when we all make mistakes, but he's—he's trying too hard."

Tyler took a few seconds before responding. "Dylan, did you ever—was there ever a point when you felt like you became a man? Sorry, I don't know how to ask that question."

I took my time to think about it. I wanted to give him an honest answer.

"When I lost my virginity. It felt like a tremendous weight had been lifted off me. From then on I knew that when someone called me a loser or a virgin, or not yet a man, it wouldn't bother me. It was the biggest moment of my life. It made me think that, if on the next day, I got diagnosed with a terminal illness, at least I wouldn't die a virgin. My life wouldn't be a waste. I had finally proven myself. It was a huge confidence boost, too. But it wasn't like it was a good experience either. It was awkward and weird. I could barely get the condom on. But it meant a lot to me. I was one of the last of my friends to do it. I felt like I had done nothing else to become a man. But what else is there you can do?"

Tyler sighed and shrugged.

"It's either that or violence. They don't call you a faggot if you're violent. You're told your whole life you have to accomplish some feat, but it's not like we're being drafted to fight Nazis with machine guns anymore. Or going out in the wilderness alone to fend for ourselves. And you have to do something to become a man. Acting tough doesn't cut it. Nobody buys that. And you can tell when they doubt if you've done enough."

We walked a few more paces before I continued.

"Then you gotta keep doing it. You have to keep proving it. Honestly, I'm getting desperate for a girlfriend just to prove it to everybody I'm meeting here. They don't know I dated two girls in high school. If I told them they'd deny it. And that's the other thing about becoming a man."

"What?"

"You have to try to disprove that other guys are men."

"Well, that makes sense."

"I'm sure you've heard plenty of it."

"Yeah, it's the reason I asked you in the first place. The same guy who picked on me to get his first girlfriend always told me I'd never be a man no longer how long I lived. That I'd never qualify. He said I was going to be a lifelong loser."

"Yeah, that guy was playing the game. That's following the rules. I mean, don't get me wrong, I don't like any of these rules, but who cares what I think?"

"When I was doing that one writing exercise for Melody about word origins I found out where the word 'bad' comes from. It was an insult for a man who wasn't manly enough. And now it's a word for anything negative. It's what made me think of that guy from years ago."

I nodded. "Every once in a while, school will accidentally teach you something interesting. That's when you pay attention."

"Yeah." Tyler started walking faster, with more bounce to each step he took. He looked like he was about to start skipping. He quickly gained ground on me.

"Hey. Wait up."

"Oh, sorry." He slowed down, but was still a few paces ahead. "I think the energy from my breakfast is kicking in."

"Don't leave me stranded out here."

Tyler turned around, shoes grinding pebbles, and walked backwards in front of me so that we faced each other. He was smiling as widely as I had ever seen him smile. His heels almost hit his butt with every step. He could sometimes get hyper after all the sugar and carbs from the breakfast.

"I think you had too much syrup."

"Sorry. I can't help it. Dylan, did you ever hear of the school shooting that happened in Arkansas in 1998?"

"I'm not sure. There were a lot in the nineties. Didn't I tell you about that one in Alaska?"

"Yeah, you did. That kid got a long prison sentence and he was bullied. But this Arkansas one was different. Two boys killed five kids at random at their middle school." Tyler held up his hand, fingers splayed, one for each victim. "They pulled the fire alarm and fired at the students and teachers coming outside. But they were the bullies. They picked on other kids."

"No, haven't heard of that one," I said.

"And they both got released from prison when they turned twenty-one."

"Sounds like they got off easy."

"I know. How ridiculous is that? They bullied kids and then practically got away with shooting up the school."

"That is crazy."

"I try not to think about it so much, it's so unfair, but sometimes I can't help it."

"Tyler, look behind you," I pointed to a broken section of the sidewalk behind him. Roots from a nearby White Oak had heaved and cracked the concrete into a jagged hill.

"Huh?" He pivoted to turn around but his foot caught on a raised section and he tumbled, landing hard on his back, his eyes wide open. He rolled off the uneven terrain and onto the soggy grass.

"I'm fine." He jumped back up to his feet. "I'm good." He held his hand up, telling me to stay away. I hadn't even moved since he fell. His face returned to that red flush I had seen in the cafeteria.

"There's no need to impress me Tyler."

He brushed off his shirt and shorts and hair. "I wasn't trying to. I was just walking backwards from a sugar rush or something."

"I meant more about the facts. I don't care if you fall all the time. But if you're looking up all those facts for me, you don't have to."

"I like to have things to talk about, so I look them up. Or else I can't think of anything to talk about if we're already hanging out. It's like studying for conversations. I've been doing that for years."

"I'm not trying to make fun of you, but you still don't have to do that. You can use your time for other things. I'd be fine with that."

"I thought you found those stories interesting."

"Yes, I do. I just don't want you burning up so much free time for me. That's all."

We started walking again, this time with Tyler next to me, walking forward. "I see what you mean," he said. "I'll try to keep it to a minimum."

We finished up the walk without saying much more. Along the way I hoped I hadn't discouraged Tyler into silence, but I couldn't bring myself to say anything else. We returned to Harris, where the glue situation still hadn't been resolved. Tyler went back to his room to chip away at citations and I went back to my room and took a long nap. We didn't meet up again until the next weekend. Even during the spring semester, when we hung out the most, it wasn't all the time. We weren't inseparable.

My circle of high school friends drifted apart during the spring. We still attended parties and hung out when our schedules allowed, but we met up less and less. A whole lot of factors led to this. Derek failed half of his classes out of sheer laziness. By the time of the glue incident, he had given up on academics at MU and decided to transfer to a technical college the next fall. He started drinking outside of parties, alone in his dorm. The last time I saw him on campus was when his roommate sexiled him and he slept over at my room in Henry's bed. He took some of Henry's beer back to his dorm in the morning. Charlie succeeded in cheating on his girlfriend at some party I didn't go to. He admitted it to her, she screamed and cried and threatened to break up with him, but after a cooldown period she agreed to stay together on the condition that he couldn't go to anymore parties without her. Charlie accepted her offer. He stopped going to parties with us at MU and started going to parties near Miranda's college with her. He said it was all worth it—the cheating, the drama, the different parties—and was glad he went through the experience. Nobody else in my high school group, including me, had ever cheated on a girlfriend. Mark scored straight C's in his classes after skipping most of them. He shouted in joy and pumped his fists when he broke the news that he had passed them all. He traveled to a party beach in Florida on spring break with some of his new friends; he couldn't tell me what happened there because he couldn't remember it, but he knew he had a good time. By April I was the only one of the group still able and willing to hang out. Mark had his new friends, and Charlie had Miranda, and Derek had his alcohol. I texted and messaged the other three to arrange more time together and they were cheerful and positive about meeting up but nothing ever came of it. Our group had effectively disintegrated at the end of our freshman year. At my high school graduation, I had expected those friendships to last well into adulthood. A last—and, I'll admit, desperate—call I made to Mark about meeting up before summer break sealed the deal for me.

"Hey Mark, so are you still free Sunday afternoon? We could have a late lunch; I know everybody'll be sleeping in till at least noon." I sat on the stairs in Harris, a place nobody used except for the fire drills.

He sounded groggy and sluggish, like he had to heave the words out. "Why are you calling me, man? Text, bro."

"I already did. I'm calling because your average response time is twelve hours."

"Where are you, bro? You sound like you're in a tank."

"I'm in the stairwell. It's all concrete, pretty weird in here. There's nobody, and it's super quiet. Too loud in the dorm. Are you getting that much busier now?"

"I'm making connections. Gonna pledge."

"And? About Sunday?"

"Hey, you should pledge too. Have to go through rush week first. The other guys at my dorm told me all about it." There was a commotion on his end of the line, full of yelling and things tumbling around. Mark cursed, said it wasn't at me, and told me he'd call me right back when he got to a quieter place.

I waited and he followed through. Now he sounded like he was inside a concrete bunker.

"Sorry about that. Some of these guys are pure assholes. Sunday, I don't know. I don't know what could happen on the weekends. Don't you hang out with that one guy? Your buddy?"

"Tyler, yeah. Still do."

"See Dylan, I knew you'd turn. How tight is his asshole? You've got to be fucking him. And I mean the up-the-butt kind."

"Yeah, but not in a gay way, just as friends."

"Oh, I see. Not serious yet." Mark coughed. "And he can deep-throat too?"

"Almost as good as your mom."

"Well, remember to practice safe sex. Condoms and loads of lube. Until you're married. Doing it raw is the only way to show commitment."

"So Sunday?"

"Look, I'll try my best Dylan. I'm going to the Rec Center as much as possible. Sundays are my best days to go there. Hey, didn't he have braces?"

"He's getting them removed once he gets back home after finals."

"Oh. I see. He's doing that for you. Then he won't pull out your pubic hair. Pretty smart."

I looked up and down the empty rows of concrete stairs, taking a moment. "Yeah, sure."

By Saturday afternoon everybody had cancelled for the Sunday lunch. Tyler had gone home for the weekend so I walked the campus by myself, exploring buildings I hadn't entered before.

Professor Melody never did make a lasting connection with either Tyler or me in the English composition class. She turned out to be another one of those dead-ends in life. I wanted her to be one of those teachers I would stay in contact with when the class was over—a casual mentor—but nothing ever came of it. Tyler submitted his final paper about allergies early to get feedback and rewrote some paragraphs. I gave him advice, and he helped me with my paper on causal links between video game violence and real-life violence; my paper argued that there were none. We both got A's and breezed through our other courses, which still mostly consisted of reviewing what we had memorized in high school. We didn't manage to sign up for any classes together for the next fall semester because Tyler had to take more engineering-specific classes. In April I got a job at a supermarket near my house—my first job since high school. I was scheduled to start once I moved out of my dorm.

Finals week of spring semester wrapped up in a lazy haze. Harris Hall, which had been bleeding students throughout the year as they dropped out or transferred, was too quiet on finals week. There were no floor meetings or parties. Students packed up and left right after their last final, which brought about a gradual emptying of the dorms. Parents and siblings drove up to help move out belongings here and there, burnt out and weary. Students disappeared every time I had a final. Henry's stuff vanished when I took one on Monday. Tyler left on Tuesday morning. I had to stay until Thursday for my last final—history. By then only Jeremy and one or two other students remained. All of the quad dorm guys had shipped out early, and their door stood wide open at the end of the hall. The quad room had huge windows with an encompassing view of half the campus, Lyndon Avenue, and miles of off-campus urban sprawl. I stepped inside the barren room more than a few times to take in the view. On Thursday before my final Jeremy caught me in there. I turned to meet his footsteps in the hollow dorm.

"Dylan, I thought you'd packed up and left by now."

"Nope still here. One more final."

"I have to stay until Friday. All the RAs have to be evaluated."

"Are you doing it next year?"

"Maybe. Trying to line up an internship."

"Did we ever find out who dumped all that glue?"

"No. Nobody fessed up to it. Sam admitted to puking in the shower but swore he wasn't responsible for the glue." Jeremy had a wad of crushed fliers in his hand. He squeezed them a few times like a stress ball.

"Technically, the rules we set up at the beginning of the year were never broken. We had puke in the showers but never shit. But it's been fun. Even with all the craziness—really because of the craziness. You had a blast, right? I mean parties and shit?"

"Some."

Jeremy looked down at me and then over to Lyndon Avenue, where a trickle of cars filtered through the lights and lanes. "Some. You need to ante up next year. You have to make the time you spend here worth your while. College is the best time of people's lives. After this it's family, bills, and working forty hours a week for the next thirty years. Probably forty years."

"Then death."

"Ha. Don't get so gloomy. You've got at least three more years here. Look, I'm a business major and it's pretty easy. Well, it's really easy, and I can do grad school right here at MU. So I'm making stories, stories I can tell, ones that I can relish years from now. They'll work for when I get into business and life. Build up that experience vault. It pays dividends."

"My parents," I sighed, "they didn't go to MU, but they love to reminisce about college. That's where they met. Went to football games and parties. They have lifelong friends they met in college. I guess they've been successful."

He grabbed my shoulder. "I'm going to play older brother here and give you some advice. That Tyler kid you hang with? I bet you'll be close for years. Don't ever abandon your social life. Living to the fullest starts with that. Oh, and whatever you do, don't miss out on life."

CHAPTER NINE

Summer

That summer, the summer after my freshman year, I started to date a girl I met after my shift at the supermarket. I won't name the supermarket, not for the company's sake, but for my co-workers, because some of them still work there.

A few weeks of pushing carts and stocking shelves at minimum wage had ground me down to a stupor. Nobody who worked there could ever remember what day it was. We always had to check our phones. There was one bright spot: After we closed the store, some of us would hang out and talk by the dark checkout lanes. This one girl would come inside to pick up one of my co-workers, and sometimes she stayed to chat and we had some fun one-on-one conversations. Eventually, I asked her out and her response was one of relief—she was about to give up on me. This was Katie. She went to MU, in the same year as me. The girlfriend of Tyler's only friend. You probably remember her interviews. The media wanted a female perspective on him and she was the closest female to Tyler willing to speak to them— none of his family members have spoken to the press, and he never had a girlfriend.

Besides my part-time job and going out with Katie, the one thing I did that summer was hang out with Tyler. Katie didn't meet him during the summer. She never personally met him until later on, a point she made in her interviews, though the media didn't air those parts. A lot of commentary was made on how my relationship with Katie affected my friendship with Tyler. It's been said that we grew further apart because I focused on her. This was never the case. She encouraged me to spend more time with him, but more out of a concern for me than him.

Since Tyler and I had left Harris, we had to hang out at each other's houses for the summer. The first day I saw his house—the same house in the news reports and specials, the same house he grew up in—the sun was baking the concrete roads into a blur. In the short drive, I had soaked my shirt in the biting June heat. And it was a fifteen-minute trip. We had lived so close for years and never knew the other existed.

Peach Grove was a small neighborhood of middle-class suburbia. The houses were all two-stories with siding. The yards were miniscule. The houses were cheaply-built, minimum-specification clones sold in the eighties and nineties. Tyler had complained about repairs his house needed, the way the siding fell apart, the uneven roof and poor insulation. His parents had bought it new to start a family and grew to regret it. The subdivision had been crammed onto the land, the houses stuffed close together, with few trees and little left untouched by the developers. Every square inch of each lot had been stripped of growth, stripped of topsoil, leveled, and the topsoil sold off. Even where I lived in Little Turtle, I had woods in my backyard that ran like a buffer zone between streets. I played in them when I was younger. No kids played outside when I drove down his street, wiping sweat off my forehead. I didn't see anyone outside. Only parked cars and plastic mailboxes and still homes.

I rang the doorbell once and Tyler answered.

"Hey." He looked calm, and smiled more than a little.

"Hey," I panted. "Don't go outside."

"They put out some kind of heat advisory." Tyler stepped aside and the air conditioning refreshed me as I walked in.

"Could you take your shoes off?" he asked.

"Sure." I slipped them off onto a mat next to a row of other shoes. Tyler was in socks.

In front of me, a hallway stretched to the back of the house and revealed a sliver of the kitchen. Running parallel to the hallway, a flight of carpeted stairs rose to the second floor.

"How's your job?"

"Alright—fine, I guess. Are you going to get one, or are you slacking off?"

"I'm applying for some. I still haven't fully unpacked from MU, and I don't have a car."

"Your voice sounds a little different."

"Yeah, I got my braces out." He showed his teeth, awkwardly drawing back his lips. They looked orderly and clean, like the house.

"Looks better."

"Gone forever. My sister says I finally look older than her."

A few seconds passed. I looked over the house again.

"Oh yeah, uh, this is my house. Plain. I've got a TV in my room."

He headed up the stairs. I followed.

The landing at the top of the stairs split into a short hallway. He led me down the left fork and through the first open door. Several other shut doors lined the hall. Over my many stays at Tyler's house I found out the house had four bedrooms—one master, one for Tyler, one for his sister, and one spare. All very cramped, like the developer had carved them out of the floor plan with a hatchet. It should've been a three-bedroom house.

His room looked like a slimmed-down dorm room. A bed tucked into the corner, a small TV on a stand near the door, a desk with a laptop, a few boxes of his dorm stuff. No posters or paintings on the white walls, unless you counted a calendar with scenic pictures of snowy mountains. A single date was marked—his moving home day. One window faced the street and the opposing row of houses. Lawns with grid patterns, driveways beginning to buckle. I checked on my parked car on the street. Nothing different. I had a feeling nothing would change about this view for the rest of the day, like it had been cast from a mold.

"Are you glad to be back here?"

"A lot more privacy, less yelling, it's quiet...yeah, you can say that."

"Wait are you dorming next year?"

"No, forgot to tell you. I'm gonna save money and stay here and commute. Of course, I need a car first." Tyler kneeled down to get his Xbox running, pulling out the controllers and untangling the wires. "Are you going to dorm?"

"Right now, that's my plan, but Charlie knows some guys who need one more for an apartment and they're offering a good deal. And it's close to campus."

"Where at exactly?"

"It's where Harris overlooked on the other side of Lyndon. We probably walked past it on those Saturday walks after breakfast."

"Wow." He smiled at the coincidence. "Start of summer and you've got everything going for you already."

"And I got a girlfriend."

Tyler looked at me, hinting at surprise. His eyebrows rose.

"Yeah, really. Her name's Katie. Goes to MU."

"Hey, congratulations," he said. "Is that the right thing to say?"

"Sure, I don't know."

"I don't want to ask a thousand questions about her, you'd probably hate that. I know my parents would bug me for every detail. Did your parents do that?"

"To an extent. But they bothered me more when I wasn't dating. Now they want me to make sure I go to more parties."

"Does she like to go to them?"

"Yeah. But I don't know many to go to in the summer. All the craziness was near campus or in it. And nobody goes back there in the summer."

"I had to go back to campus to buy a parking permit last week and it was a ghost town. It's deserted, just like Saturday mornings."

"Which garage are you parking at?"

Tyler handed me a controller.

"North. It's the big one. Permits are crazy. Over a thousand for the year."

"Ouch."

***

We settled into gaming and lost track of time. There were dozens of more questions I could've asked him or changes in my life that I could've told him about, like what kind of job he was looking for, how much my apartment would be, or if I could help him search for a car, but those didn't seem urgent. I wanted to get lost in the game with him, and the same went for Tyler. How we played worked like the spring semester, and a few facts emerged within three or four missions. It felt like we were right back in the dorm, except his bedroom had more comforts: air conditioning, a ceiling fan, and a quiet atmosphere.

The timeless, blissful void of the afternoon broke when somebody yelled for Tyler from downstairs. He paused the game and fumbled around with the controller, unsure of where to set it down. "I'm sorry. Hold on." He left the room and I heard his feet pounding down the stairs. I checked my phone. Katie had texted me a picture of fast food, claiming that it looked more attractive than I did. I tried to come up with an insulting, clever reply, starting and restarting, until feet pounded back up the stairs. Tyler poked his head in.

"You want anything to eat? Or drink? We've got plenty of stuff."

"Um." At our dorm rooms we had gotten so used to offering drinks and food to each other that by spring we stopped offering because our two fridges had become shared.

"Maybe something to drink."

I followed him downstairs and through the hallway. More sunlight washed out the kitchen and it took time for my eyes to adjust to the exceptional brightness reflecting off the white tile and chipped countertop. A window over the sink and a larger window in the dining room let the angled sunlight pour in. Tyler's mom stood by the sink, facing the window, examining a paper in her hand.

Tyler circled around the island to the fridge in his socks. A laptop, bills, and a checkbook sat neatly arranged on the island. He had forgotten to introduce me to his mom.

Tyler slammed the fridge shut and purposely slid around the island. He looked so comfortable. He moved freely and with flair, setting a jug of lemonade down and turning around to grab cups from a cabinet. On campus he had seemed so stiff by comparison, too aware of his own movements. I had never seen him so confident and un-self-conscious before.

"Hi, Mrs. Eberle?" I asked.

She turned, blanking out until she realized that she didn't recognize me. Then surprise. "Oh. Dylan. Hi. Nice to meet you. Tyler told me about you." She eyed him.

He looked up. "What?"

"Well, it's nice to meet you," I said.

"Tyler said you met in the first week of classes?"

"Yes."

"It's a shame I didn't get to meet you until now. You guys have been friends for nine months already." She had a commanding, clear voice and wide eyes, and was a little taller than me. I had always thought of Catholic mothers as small women with petite voices. If you paid attention to the news reports, you might have still missed her picture. She never had any social media accounts and wasn't fond of getting her picture taken. The only shots of her that came out were from random people who recognized her while she did errands.

"We were always on campus and neither of us had cars, so it makes sense I didn't see you. Tyler hasn't met my parents yet."

"I like to know who my son hangs out with. Tyler doesn't tell me much about what happens at MU." She paused to eye him again. "But from what I've heard, you sound like a nice boy and a good friend."

"Thanks," I said.

"We've got apple juice, lemonade, pop, and ice water," Tyler said.

"Ice water," I said.

"Lemonade for me," Mrs. Eberle said.

Tyler poured lemonade for himself and his mom.

She questioned me about my major, where I lived and other innocent things. She never ventured into any of the partying or drinking, though I got the sense that she trusted us to be responsible and still have a good time. After fixing our drinks, Tyler looked annoyed and impatient as his mom spoke, but he stood by and listened. I didn't mind getting to know her. I found out she had gone to college, though not MU, and had enjoyed it very much. She hoped Tyler was having fun there. He didn't let her know much when it came to anything outside of academics.

"Tyler, why don't you grab your sister and see if she wants anything."

"Let me guess where she is." Tyler moved out of the kitchen and opened the nearby sliding door, squealing it over the plastic tracks. A moment later he returned, his sister in tow. She was very skinny, like Tyler, and wearing a two-piece green swimsuit. She flew right through the kitchen, into the hallway, and didn't notice me.

"Sweetie, put on more sunscreen," Mrs. Eberle told her.

"Do you have a pool?" I asked Tyler.

"No, she's sunbathing. Does it all summer. Our neighbors have a pool but they never use it."

"And she's going to be sunburnt if she keeps it up like this," Mrs. Eberle added. She undid her ponytail, scratching her head and unfurling her dark hair. She had a habit of putting her hair in a pony-tail. I saw it a lot over the summer and sophomore year.

I went to the dining room to see the pool through the window.

"You can't see it. They have a privacy fence," Tyler said.

"Is it above-ground?"

"Yeah. It's a small one."

Tyler's backyard lay flat and unremarkable. A tall wooden fence marked its end from a house behind it. The sun had bleached the wood bone-white. The fence, cracked and showing signs of dry-rot, resembled the fossil of some giant, maybe the backbone of a dinosaur. Beyond that, more houses clad in siding crested over the bones.

A patio extended from Tyler's house. A pink beach towel covered one of those outdoor lounge chairs and a pair of pink sunglasses rested on the towel. Next to the sunglasses sat a Nicholas Sparks novel, its pages crinkled.

"Here." Tyler passed me a cup of ice water. I nearly downed it without taking a breath. Tyler made another for his sister and poured lemonade for his mom.

A distant toilet flushed and his sister reappeared in the hallway. Her body was drenched in sweat. It looked like she had gone swim-ming. I found out later her name was Chloe, and she was almost sev-enteen. No braces adorned her teeth and no acne blemished her face. Brash and extroverted and popular at school—the polar opposite of Tyler. She had more than enough social media accounts filled with pictures and selfies. And because she was not a minor when it hap-pened, the news had no problem sharing her pictures. Her life went viral before she could shut down the accounts.

"Here." Tyler offered her the ice water.

She shuffled forward, dragging her feet on the tile, and snatched it from him. Then she left, headed for the patio. Tyler refilled my ice water.

"So Dylan, do you have a girlfriend?" Mrs. Eberle asked. She looked right at me for the response and sipped her lemonade, eyes cresting over the cup.

"Yeah, I do."

"Mom, we're gonna go play some more now," Tyler said. "Dylan, you can bring that up to my room." He pointed at my drink.

———

A majority of our summer visits ended up like that. Hanging out at Tyler's house and sometimes my house worked better than the dorms. Less stress to deal with, fewer interruptions from the hallway, and no loud parties right down the hall. Details about his mom and sister emerged in chunks, usually in indirect or accidental ways. I'd overhear a conversation about his mom's job or Chloe's friends or an argument about her Friday-night-disappearing acts. Mrs. Eberle worked as a full-time paralegal on an odd schedule, which allowed her some weekdays off. Tyler kept asking for his own car, so he could drive to a job to pay for it, to her annoyance. He never did this while I was there; I heard about it from Mrs. Eberle. Chloe stayed committed to her backyard tanning and our paths rarely crossed. All three Eberles attended church every Sunday morning and ate out for lunch afterwards, sometimes with Tyler's grandparents. Occasionally Mrs. Eberle would give Tyler and Chloe little impromptu oral quizzes on Bible readings or the books of the Bible or the doctrines of Catholicism. Tyler always aced them; Chloe had trouble. But I didn't think of the Eberles as a deeply religious family. Religion didn't come up much and the quizzes were more tests of knowledge and memory. The few times I did eat supper with them, religious discussions never came up. Overall, the family was average, ordinary, to me.

Tyler never brought up his father during all of freshman year and I never saw him at the house. Through most of the summer I explained away his absence in my head, assuming he was a traveling businessman with a lot of work responsibilities which kept him away from home. The blooming possibility that his parents could be divorced festered in the back of my mind, gaining steam toward the end of the summer. I thought Catholic couples didn't get divorced. For it to be okay in the eyes of the church, they needed a special annulment, and that wasn't easy to get. Another possibility was that he had died. And I did not want to deal with the heavy awfulness of making Tyler bring it up by asking him where his dad was.

That fear of asking broke one night late in August at Tyler's. The whole summer up to that point had been uneventful with him. It all felt like a continuation of spring semester in Harris transplanted to our homes. We never met up anywhere outside of them. We didn't go to the movies or parks or any other places. Sometimes I asked him if he wanted to do something else—he politely said no every time. I came to understand this. Tyler had had enough of dorm life. He saw it as too chaotic. He wanted to stay home as much as he could before sophomore year began. And I couldn't blame him. His mood seemed to improve throughout the summer. He was more upbeat and energetic than he was on campus. He had no problem striking up conversations with his mom and sister or even arguing with them. I had never seen him argue with anybody during freshman year. At MU I had assumed he had a quiet, low-key personality all the time. I had been wrong about him. But either way, we grew closer, inch by inch, week by week, all of it a slow build-up to that one night late in August, when the dam burst.

CHAPTER TEN

Late August One Night

The shadows extended over the street, swallowing lawns, parked cars, and sidewalks. Tyler's home cast its shadow, dousing the house across from it in gloom. Porch lights flickered on, trying to dispel the inevitable night. I backed my head away from the open window. Legions of crickets chirped.

"I agreed to the apartment. It's official," I said. "No more dorms for me. And I can keep my car there on the street."

"Sweet." Tyler was at his desk, using his laptop. "Have you met any of them yet?"

"I've talked to one of the guys. He seems alright. I still have to sign the papers."

"Hey, you'll get more freedom. You can drive around. Don't have to rely on the meal plan."

"Plus, more personal space. Should be awesome."

"And now that I have a car too, I can drive down to you. Or if parking's tight I can walk from campus."

"I'll have to let you know how parking is. How's your job?"

"Mind-numbing. My boss still doesn't think I'm aggressive enough with the forklift."

Tyler had started a job at a warehouse moving, organizing, and cataloging boxes—fifteen hours a week at minimum wage. The happiest I ever saw him was when he told me he got that job, his voice cheery, with a raging smile and bright eyes. His mom bought him a used car on the condition he would pay it back with a portion of every paycheck he got. He was learning how to operate a forklift and some other machinery, but his boss thought he was taking too long to pick up on it because he was too afraid of damaging inventory. I told him not to worry.

"It's nothing to sweat over. You'll adapt. I had to adapt to angry customers who want to bicker about where certain food is located."

"I don't think I could do a job where you have to deal with the public. Anything customer service scares me," he said.

I checked my phone. Katie had texted.

"Katie's at work. She's bored."

"Does she have an apartment for this year?"

"No, a dorm. But a nicer one. In Sherman Hall. They're the premium dorms." I went back to my phone, texted Katie that I was with Tyler and turned it to silent.

It had been a week or two since I had last seen Tyler, and after we caught up on our jobs and living arrangements, we each had a litany of new facts to share, gathered over the summer. We talked about how the Romans nailed Jesus through his wrists when he was crucified, not through his hands; how extremely unreliable the M16 rifle was in the Vietnam War because of lobbying; how the United States overthrew democratic governments in other countries and replaced them with dictatorships; the Children's Crusade; the many times the world almost had a nuclear war. After shocking each other with what we had found, we paused. The crickets and humidity pressed into the room. Tyler's ceiling fan clicked or creaked as it spun. He told me the noises made it hard for him to fall asleep and if he turned the fan off, he soaked the bed in sweat.

"Have I told you I have a balancing kit for ceiling fans?"

"I don't think so. But it's fine. I don't need it."

"It sounds like you do."

He didn't respond. We sat for a little with only the ceiling fan making noise. Gaps like these would come up more in our sophomore year. Not awkward, just mental breaks. We had more on our minds. Tyler stressed over his job. He beat himself up over it.

"Have you watched the Roger Williamson video?" he asked.

"Which one is that?"

"A Formula One wreck in the seventies. Here, I'll bring it up. Back then drivers died all the time in races. But this one was on camera and like, awful in the worst way."

"I've seen crashes online. I might've already seen it," I told Tyler, now hovering over him.

He played the video, and it was brutal. I hadn't seen this one. A car wrecks, slides upside down, and comes to rest fully on fire with the driver still in the car. Another driver stops his car off the track and runs over and tries to flip the car over but can't. Some track officials come over but they won't help him flip the car over. All they do is give him one fire extinguisher, which doesn't do much.

Tyler pointed at the screen. "The driver who was trying to help said he could hear Roger screaming. After trying and trying to save him he couldn't stand it anymore and gave up. Nobody would help him."

The driver walked away from the burning wreck in despair.

"Crazy," I said.

"It's real tragedy right there in front of you. This is a few minutes long and it makes you feel more than most movies do."

We did a little more research and found that David Purley was the driver who had stopped to help Roger Williamson, his friend. He even signaled to other drivers passing by for them to stop, but they didn't. The track officials didn't have fire-resistant clothes, but we thought they could've still helped. Purley later retired from racing. He took up flying and died in a plane crash at age forty.

Footsteps approached and Mrs. Eberle strode into the room. Tyler kept his bedroom door open if his mom or sister were home. If they wanted to come in, they could. I never asked him why he did that. It seemed like a longstanding house rule Mrs. Eberle had made so she could keep an eye on her children, and I didn't want to force Tyler to explain by bringing it up, but I had noticed Chloe liked to keep her door closed.

"Hello Dylan." She gave a pleasant smile.

"Hi."

"Sorry to interrupt you two, but did you finish the laundry?" She looked at Tyler.

"Yeah. I put it in the dryer. Forty minutes."

"Did you take it out?"

"Not yet. I didn't get the chance. Dylan came over then."

"You have to take it out and finish it tonight. I'll be leaving soon and when I come back it better be done."

"I'll get it done." Tyler didn't show annoyance or frustration. It was all a matter-of-fact for him. He accepted the instructions as fate.

"Oh, and Chloe said she needs help with her summer reading project."

"Now?"

"She's not allowed to go out until she gets her opening paragraph and thesis written. And there's a boy who has been texting her a lot."

He looked down. "That means she'll be begging me for help."

"Are you guys leaving? You should get out of the house. I don't think it's good to be cooped up in this room all the time."

"Mom, I've got work tomorrow," he said.

"That didn't stop me when I was your age. I'd stay out till three and then drive to work and sleep in the parking lot of that golf course I worked at, then work eight hours."

Mrs. Eberle held a bottle of wine in her hand by the neck. She had on a light jacket and jeans, black socks over her feet. I could smell perfume. An attractive woman in her forties, she looked excited to go wherever she was headed.

"Are you going to keep your hair in a ponytail?" Tyler asked.

She reached back and grabbed her hair to check. "Oh, no, almost forgot." She turned and left the room.

"Sounds like you've got chores."

"I procrastinated all day. Sorry about that. I mean for the laundry, just couldn't get myself to do it. But Chloe should've started her paper earlier this month."

"Aren't you going to do it?"

"Well, you're here."

"I don't care. Sounds like you're almost done with the laundry anyway. Where's your dryer? I don't think I've ever seen it."

"It's in the basement. You're sure you're okay with this?" He looked up at me, the light from the ceiling fan almost glowing off his face. The traces of his acne were all but gone.

I smiled. "Your mom did say we should do something different."

Down the hallway we heard a shower running from the bathroom by the stairs. Pop music blared over the crashing water. Not blaring like loud, but like a small speaker had been turned all the way up, distorting the loudest parts of the song.

"There's Chloe," Tyler said.

"Does she have a habit of playing music while she showers?"

"Once she got a Bluetooth speaker to connect with her phone, yeah. But she only got that a couple weeks ago. I think it might be from that boy who keeps texting her."

Down the stairs, we circled to the kitchen and went down another flight to the basement. I had never been to his basement before. It was plain and unfinished and pretty empty. Boxes and plastic tubs stacked in corners collected dust. Tyler led the way to the washer and dryer in the corner. He yanked a cord to switch on a naked lightbulb. I spotted a long crack in the nearby concrete wall with dark stains below it, crumbled concrete on the floor below. He insisted he do the work himself, so I wandered around breathing in the cool, dry air. At first I thought he wanted to complete the laundry himself because he felt responsible for it, but the laundry included his sister's and mom's clothes and their underwear, so I watched the rest of the basement as a courtesy.

I liked unfinished basements. My friends had had them when we were younger and they made great indoor battle arenas, mini roller-hockey rinks, and hiding places. Over the years, their parents saved money and had them converted into entertainment centers and bars. After that, we had to stick to video games or movies on rainy days. I guessed Mrs. Eberle never recuperated financially from the housing crash or had no need to finish the basement. I wished I had known Tyler earlier, so then we could've played in his basement as kids and all through middle school.

Tyler carried a basket stacked with clean laundry up the stairs and I turned off the lights on our way up. Mrs. Eberle leaned against the countertop in the kitchen. Her bottle of wine waited near the sink and the dimming window. She looked over something on her phone. Her hair was no longer in a ponytail. It draped over her shoulders.

"I thought you were going," Tyler said as he rounded a countertop toward the hallway.

"No, got ready faster than planned. Your sister's ready."

I trailed Tyler down the hallway, caught between them.

He paused and called back, "She'll have to wait."

Up the stairs to the second floor, Tyler's bony arms strained under the bulky load. I wanted to help but I knew he wouldn't let me. Chloe appeared at the top of the stairs with a towel wrapped around her body. I looked down at my socks. Neither Tyler nor Chloe seemed to mind me as they worked out a plan to meet in the kitchen to start working on her paper. I didn't sense a deep rivalry between the two. They didn't raise their voices; Chloe's voice was speedy yet clear, while Tyler's remained calm and meek as he explained his need to hand out the laundry. Chloe dug out her clothes from the basket and continued past the stairs. As her steps receded, I looked up in time to see Tyler go down the hall and out of sight. Stranded on the stairs, I did an analysis on the risks and rewards of catching up to Tyler. If I saw Chloe up close in her towel, she might feel violated and I didn't want her thinking of me as some creep. On the other hand, I could get to see Mrs. Eberle's room, but that somehow also seemed like a privacy no-no. The master bedroom door was always closed. Mrs. Eberle had never been suspicious of me and was always happy to see me—I didn't want that to change. The master bedroom had taken on a sacred aura in my mind, the one place in the Eberle household that guests could not enter. And I never did.

I made the stairs my temporary hang-out spot for several minutes. It still beat standing alone at a party. I pulled out my phone and didn't have to worry about someone giving me strange looks or bumping into me. Only the scurrying upstairs and Mrs. Eberle running the sink broke the peace of the middle ground I occupied.

When we regrouped Tyler apologized for leaving me and apologized for stopping our time together to help Chloe, and would continue to apologize for both things the next couple of times I met up with him. I told him that I welcomed the challenge of coming up with a thesis for a high school paper. A chance to tackle one now with a year of college under my belt sounded interesting.

Chloe brought down her laptop and papers and set up on the kitchen table. We turned on all the lights and the windows turned black. She began explaining as we set up for a study session like Tyler and I had at MU, retrieving a few snacks and organizing the papers. Mrs. Eberle watched in amusement.

"Okay, listen Tyler." Chloe turned to make sure he was listening. "Mrs. Havert gave us a list of books to read and we had to pick one. So I chose this one because they made a movie about it and it's not one of those super-old movies."

"Which one? You didn't tell me which one you picked."

"This one." She pointed at a sheet. "*Into the Wild.*"

"I know about that," I said. "I wish my high school teachers let me pick a book from a list. We were just assigned ones to read."

"Great, so you can help us," Tyler said. He turned to Chloe. "So where's the book?"

"Over here." She got up and searched her backpack. She tossed it on the table.

"So how was it?"

"Are you kidding me?" Chloe looked appalled at his question. "I read about it online and watched the movie."

"But you'll read those romance novels."

"Sometimes. And those are different. I never read anything for school."

"Okay, tell me what's it about."

"This guy, he graduates college back in like 1990, his parents give him money, he gives that to charity, and goes hitchhiking all over America for two years. Then he hikes up to Alaska and lives alone in the wilderness, gets trapped there, and starves to death. And while he was traveling, he would explore places, out in the west, by hiking and canoeing and camping."

Chloe sat down at the table and Tyler stood next to her as she opened a new document. I examined the list of books she had to choose from.

"Did he work at all?" Tyler asked.

"He picked up odd jobs along the way. He stayed in one place for a while a few times and visited some cities. And sometimes he rode on trains to travel."

"And what're your ideas for the paper?"

"Right here." Chloe handed him a sheet of prompts made by the teacher. "She emailed the whole class these, a couple for each book, and I have to pick one."

Tyler scanned the prompts and then let me look over them. They each focused on one theme of the story and asked a lot of open-ended questions, so it gave some freedom to come up with an argument. One of them did bring up the ethics of his decision. The guy's name was Christopher McCandless. I had already seen the movie and knew about the real-life story. I didn't think Tyler watched many movies, and he gave no sign that he had even heard of this story or the movie. Mrs. Eberle walked over and picked up the instructions for the paper. Chloe set up the format and header for her essay. She tapped her fingernails on the laptop as Tyler consulted me about ideas. Our recent experience in Melody's class did help out. We selected topics that would have many examples in the text to pull from, as well as specific points to make up the body paragraphs.

"How about covering nature in the book? It's something great to explore but dangerous."

"Sure," Chloe groaned.

"Or there's Christopher's isolation. You could write about how he left his parents and sister to be alone, and the people he met along the way."

"I guess."

"Don't you care?" Tyler asked.

"But I want to be a designer. I don't need to learn how to write a paper about a guy who died years ago."

"Chloe, you are going to write that first page," Mrs. Eberle said. "If you don't contribute and come up with some ideas for your brother so he can help you then you can say goodbye to any plans you had for tonight."

She conceded and chose the theme of isolation. Tyler guided her through a few claims she could make and how to support them with quotes and reasoning. Mrs. Eberle, after reading the instructions, interrupted.

"What was wrong with him?"

"Who, this guy, McCandless?" Tyler said.

"Yeah, was he mentally ill?"

I butted in. "Because he went out on his own?"

"I don't see how someone in their right mind could do this." Mrs. Eberle looked worried scanning over the prompts. "How could he go to Alaska without the preparation and think that was a good idea?"

"He just did what he wanted to do," Tyler said. "It sounds like he was searching for something we don't want. That's why we have to write papers, to try to understand."

Mrs. Eberle sighed. "How could he walk away from his life? He abandoned so many things. He got a college degree, his parents gave him money, he had everything in front of him. Something in him had to be off."

"If you ask me," I said, "he's the sanest person I've heard of. I like what he did. Gives up his possessions and goes out on his own. Doesn't fall in line with what everyone expects of him. That's rebelling. It's not pretty, but I don't think it's supposed to be. He went against the grain."

"I think he had a death wish," Chloe said. "It was his one last vacation."

"A vacation that took two years?" I asked.

Mrs. Eberle laid the paper back on the table. "He died when he was twenty-four. That's too young. And his family didn't know where he was or what he was doing the whole time. I'm sure he worried his parents to death."

Though I didn't know Mrs. Eberle that well and wanted to remain polite, I couldn't let this one rest. I admired McCandless. I considered him one of my role models. "Yeah, he abandoned his car and took the license plates so no one could find him. It makes you wonder why. But you have to look up his whole story. His dad had another family.

He was still married to his first wife when Chris was born to another woman. He had two families at the same time. Chris's sister wrote a book about it. She said their father was abusive. I bet that made a big difference in Chris's decisions."

"If he was running away, he didn't have to risk his life doing it. He could've taken precautions. That paper said he went to Alaska with none of the right gear."

"Yeah, he got a little too ahead of himself. But like Tyler said, he did what he wanted to do. Would you rather have him do what his parents wanted him to do, living unhappily? And lots of people have done what McCandless did, back then and now. Some have lived most of their lives in the wilderness. A guy named Richard Proennecke lived in Alaska alone for thirty years. Chris is a famous example because he died young and this book was written about him. Are all those other people mentally ill?"

"I do think people should take risks in life, don't get me wrong, but keep them in proportion. He could've had a lifetime of planned travelling and taken risks elsewhere, like with dating, partying, and spending quality time with friends—which he missed out on. Then stay in contact with his family, explain what he was doing and weigh the risks. Like a mature adult."

I took a second to think. I didn't want to take this too far. The tension was rising, and arguing with a friend's mom carried with it a deep awkwardness. When Mrs. Eberle spoke she looked at Tyler and Chloe as much as she looked at me, like she was lecturing them. They both watched our debate closely. I was challenging her in a way that neither of them had challenged her before.

"What you're saying is that he didn't take the right kind of risks, the pre-approved risks he was supposed to take. He broke from what was acceptable and now gets seen as mentally ill. Is it so bad to want something wildly different?" I decided not to push the argument any further and called it off. "Alright, there's your paper Chloe, I hope you were taking notes." I smiled at her. They all laughed. That was the first and only argument I had with Mrs. Eberle. Though I did look up to McCandless, Tyler had to help with Chloe's paper, Chloe needed to write it, and Mrs. Eberle had to leave. I had taken up enough of their time and interfered too much.

Chloe resumed typing an opening paragraph for her paper. Mrs. Eberle offered me something to drink and insisted that she get the drink for me. She and Tyler never failed to offer food and drinks when I came over their house. They kept the fridge and cabinets full. Yet they all managed to stay skinny. The only thing the kitchen lacked was a large supply of alcohol. My dorm fridge had held more beer and liquor than the Eberles' did.

Mrs. Eberle handed me a can of pop and headed back to the other side of the kitchen to help Chloe and Tyler. I opened the can and sipped the carbonation surging up. I had never paid much attention to the fridge door over the summer. Old cartoonish magnets and pictures and report cards stuck to the door in a collage that had once been organized, but over time been bumped and scooched into a mess. Most of the pictures showed the Eberles when they were younger and on vacation. A lot of snapshots of a tiny Tyler in swim trunks standing next to a pint-sized Chloe and a tan Mrs. Eberle. I scanned over them, watching Tyler and Chloe grow up at different landmarks and cities, smiling in the sun or under the lights, grasping toys or bags, revealing a silent slice of excitement. The pictures lasted all the way up until their adolescence, where they stopped. The earliest ones restarted from there, showing a toddler Tyler and a glowing Mrs. Eberle hovering over him. No Chloe yet. The one adult male in any of the pictures was his grandpa, his arms wrapped around the shoulders of Tyler's grandma. They all had small noses and a vague similarity of soft faces and thin bodies.

"Dylan what do you think of this?" Tyler asked me from across the kitchen.

"Yeah Dylan, you're the expert. I should use you to write the paper," Chloe said.

"That's twenty dollars per hour. But if it's a rushed paper then it's double that."

Tyler and Mrs. Eberle smiled and Chloe sulked for a second before turning back around to her laptop. Mrs. Eberle hinted to me about possibly tutoring Chloe during her senior year because her grades had been lagging. She said Tyler and Chloe, as brother and sister, couldn't work together for extended periods of time. They didn't fight anymore; what happened was closer to a stalemate of refusing to help. Chloe opened her mouth to protest the idea but Mrs. Eberle had a slight gasp at her watch, said some goodbyes, issued a warning to her, and headed to the garage.

We waited until the garage door shut and the sound of Mrs. Eberle's car faded into the night. The kitchen felt emptier. Chloe rushed the rest of her opening argument, pulling every scrap of information we gave her. She rounded off the first page in a flurry of disorganized writing and ignored Tyler's advice to revise the ugliest parts. Tyler and I stepped back as she saved the document, slammed her laptop shut, and raced upstairs to finish getting ready to go out. He smiled at me and I returned the feeling. My sisters had done the same thing when I was a kid.

Tyler got himself a pop and brought out some pretzels. We munched and sipped while standing at the island. He wanted to watch Chloe leave. I didn't know if she was allowed to use Tyler's car, or if someone would pick her up, because she didn't have her own car.

"When does Chloe start school?"

"End of next week."

"That's only a little before we start. You ready for our second year?"

"With driving it'll be easier. And I think it'll be better for studying, you know, with less distractions. I'll be able to concentrate here."

"Should I barge into your room and start a party like Jake did? And bring some friends?"

Tyler smiled. "You don't have to do that." He crunched down pretzel after pretzel, only breaking to swallow or talk.

"We can set this up for a rave. Tear down your neighbor's fence and start a pool party."

Clattering and movement from Chloe's room could be heard over our chewing.

"Will Chloe get her paper done in time?" I asked.

"Sure, whatever doesn't get done by the night before it's due she'll stay up until it's complete. I thought that was crazy until MU. You know all those guys on our floor who wrote a full paper the night before."

"That's almost everybody who does that."

"And I still can't believe some of them skip most of their classes and only attend the last week. You can't catch up on a semester like that. I don't know how anyone does it, and they pass. That's the worst part."

"What do you think about this assignment for Chloe?"

"It's a great subject to write a paper about. If I had read the book, I would've used it for Melody's class. There's so many ideas."

"You think McCandless did the right thing? Or maybe that's not the right question. People go a bunch of different ways with what he did. Some admire him, others thought he was suicidal, or insane, or just dumb, or too idealistic."

Tyler took a second to finish the pretzels he had in his mouth. "He was an adult, right?"

"Yeah, he was twenty-two when he left home."

"I think that should be old enough to be aware of what happens down the road. It's not like he was a kid. He did what he did, had a different set of goals in life. Just not the ones we're used to. And some don't like it." He shrugged.

"I've never told my parents this—I doubt they've even heard of him or the book—but I'd be interested in doing something like he did. I don't have any concrete plans for it. I dream about packing up one day after college and leaving, going wherever. Go where I want, meet people, see something different for once."

Tyler seemed to relish that vision too. His eyes lost focus. We fell into silence, running scenarios in our heads. Driving alone on an empty expressway, sun bright, windows down, forests lining the roads, and gray mountains dipped in snow cresting over the horizon. I could smell the fresh air.

Chloe almost tumbled down the stairs in a volley of thuds. We ran to check on her but she recovered swiftly, swinging a purse over her shoulder and refusing to accept Tyler's help.

"I'm fine. I said I'm fine and I'm fine. God, I'm going to wait for him right outside the door."

"You're not hurting?"

"No. Leave me alone, you sound like mom."

"Okay. Alright." Tyler opened the front door for her. Chloe stepped out and slammed it behind her.

"She's only like that when she's going out." Tyler scratched the back of his head. "Um, can we go to my room? My mom says I have to keep an eye out for her." He shrugged and glanced at his feet.

"Well, sure. Should we clean up in the kitchen first?"

"That's a good idea. I'll go do it."

"I'll help."

"You don't have to."

We tidied up the papers and cleared the island of its dusting of crumbs. I wrapped up the bag of pretzels to take upstairs. My socks slid on the tile floor. The blackened grout and white squares reminded me of a chessboard. Veins of gray flowed through the ceramic, disrupting its simplicity and neatness. Tyler washed out plastic dishes and stuck them in the dishwasher.

"Ready to go?" I asked.

"Yeah."

The house seemed even bigger without Chloe in it. Giant and hollow. The upstairs hallway stretched out deeper and wider under our socks.

"You like living here?"

"I don't know how well I can answer that. Other than Harris, I've lived here my whole life. I don't have any other house to compare it to."

"I used to live in a smaller house. There's less privacy. You feel like you have less personal space. You hear too many things you shouldn't. But I didn't realize it until I moved out and looked back."

"It can be easier to see some things at a distance."

Tyler's room welcomed us back with summer air. Humid and warm. I took a deep breath. There was a whiff of dying leaves. Tyler shut the door behind him. He moved his desk chair to the window. I sat on his bed. He didn't turn the light on. The uncountable porch lights, garage lights, and indoor lights in the neighborhood gave us a good view of the whole street. We couldn't see Chloe because there was a small roof over the front door. You might remember how his house looked from all of the news footage. Some broadcasts took place on the street we were looking at.

With the bedroom door closed and only one window it felt like we were right back in Harris Hall on a Friday night, minus the noisy hallway. We kept watch over the motionless street, not talking. The crickets held any awkward silence at bay. We alternated taking swigs of pop. It was peaceful. Those were the moments I looked forward to most in friendships: the sublime. Tyler and I reached those heights several times. Sitting there in the stillness, guarding nothing, a satisfying blankness. I didn't know how long it lasted and I never checked his clock radio for the time. We had both emptied our pops before a car pulled up to the house. Chloe darted to it across the lawn and ducked into the sedan. It lurched forward and away.

"When do you think she will be back?"

"Early in the morning. Long after my mom comes back and you're gone and I'm in bed."

"Has she gotten into drinking yet?"

"Not that I know of. I think it's more about boys than drinking."

"Oh."

Not more than a minute later, a different car crawled into view. It slowed and turned to the house right across the street. A silver two-door Audi. The polished bodywork seemed to ooze over the tires in the glossy porch light. A tall young man in a suit exited the driver's side and a young woman exited the passenger's. Even at a distance, lit by weak porch lights, she looked stunning in a tight red dress.

Tyler rested his head against the window frame. His body was loose and splayed out on the chair, a big difference from his usual tight and hunched stance. "That guy, he's Joe. I grew up with him here. He's three years older than us."

"Does he go to MU?"

"Yeah. He got a big scholarship too, scored better than I did on the ACT. I know he wants to go to some impressive business school to get his master's."

Joe rounded his car and embraced the woman, grabbing and then caressing her waist. She held his shoulders and they began to talk in voices too soft for us to pick up.

"Who's she?"

"I don't know. He always has a girlfriend. She seems new."

"She seems gorgeous. Wow."

"Yeah. Joe was in—" Tyler shifted his head on the window frame. "—in our class with Melody in the spring."

"Really? I don't recognize him."

"Well, you know how we always sat by the windows? He was always on the opposite side."

"You never spoke to him in class, did you? You never pointed him out to me."

"Nope. I haven't spoken to him in years. We looked at each other once in class, and that was it."

"An old friend who's now a stranger? I get that."

"No, not like that." Tyler made a devious, knowing smile as he tilted against the window frame.

"What is it?"

"Remember that kid I told you who got his first girlfriend by picking on me and that impressed her?"

"A little bit, yeah."

Tyler nodded in Joe's direction. I hadn't seen Tyler like this before. He seemed very confident in what he was telling me, almost enjoying it.

"Oh, okay. That's who Joe is."

"Yep. One time he invited me to this party he was having in his basement. It was all of his friends from school. I didn't know anyone. That girl he impressed was there. They were drinking beer and talking about who had had sex. I was in the seventh grade, you know, I was terrified. They were public-school kids, all older, and I had never been to a party like that. I was too stupid at the time to realize Joe had only invited me as a way of getting that girl's attention. About an hour in Joe had me stand in front of his friends to introduce me, being really nice and polite. I honestly believed he was trying to make me feel included. Then, when his friends were telling me their names he reached over and pulled my shorts down to the floor."

"Shit."

"The good news was, my underwear stayed on. The bad news was I was wearing tighty-whiteys."

"Oh boy."

"It wasn't good. At all. This was when everybody wore boxers. I almost wish he had taken my underwear down too. Cause I had never heard so much laughter in my life. Joe fell down on the floor and started punching the carpet he was laughing so hard. Their response shocked me so much I think it took thirty seconds before I pulled my shorts back up."

"Assholes. If you were wearing boxers they probably would've gone down with your shorts."

"I guess so. I had a belt on my shorts, but I wore it loose so the shorts wouldn't ride up too high, cause then they'd have made fun of me for that."

"You try to fit in and you pay for it."

Tyler nodded. "I didn't even leave the party right away. I didn't want them to think of me as a coward. I can't be a coward. So I hid in a back corner. After they calmed down some of them started making out. Joe and that girl made out. That was the first time I saw kids around my age kissing."

Joe and his girlfriend began an impromptu slow-dance in his driveway. Tyler watched them while talking to me.

"I've never told anybody that story."

"You kept it secret all this time?" I asked.

"It's never been a secret. Joe and all of his friends told everybody they could at their school. Kids at St. Anne's heard about it too. I got a lot of odd looks at school. A rumor went around that my underwear had come down too and that my, uh…that I was very small down there. I pretended that the whole thing didn't exist and hoped it would go away, which it never completely did."

I asked Tyler for Joe's last name in case I had heard of him, but I hadn't. Joe had gone to a different public school than me.

"If it's any consolation," I said, "I never heard of a kid who went through that. The rumors never spread as far as Little Turtle."

"Oh. I became pretty famous at Joe's school, even though I never went there."

"So is Joe still a jackass?"

"I don't know. That party was one of the last times I ever spoke to him and we live across the street from each other. I know he gets good grades, always has. He liked to use his brain to get at me more than his muscles. Planned stuff out." Tyler stopped there. He seemed caught up in the dancing on the driveway.

"How long have you known him?" I asked.

"Oh, for years. Both of our parents moved into these houses before we were born. I remember him when I was in kindergarten."

I took in a deep breath and exhaled in a big sigh. "Tyler, I wish we had known each other growing up. If only we lived a little closer, and my parents sent me to Catholic school, we could've been great friends. Maybe Joe wouldn't have done such a horrendous thing to you."

"That wasn't the worst thing he did to me. No. We played together for years, along with some other kids on the street. And every time he made it about putting me down. Some of the neighbor boys and girls would sometimes join in on it. And he turned everything into a competition: tag, capture the flag, kill-the-man-with-the-ball, basketball, squirt-gun fights." Tyler smiled to himself. "He always won. I always lost. He was smarter, older, stronger, and taller than me. Every once in a while I'd be good at a game, so he would change the rules until he had an advantage and then win. If I challenged the rule change, he'd challenge me to a fight, so I'd back down. He loved competitions. That was how he justified beating me and hurting me. When I went to my mom crying or bruised it was all because of a game. Joe never straight-up beat the crap out of me. My mom would never have been okay with that. All the adults liked Joe. They thought he was a good kid. But he was a ruthless dictator, hell-bent on crushing me."

"I know where you're coming from, Tyler. I never had one single kid who picked on me a ton. But I did have some rough times in school. Got picked on because—because I was there. They shoved me around. I got sick of being called a cocksucker, retard. Saw it happen to other kids every day too. There was a boy with a locker next to me who had his head crushed into the locker when he bent down to get his books. Sometimes he fought back. You ever see any fights?"

"A couple."

"Every fight I saw was a bullied kid who went ballistic. It's like he'd had enough and saw red and attacked the bully with everything. Everything. It was awesome. I always secretly cheered him on. Shit, if it was a bully who'd picked on me who was finally getting a taste of his own medicine, I wanted to join in on it. Those were the best."

Joe and his girlfriend had stopped dancing and were talking to each other in soft voices again. They giggled and pressed their noses together.

"He's the only person I truly hate in this world."

I didn't say anything. Tyler was still speaking in his normal voice and I couldn't hear any malice in it, which really worried me. I couldn't remember a time when Tyler had spoken that way about anybody. If he had cursed Joe and turned red in the face from rage, I would've been less worried. But he was so blank, staring out of the dark room like he had at the fall party during beer pong. He spoke about Joe as if he was detached from any of the emotion he described.

"Joe did mess up once though. Big time."

"How so?"

"One of his favorite games to play was paintball. Joe, me, and some other kids from around here, we'd ride our bikes to some woods nearby. The woods is gone now. They cleared it out and built houses there, but Joe loved to play there, not just paintball. He was our unofficial leader, and he chose what games we played. It seemed normal enough on that day—he picked paintball and everybody went back to their houses to get their gear. We had played it several times before. My mom wouldn't let me have a paintball gun or any of the equipment, so Joe let me borrow his old stuff."

"Your mom was okay with you playing paintball?"

"I didn't play at first. I told Joe that I'd asked my mom if I could play and she said no. But really, I didn't even ask her, because I was afraid she might say yes, and I was terrified of what Joe would do to me with paintballs."

"Yeah. And you couldn't tell Joe that you didn't want to play—"

"Because then I'd be a coward. A boy who didn't want to play because he might get hurt was basically committing suicide. They'd still be calling me a faggot if I'd done that. There was even a girl who played paintball with us a few times. I relied on the excuse that my mom didn't let me play. But my plan only worked for a while. Joe went to my mom one day when she was doing yard work and made a case to let me to play paintball. I guess he found out that I had never asked her. He explained to her that he had a spare gun, helmet, and pads and that he would watch out for me."

"He convinced your mom?"

"Yep. He was good at convincing. He was very friendly to adults." Tyler lifted his head off the window frame and sat back in his chair. He looked at me. "The next day she told me what happened and that I was allowed to play paintball. So I lost my excuse and I had to play."

"How was paintball?"

He shook his head. "I had to use all his old stuff. The helmet, mask, and pads were fine, but his gun was awful. It jammed all the time and was pretty inaccurate, like the M16. His new gun was nice and powerful. He won a lot and I lost a lot, but sometimes we'd be on the same team. Despite all of that I started to like paintball, running around, you know, crouching behind trees and logs, and getting to shoot the other kids, but none of them ever stood up for me, or stood up to Joe."

"I see. He targeted you over the others?"

"Definitely." Tyler gave a big sigh. "I still had fun, until he started freezing his paintballs."

"That's dirty. I've heard of kids who did that."

"And he was the best shot out of all of us. His two favorite places to hit me were my head and my crotch. I had to hold back tears sometimes. He would cry from laughing so hard. But everything he did was still in the limits of the game. He could still rationalize everything. He would say that it was all part of the game, the competition, that it would get me used to what real life would be like."

"What bullshit."

A distant door slammed and we both leaned forward to see that Joe and his girlfriend had gone inside. Lights turned on inside Joe's house. The porch light by the driveway remained on.

"The mistake that he made was when he went outside of the paint-ball game to hurt me. I have to back up the story here, sorry," Tyler said, flashing his old innocent smile and readjusting himself on the chair. His expression settled into that blank look again. "When we had squirt-gun fights and I did well, and soaked Joe pretty good, once the fight was over he would shove me to the ground and hold me there and everybody else playing would come over and empty their guns on me. I had, I guess, you could call 'asked for' that as a price I had to pay for winning. He was only making things even. So he had gone outside of the game before, but squirt guns only got me wet. He didn't do that for paintball. I'm sure he had calculated the risks were too great that I could get really hurt and he would be exposed for what he was doing to me."

"Did you understand all of this back then?"

"No. It took years of going over all of those events to figure it all out. I don't think I got his strategy until late in high school. He had me figured out. He could tell when I was close to my breaking point and ease off of me, no matter what game we were playing."

I nodded. I had to keep reminding myself to let him say what he wanted at his pace.

"So, yeah, his big mistake with paintball—I don't remember it. I only know about it because of the other kids who were there and saw it all happen. It was in the summer. We played a few rounds and I got Joe right in the neck and he cried out in pain and it left a big welt. His eyes watered. Then we played some more rounds. Joe even stopped one round when my gun jammed and helped me fix it, something he never did. Then, later, when we were all getting tired, he called us together and told us to take a break. It was hot and humid, and he told us to take off our pads and helmets to cool down. He didn't. He said he was strong enough to deal with the heat. After we took off our pads and helmets and set down our guns I leaned on a small tree. Joe stood in the middle of our group. And he still had his gun. Without warning he raised it and shot my crotch and then started shooting as fast as he could at me. He didn't say anything. He didn't laugh, no smile, nothing. He had a hopper full of paintballs and just unloaded on me. I turned and ran away as fast as I could and he got me in my back and butt. They said there was a ditch in front of me that I was heading to. But there was a big exposed root that I tripped over and I went flying into the ditch headfirst. Nobody saw where I landed, but my head hit something hard, either a rock or another root and knocked me unconscious."

"Oh my God."

"The other kids ran over and tried to wake me up but I didn't. Blood was running down my face." Tyler looked down. "Like R. Budd Dwyer. Joe walked over with his gun and yelled at me, 'Get up weakling, stop being a faggot!' I think he didn't believe it. One of the kids had to run to a nearby house and call 911. Joe went back to the other guns and emptied his hopper and told the other kids that it was an accident. Said he just wanted to even the score from me hitting him in the neck and he didn't mean to really hurt me." Tyler stopped there and stared down at his legs, head hanging from his shoulders. "Sometimes I think I remember parts of it, in little flashes, but I'm sure that's my mind imagining it. It's not too hard to see Joe doing something like that. There were other times when he would go quiet if he felt he had been wronged and then lash out at me. Anyways, I had a severe concussion. Six stitches for a gash on my head. Technically I had a skull fracture, too—but only a hairline crack, plus bleeding in my brain. The doctors said I was lucky I didn't split my head open. Oh, and I don't remember the hospital either. My mom had to tell me everything later. She was—was beside herself. It was the most upset I've ever seen her; it's the closest I've ever been to death." Tyler cocked his head up to me, his mouth hanging slightly open.

"How did you recover from that?"

"The doctors were worried about brain damage, at my age. I was still young, still had a developing mind. I had headaches, and the memory loss. I had trouble thinking for a while, like my mind was foggy, but that was expected. I'd get angry for no reason. Just full of rage out of nowhere. I couldn't play video games, wore sunglasses inside. At least I got to miss a lot of school. And I'm never absent from school."

"I've never had a concussion. Got bruises from other boys hitting me, or trying to fight me. And then broken bones—from accidents."

"That's another thing. I've never broken a bone, but bones heal and grow back stronger than they were originally. With a concussion, that's brain damage, that's permanent. My mom did say I was a little different after it. Like I was a little darker, bitter."

We fell silent. The lights in Joe's house were still on. Outside crickets chirped, interrupted by a few distant cars.

"Joe apologized once I had recovered. He came over and said sorry to my mom, but not to me, and I was there. She yelled at him. He had broken his own promise to her that he would watch out for me."

"Oh, I bet you were pissed."

Tyler shook his head. "No, I was more sad than anything. I kept asking what I had done to deserve this. What had I done wrong? Where was karma? And besides, my parents didn't like me getting very angry at anything. They said anger never helped."

"Did she accept his apology?"

"Yep. She made me forgive him too. I didn't want to, but my mom reminded me about forgiveness and what it meant to be Catholic. Joe seemed very sorry for what he did, but he liked to appear genuine, like he had at his party, and then trick me. I think he was there to do damage control, and it worked. The adults on the street still liked him.

They viewed it as just two boys who got into a fight over a paintball game. His parents took away his paintball guns for a while, then gave them back. I was never allowed to play paintball again, even if Joe wasn't playing."

"Did you hang out with Joe after that?"

"Not at first. I stayed in my house as much as possible. Joe and some of the neighborhood kids would come around and ask me to play but I'd say no every time. I didn't want to go out there at all, even if they weren't playing some stupid game. My mom understood, at first. Later she said I had to play with other kids again and socialize, that I couldn't stay inside all the time and be a recluse. I argued against it. I said Chloe never had to play with Joe. But she played with other girls on the street. So yeah. I gave in and played with them again. I regret that big time. If I had stayed inside, I would've never have gone to that party in seventh grade and been humiliated." Tyler sighed and looked out the window.

"I know what Joe did to you sucked, and I hate him now, but I gotta say, you don't sound like you hate Joe. I thought you said you truly hated him."

"My mouth's getting dry. I usually don't talk this much." He cleared his throat.

"Do you want to go down and get a drink?"

"Yeah, I think—think so." Tyler started to get out of his seat but then stopped, and hovered, staring at me with a panicked look, and then sat back down. His hands gripped the armrests. "I shouldn't have said that I hate Joe. I didn't mean it. I just stay away from him. I get enough of him in my nightmares. He chases me and catches me every time and pulls me down. He stomps me and stabs me, or shoots me, sometimes with a real gun. I can feel the blood surging up my throat. He watches me die. I would've dropped Melody's class when I saw he was in it, except you were in the class and I didn't want to explain it to you."

"Oh." I wanted to offer words of solace but that was all I could muster.

"I'm going to get a drink now." He stood up and walked straight out of the room.

As his footsteps receded down the stairs, I turned on the light in his room. It felt too dark after that talk. I looked over his room again, noting the bookshelf half-filled with books and half-filled with toy cars and LEGO sets coated in dust. Trophies, medals, and ribbons rested on his tall dresser in an orderly array. Some were for childhood sports teams, others for academic achievements. One for an essay contest leaned next to a thick stack of 1st Honors ribbons from St. Anne's. His dorm possessions from freshman year had been put away, and the only messy space was the top of his desk: a pile of candy, change, keys, pens, paper, and flash drives next to a sleeping laptop. His closet door was closed. He had a lot of old stuff in there, like old toys and school papers and old video games and controllers. I had seen all of it earlier in the summer. Almost everything in his room came from a time when Joe was still bearing down on him. I thought of telling him to get rid of some of this old crap, make even more distance between him and Joe, but I didn't want to tell him what to do. He had gone through enough. Instead, I wanted to say sorry for making him have to take a class with Joe, even though I had no idea who Joe was at the time.

Tyler returned sipping from a glass of ice water. The ice clinked with every movement he made. We both sat back down. Tyler had his legs pressed together, holding his cup awkwardly above them.

"What did your dad do when he found out you got a concussion?"

"Didn't say much. He said he got into fights too. Said I should consider myself lucky and not complain about it."

"Not to be mean to your dad, but that's heartless."

"It's okay. I don't see him that much. My parents divorced when we were little."

"Does he live around here?"

"Yeah, not that far from here. With his girlfriend. I have a key to his house; I can go over whenever I want."

"Do your parents get along?"

"Well, they're nice to each other, but they're distant. Kind of like a business relationship I guess."

"I see."

Tyler sipped more from his glass. "I just want to say thanks for doing all of this."

"Don't think of this as a favor. I'm not trying to score karma points."

"I've imagined trying to talk to somebody like this and they would laugh at me and make fun of me for it, like Joe would. Anything I told him he'd turn against me. I haven't had a talk like this with anyone. And Joe's been somebody I haven't talked about since I stopped hanging out with him."

"Is your plan now to try and forget about him?"

Tyler looked down and then across the street. "I'm not sure. I don't think that will work. I still see him, still hear about him. He's a success story. When we were kids all the adults thought he would grow up to be a good man. I guess that's become true. Scholarship, a girlfriend, tons of friends. Everybody thinks he's going to be big in the business world. They say he's ambitious and outgoing, got the right stuff." Tyler bit his lip and crossed his legs. He scanned the room until his eyes settled on me. More wanted to come out of him. I could feel it. More secrets, more memories. I think he was afraid of sleeping that night because he knew Joe would be visiting him.

I bit my lip. "Why don't we start back up on *Resident Evil?*"

CHAPTER ELEVEN

Ceramic Shards

Sophomore year started slow. I moved into the off-campus apartment with the three guys Charlie had told me about. The apartment was a nice improvement from my old dorm: It offered more space, more privacy, and better sanitary conditions than Harris Hall. It had air conditioning and a tiny kitchen. I parked my car right outside on the street and used it to drive to work or take Katie out on dates. On some weekends and holiday breaks I drove back to my house and ate with my family. To get to classes I had a short, pleasant walk to campus across Lyndon Avenue. It was liberating. The campus no longer held sway over my life. It made living in a dorm feel all the more like prison.

My roommates watched a lot of television when they were in the apartment. Netflix, sports, reality shows, cartoons—they didn't seem to be too picky about what they watched. They left and came back at intervals I couldn't keep track of. But they wouldn't disappear for days at a time. It was a relief not having another Henry. With one or more of those guys around we could always fill the air by talking about classes or random things. It kept my mind off the mounting stress. They saved their partying and drinking for places outside of the apartment. It was a nice arrangement. Beer filled the fridge and liquor lined the top of the cabinets. The apartment served more as a quiet supply room than anything else.

I took on a heavier class load—five classes total for the semester, including an introductory psych course as an elective. Homework took a little more time but wasn't any more difficult. Tyler, who was commuting from home, had more intensive engineering courses, along with more calculus and physics. One class involved a semester-long group project to build a small robot that looked like an RC car. A computer engineering major on the team would program it to perform simple tasks. At the end of the semester the class would have a large competition where teams would receive grades based on the robot's ability to complete challenges set up for it and how fast it did them. The project consumed more and more of Tyler's time as the semester wore on. And with my dates with Katie and both of our jobs, we had far less time to hang out in the fall. We met up maybe once a week if we were lucky, sometimes at my apartment, sometimes at Tyler's house, and sometimes on campus, basically whatever place was most convenient for our schedules.

The time we spent together then felt, oddly enough, obligatory. After all of the fun in the summer and how much we learned about our families and shared our personal histories, the onset of a busy sophomore year reset our priorities. We had to text each other a lot to find common free time and both of us canceled a bunch of scheduled meet-ups. The slow, unpressured time we had our freshman year to ease into conversations and talk about any random subject vanished.

The one exception to the trend came in October. Tyler told me that his dad owned several guns, and his dad's colleague owned a small piece of land further out, beyond the suburbs. He was allowed to take his dad's guns and drive out to the land and go target shooting and he invited me to go along with him. I agreed; I had never fired a real gun in my life and wanted to see what it was like. And my parents jumped at the idea when I told them about it. They were glad I was doing something with Tyler other than playing video games.

I have to make a brief note here to clear things up. After I had been identified as Tyler's only friend by the press, many early news reports claimed that we had started target shooting soon after we first met at MU. Rumors also circulated that we had a gimmick of printing out pictures of other students at MU, shooting at them and then bragging about it, which the news outlets also broadcast. Later follow-up articles corrected these mistakes, but those follow-ups didn't make headlines like the earlier articles did, so many people have continued to believe those falsehoods. I want to make this clear: Tyler and I did not go target shooting until October of our sophomore year, and we did this once. Before that time, Tyler either went by himself or with his dad to the property. And, we never printed out pictures of MU students for target practice. We never even talked about doing that.

Tyler borrowed his dad's rusting Nissan pick-up to drive us to the property. He had gotten a few lessons from his dad in high school on how to use its 5-speed manual transmission but not enough to feel comfortable with it. He explained this to me after he picked me up, apologizing for his lack of skill. He stalled it at the first stop sign. His face turned almost as red as the sign. I wanted to tell him that it was okay. During the whole trip he struggled with the gears, his skinny arm yanking on the shifter, sometimes moving it to the wrong gear, his left foot working the clutch in uneven movements, unsure of how much force to use. It was an uncomfortable, lurching ride. I wanted to help but I had never driven stick. Instead I tried to keep a conversation going, and to do that I had to keep asking questions. I didn't get much information from him, except that his dad was on a business trip in Savannah, and the truck was the designated vehicle for driving to the property because they had to take a pitted dirt road to reach it.

The property was about a forty-five-minute drive out from Peach Grove, but our drive took longer because we made two stops along the way. The first was the drive-thru at a McDonald's, where Tyler stalled the truck twice. A middle-aged woman with bloodshot eyes handed him the change and a few seconds later added, "Have a nice day." When Tyler turned to look at her and give a reply, he spilled the change inside the truck, sending coins under both seats.

"I'll get them," he said, reaching under his seat.

"Don't worry about it, there's cars behind us." I reached under my own seat. I felt something hard and pulled out a CD case. It was Korn's first album.

"Your dad listens to Korn?"

"No, I do. That must've fell under the seat the last time I drove this."

Once we collected the change, got our food and parked, I convinced Tyler to play the CD as we ate. It was the first real insight I had into his musical tastes. I guessed he would've liked classical or whatever they played on the radio, not the rage and vulgarity of early Korn, music that my parents called "satanic." He said his parents called it "satanic" too. I liked it. We devoured our lunch without saying much, watching the traffic on the expressway and letting Korn fill the dusty cab. It was an odd experience, in the middle of the day, in a cracked and potholed and desolate parking lot. We finished and sat there, listening to more of the CD.

Before the trip, Tyler suggested stopping at a flea market to pick up some small ceramics to use as targets. He said he and his dad did this when they went up, because the ceramic made a satisfying sound when you shot it. I said sure. The flea market was right up the road from our lunch. Tyler had two cloth bags with him, and we split up and bought a small mix of cheap statues, figures, and crosses within minutes. We met back up at the truck.

"Look at this, Dylan." Tyler came up to me holding the handles of his bag apart.

"What? What is it?" I peered in.

He had about ten weathered and stained angels in different poses, complete with wings and halos.

"Scored a great deal. They look like those angels you see in paintings about stories in the Bible."

"Sweet. Those will work. Think we got enough?"

"Yeah, more than enough. We won't go through all of them. They should last a couple of trips."

We loaded the bags into the cab with us. We didn't want them breaking in the bed where Tyler had put the guns and ammo. After a few stalls, he got us on the state route heading north and right into rural fields and woods. It reminded me that most of America is fields and woods. I had been spending so much time on the islands of people called cities and suburbs that I had forgotten what was outside of them. We turned off the CD and rolled down our windows.

———

That October had beautiful weather. We cruised down thin back roads with nothing but farms or forest canopy lining the way. The whole scene lifted my mood. The leaves had all turned bright autumn colors. The sweet dry breeze swept the smell of burgers out of the cab. Leaves cascaded onto the road in front of us and the wind swept them in wide arcs like a herd fleeing from a predator. Tens of thousands of branches lifting and dipping in unison. I closed my eyes and it sounded like a beach and its crashing waves. But the property wasn't too far into the country. Right when I had adjusted to the sights and sounds Tyler pulled into an unmarked private drive. A rusted metal gate blocked the way.

"Here we are."

"This is nice."

Tyler smirked. "I don't think it's nice. The road's bumpy and we don't do anything to clean it up. My dad says his friend will come up here sometime and cut down the vines choking all these trees, but he's been saying that for years."

Tyler got out, unlocked the gate and swung it open. He didn't bother to close it once we drove through. The asphalt quickly petered out and became hard-packed dirt scarred by roots. Gravel filled some holes. There was a mini concrete bridge over a glistering brook. The bridge had so many cracks it looked like it was breaking apart from the inside out. No one had done any repairs to the private drive during our lifetimes.

Not long after the bridge, a clearing opened up before us and the road ended in the scattered remains of half-buried gravel. We parked and the rough pebbles crunched under our feet as we circled to the tailgate. Tyler had tucked plastic buckets full of ammo, empty pop cans, and beer bottles into the corners of the bed. The buckets held down the corners of thick blankets that covered the canvas bags spread out on the bed. I had no idea what the laws were for transporting guns but it did feel strange to haul a bunch of them in a truck bed on a state route. Anybody who would've looked in the truck's bed and had an ounce of curiosity could have figured out what we were doing.

"Yeah, right behind this tree. Right behind here. That's where we kept them." Tyler stepped around a pile of rocks. We were feet inside the woods that surrounded the field. Tyler's truck sat in the distance. He rolled up his coat sleeves, reached down and hauled two decent-sized rocks out of the tree line and into the field. I rushed over to pick up two more rocks from the pile. The ones on the bottom had sunken halfway into the ground. Loads of seashell fossils and what looked like coral embedded in the rocks gave them a gray and rough surface.

I followed Tyler into the field. We called it a field but it was closer to a meadow, bristling with tall, wild grasses browning as the days grew shorter. Our jeans scratched against those grasses. Tyler struggled to control the shifting weight. His arms shook. He laid his two rocks on one of the upside-down buckets from the truck and I stacked my rocks on one nearby. We dusted off our hands and centered the rocks on the buckets. They made two short pillars in the field, like dual monoliths of once-great stature now eroded to a pulp.

"Know why all these rocks have fossils of seashells and coral?" I asked.

"I'm not really sure."

"This area, the whole Midwest, was at the bottom of the ocean millions of years ago. These fossils are from the Ordovician, long before the dinosaurs. They're ancient. You're touching something that's hundreds of millions of years old."

Tyler inspected the ancient stones, tracing his fingers over the edges of sea life from eons ago, fossils that were already fossils when the dinosaurs ruled the earth.

"They're graveyards," he said.

"These won't last much longer. Now that they're above ground, the elements will wither them away."

"Why aren't there dinosaur bones around here?"

"The land was eroding then. Been eroding for a long time. Nothing fossilizes. Nothing stays."

Tyler walked back to the bright woods, looking over his shoulder several times to see if I was following, which I was.

"How much of this land does your dad's friend own?"

"About ten acres. He said it was cheap. I want to spend more time here. There's other things to do. Ride mountain bikes—the woods aren't that dense and I could clear little trails. I explored some of this when I was younger, but I've always wanted to...walk, you know? Walk for so long I forget where I am and it doesn't matter. That kind of walking would be nice." He went into the woods, going deeper, past where we picked up the stones. A few steps behind, I ran into the vines and low branches that he dodged.

"I've had dreams of that kind of walking. That would be so relaxing. You think you could do it around here?"

"Maybe. I've looked this area up online and it looks like a chessboard from the roads crisscrossing it. But I still would like to try."

He appeared from a clump of trees and bare bushes carrying a long two-by-eight board. It was rotted to the bone. Not a two-by-eight anymore—dirt and moisture had taken turns consuming and dissolving the warped carcass for years. It must had been a real horror show for the still-living trees that had to stand there and watch.

"We'll lay this across the rocks and put the targets on this."

We set up the pop cans and two-liters as the first row of targets. The wind knocked them right over so we gathered some pebbles to weight them. The more satisfying targets of ceramic we saved for later.

Tyler retrieved the guns and ammo. He laid the weaponry on other buckets maybe fifteen yards from the targets. I held the safety glasses and earmuffs. He had a .22 lever-action rifle, a revolver, and a .410 break-barrel shotgun. The boxes of the .22 bullets rattled on the plastic buckets. The boxes of the shotgun shells did not.

"Only three guns?" I wanted to fire all sorts of types, as many different ones as I could.

"Not three, four. My dad does have more than these but he doesn't have any ammo for the others right now. Next time I'll bring new ones."

"I only see two types of ammo."

"The revolver and the rifle both use the .22 rounds. It makes the ammo easier to keep track of. And cheaper. And I thought you'd like that shotgun."

I did. It had that vintage look. Like something that could've been made more than a century ago.

"And what's the other one?"

"Thirty-aught-six is the fourth one, the fourth gun. Bolt-action. It's still in the truck."

"It's got a lot of kick?"

"Yeah. By far the most out of all of these. It's like getting punched in the shoulder. Is there one you want to start with?"

"I'm not sure. I don't know which one is best for starters."

"You can go ahead and pick them up. See which one feels comfortable. Just don't point them at me, or yourself." Tyler backed away from the buckets. He rubbed his hands on his hips.

All three had the appearance of well-used and aged tools. They reminded me of the hardware in my dad's garage, inherited from my grandpa, who used them for years, and barely used by my dad. Dull black steel, chipped and scratched wood, yet hardy and reliable, as if age and wear had toughened their parts instead of weakened them. The shotgun and rifle were both much longer than I had expected, but light. I picked up the revolver and held it loosely in my hands. The cylinder was out.

"I double-checked to make sure they were empty before I left," Tyler said. He reached his left hand out toward me. I gave him the gun.

He showed me how to use it, explaining first and then demonstrating the right way to use each part. He asked if I understood what he had explained. He took care to repeat his instructions, more to assure himself of what to do than to tell me. The one difficulty we had was that Tyler was a southpaw and I wasn't. He said almost all guns were built for right-handers, so it would really be easier for me to use. After loading the revolver, he offered me the chance to shoot first. I declined and let him go.

"I can wait. I'm fine with letting you do most of the firing today," he said, smiling and squinting in the sunlight.

"No, I want to watch first. See how you handle it."

"Oh, it's not much. The .22 is one of the smallest calibers."

We donned our earmuffs and safety glasses. Tyler stepped up— feet hidden by the tall grass. He pulled the hammer back, raised the gun, holding and supporting it in the way he had shown me, taking his time to line up the sights, slowing his rapid breathing, applying pressure on the trigger, and fired. I flinched. A two-liter tilted back and fell off the rotting board. The gunshot wasn't too loud and his skinny arms absorbed the recoil just fine.

Tyler never stopped to look back at me as he fired the remaining bullets. He nailed another two-liter and missed the rest. He took his time for every shot, concentrating, his body still, not moving to a new target until he hit his current choice. By his last shot I didn't flinch from the sound. Once he finished, we both removed our earmuffs.

"Your turn." He aimed the gun at the ground and passed it to me.

I picked out the empty cartridges and pushed new ones in. "How was your first time shooting?"

"I was so nervous. I about closed my eyes when I fired—missed wildly. You could hear branches in the woods breaking. My dad laughed. He said I would be good for shooting the vines down. I was squeezing the gun so tight I could see all the tendons in my hands."

"Did it take you some time to get used to it and shoot consistently?"

"Oh yeah. I'm slow to adapt to anything like that, anything risky." Tyler shrugged. "Yeah, you probably knew that. I can read tips online of how to hold the gun and the steps for aiming, but shooting it in real life is the best way to improve. I didn't hit anything that I tried to hit on my first day."

"I'll just hope playing all those video games are worth something. They have to help with hand-to-eye coordination."

"They might. Don't forget your hearing protection."

Tyler stepped back, though more to the side so he could watch my hands and arms as I brought the revolver up into my line of sight. My hands trembled along with the gun as I made sure to hold it in the exact way Tyler had explained. I lined up the sights with a two-liter I had already picked out, closed my left eye, put the logo in the middle of the two sights, and eased into the trigger, gradually applying pressure and eyeing that logo. It took a great deal of focus and steady arm strength. My elbows had started shaking when the trigger yielded and a tiny shock of recoil traveled up my wrists and arms. The gunshot resonated through the woods. The barrel rose for a teething second and blocked my view. I had missed and had no idea where the bullet went. I glanced at Tyler, who nodded and smiled. Then I reset my aim at the two-liter.

My head never turned back to Tyler for the rest of my shots. The anticipation of knocking one of those targets over locked in my focus. It was a real challenge to hold everything still and try not to brace for the shock. I missed every time except for the last one: I nicked the two-liter, rocking it back and forth, but it did not topple over.

"Close!" Tyler yelled. He sounded distant through the earmuffs.

We tried the rifle next. Tyler explained how to load and aim it in his thorough way. It could hold ten shots in the under-barrel.

Tyler went first, turning the safety off after he aimed down the field, firing at a slow pace, cocking the lever each time, knocking off three pop cans, though some required more than one hit to fall over the backside. Without taking off our earmuffs, without any words, he gave the rifle to me and I loaded it. I found the rifle much easier to hold and aim. The lever was awkward though, and I realized it would take a lot of practice to get used to it. I was able to send the two-liter sailing and even took a chunk out of one of the final pop cans standing. Through some basic hand signals, I told him I wanted to stick with the rifle. We each went again and our combined efforts knocked everything off the board.

Before we reset the targets, Tyler let me try the shotgun. It was a breeze to load and reload, like any double-barrel I had seen in a movie or video game. We each fired into the field a couple of times, not aiming at anything. The recoil kicked harder than the .22's and made my heart race the first time it shoved back into my shoulder.

With the shotgun resting on the bucket, its barrel now hot to the touch, Tyler asked, "More targets?"

"Hell yes."

———

We set up a crowded line of small ceramics from the flea market for our second round of targets. Placing them on the rotted board made me excited, almost giddy. I had fired real guns for the first time in my life. If anybody asked me if I had ever fired a real gun, I could say yes.

I would no longer have to lie or admit that I hadn't. I knew what it was like now: the loading, the aiming, the pressure of the trigger on my fingers, the force of the recoil, the smell of the burnt propellant, and the wisps of faint smoke that rose from the barrel.

Aiming for those ceramic vases and figurines and straining to get off the right shot sucked me into a near-trance of single-minded attention. I understood why people could do this over and over. It melted everything else into oblivion. Striking the target became my sole objective. I could forget Tyler, standing there by me, watching the board for results. The cool wind shaking the branches in the woods and flapping my hair like loose shutters didn't matter. It reminded me of building with LEGOs when I was a kid. I couldn't make the car or castle or ship the way I saw it in my mind. I'd tear every piece apart and rebuild it from scratch, hours passing like they were minutes. But when I did create what I had envisioned it gave me a deep feeling of accomplishment. I felt that same way when I hit one of those ceramics—the shattering, splintering shards exploding outward, and the lavish clay sounds, like a plate smashing on tile, gave me as much satisfaction as any A on a test.

I didn't hit many of the ceramic figures. I was a terrible shot. I missed far more than I had expected. But Tyler didn't say a word about it—not even a light-hearted joke. He gave me feedback and advice on how to improve my shooting and never grew bored or frustrated. He even loaded the other guns when I was firing one so I wouldn't have to reload them. I kept offering him the chance to shoot but he only went a couple of times. His accuracy was a step above mine, but nothing impressive. He didn't have a ton of experience with firearms, just enough to be competent with them. His dad had taught him the basics, nothing more.

After several more rounds of firing, we decided to take a short break and removed our earmuffs and safety glasses. We had worked up a sweat from standing stock-still in the sunny field, so we walked over to the board and sat down wordlessly. The sun was arching downwards in the west—tree shadows crept toward us. The wind still blew through the woods and grasses. We couldn't have picked a better day. Tyler looked worn out but content. Slouched-over, knees together, his shoes ground the pulverized ceramic chunks into the dry dirt. The remains of our targets around the board looked like ashes and charred logs from a scattered fire.

I broke the quiet by asking Tyler if he wanted to have a little competition to see who was more accurate.

"I'm good." He sighed in a great heave. He didn't look at me.

"What are you thinking about?"

"Joe."

"Can't get him out of your head?"

"These guns make me think of him. He'd come up with paintball accuracy competitions. He'd make me face off against other kids. You know, he loved to pit me against other kids on the street if he could— it wasn't always me versus him. I think he did that to keep his enemies divided. I didn't get along with other kids on my street, even though he tormented them too."

"What did Joe do to the winners and losers?"

"The winners got to escape all of his insults. The losers were faggots. If you lost any game, or quit, or refused to play, you were a faggot. Kind of like you were downgraded, knocked down a peg. That and coward. Sometimes he would use coward instead. I lost so many times he said I deserved something worse, so he started calling me a lifelong virgin."

"That street was his own little kingdom."

"Pretty much. He had a lot of fun with it. His favorite game, other than paintball, was push basketball, where we'd play on his driveway, and you were allowed to foul by shoving as hard as you wanted. Because of our size difference, every time I pushed him he didn't budge. When he pushed me, I'd leave my feet and land on my back, and the back of my head would smack against the concrete. Then he'd say, like he was trying to give me advice, 'Come on, get up, don't be a faggot,' after he scored. I didn't win a single game against him."

"Did you shove as hard as you could?"

"I couldn't bring myself to do it. It wasn't in me. It all felt hopeless. I couldn't win and I couldn't quit. That went on for years. I kind of got used to it, just accepted it."

"Were you good at basketball? I mean, could you have beaten him without the shoving?"

"I don't think so. He was the one who taught me how to play. Almost every sport and game we played, he taught me—how to shoot a basketball, throw a football, a Frisbee. He taught me everything about playing and talking with other kids my age. Everything except where the word 'faggot' came from. I always thought it meant a boy who was a loser and a quitter. I didn't hear kids use it in a way against gay people until high school."

"I don't think I heard it used that way until my middle school years."

"It confused me. Joe never sat me down and explained to me what any bad words meant, or what they could also be used for. Nobody else did either. And my family didn't have internet back then for me to look things up."

"I know what you mean. MU needs a class on words you're not supposed to talk about. A one-credit hour course. Get everybody on the same page."

We fell into our own thoughts for a few minutes. The air was cooling, prepping for the night. We were probably the only two people within a mile in any direction. It reminded me of that night in August, having that heart-to-heart, except this time we were breathing in cool, dry air. Tyler looked uncomfortable, arms almost hugging his knees, watching the woods, squinting in the fading sunlight.

"Did you ever tell your mom what Joe was really doing to you? That he played these twisted games for his own amusement?"

He shook his head. "I wanted to handle it myself. I didn't want to rely on Mom. Joe would make fun of me for it, too. He said the only way I could get better was by tackling his games myself. Going to my mom would be admitting weakness. Plus, there were a few games I did like. Sometimes we would get wiffleball bats and have sword fights with them. I was pretty good at that. It was loads of fun. When we met up, I always hoped that Joe would pick that to play. But he changed the rules so that we used garbage can lids as shields and we had to stay in a small area. That favored his strength over my speed."

"He kind of controlled you, didn't he?"

"Oh yeah. He would say I was his bitch in front of girls. He knew I wouldn't do anything about it. Any outburst I had he'd use against me. Sometimes I worried that he could read my mind. He knew me too well. So I learned to not express anything around him. By being stoic, I could kind of hide from him in a sense. It became a habit that I did automatically—I still do it. All of this is clear to me now, but it's too late to do anything about it." Tyler's sentence trailed off to a whisper. He didn't look at me.

"You know what? Crap." I snapped my fingers.

"What?"

"I'm sorry. I forgot. The fourth gun. We haven't fired it. We could use it on those clay angels you got."

Tyler reached down and grabbed the cloth bag resting beside the bucket. He pulled out one of the angels. The figure was sitting on a tree stump and had its head buried in its hands. He set it down on the board and pulled out a few more, all in various poses, some kneeling, heads cast down, others standing and gazing skyward.

"You know what?" I slid over and picked up the first piece he had taken out. "These are pretty nice. Well-made."

"Yeah. They really caught my eye at the flea market."

I examined the figure. Small enough to be held in one hand, the angel and the stump had a worn, textured look, not glossy, like it had sat in someone's garden or on their windowsill for years. The stump had chips in it. The angel's wings were folded against her back. I wanted to keep it but felt stupid for liking it. I had never collected any statues or figures. But it looked striking. Something powerful made that angel despair. And it wasn't overtly religious—I didn't see any crosses or other symbols on it. An angel with a burden.

Tyler watched me look at it. "If you want to keep one, go ahead."

"I guess I'll take it. Do you like them?"

"Yeah. They're cool. You can take more."

"This one's fine. We don't have to shoot any if you want to keep the rest."

"No, well, actually I kind of want to pack up here before it gets dark and head home. There're no lights around here. At night it gets pitch black. Is that okay?"

"Sure. It's your call. You've been out here before and they're your dad's guns."

"I'll bring the fourth gun again next time. Sorry."

We disassembled the target stand and packed up the guns and ammo. We drove back along the country roads in the afterglow of dusk, talking about the guns and the targets and how nice it was to take a break from campus and the suburbs. When Tyler dropped me off at my parents' house, where I was staying for the weekend, nighttime had set in and brought a chilly breeze with it. We talked a little in the driveway about going out to that property again but we both agreed we were too busy in the next few weeks to pick out a future date. We gave awkward goodbyes. I stood in the driveway and held the clay angel at my side as Tyler shifted into reverse. He seemed too small in that cab as he backed out, not quite sizable enough to handle the truck's weight, as if he wasn't qualified to take it all the way to fifth gear.

———

We kept trying to make it back up to the property before winter, but it didn't work out. Tyler's engineering project consumed more of his time, and as finals neared, I couldn't carve out a couple of hours from my schedule, let alone a whole day for target shooting. Our classes and work engulfed our lives. We stopped texting each other in November. That went on for weeks until finals in mid-December, probably the longest we had gone without texting since our Chemistry 101 study sessions. The day before I moved back home for Christmas break, Tyler texted me, asking if I wanted to meet up one last time. I said of course and let him pick the spot. He chose the top level of Polk Garage, the tallest parking garage on campus, famous for offering a great view of half the campus.

When I made it up the steps to the top level he was already there. He was leaning against the concrete wall, gazing out at the world like the captain of an abandoned ship. Not a single car was on the top level, and no one else had come up in the bitter and gloomy December afternoon. It was us two.

Thick clouds obscured the sun and darker ones approached from the west. The weather had stayed mild enough to keep the snow at bay, but that didn't rule out a cold, miserable shower. Tyler didn't smile at me as I approached. He barely glanced over his shoulder. Without much of a greeting he dove right into explaining why he had been too busy to go shooting again. In a slow, deliberate speech, like he had rehearsed it, Tyler told me how his group engineering project to build a robot car had morphed into a practically solo project. His project partners had refused to meet up or work on it during the weekends, forcing a much slower development speed. Tyler picked up the slack for his group by working alone on the weekends, completing his own tasks as well as what his partners hadn't finished. However, there was still too much work to be done. The student responsible for the programming had bailed and Tyler could hardly code. At the beginning of finals week the projects were due. The finals for that class consisted of testing each team's robot on a small course in a competitive demonstration outside. Their robot's performance was embarrassing, struggling to accomplish the most basic objectives, drawing laughter from the other engineering groups and curious onlookers who had stopped to watch. Tyler said he would've invited me to watch but he knew it would fail. So even though he only had the responsibility of designing and building the chassis and that part functioned just fine, the grade was assigned to the team, not to individuals, and he received a D-minus along with the members who, Tyler knew, didn't want to fall behind on their partying. I tried to offer support as best I could. He let me know that he had never received a grade below a B in his entire life. Now his GPA would have a permanent dent in it.

"You could've told me about it back in November or sometime. I would've helped you."

"No. I thought I had it. I had never gotten a bad grade on anything that important before, ever. I didn't think it could happen to me. No matter what else happened in my life, grades were always my one positive."

"At least you learned a lot, way more than you were supposed to."

"I guess." Tyler stared down at the empty sidewalk below.

"It's useful stuff, isn't it?"

"Maybe. Even if it's useful, I'm not good at it."

We watched the campus. A few students dotted it. Neither of us spoke. Then Tyler broke the quiet.

"You heard of the Port Arthur massacre?"

"The one with thirty-five people killed? Yeah."

"Do you know the full story on that? It's crazy."

"No, just that it happened in the nineties in Australia."

"So, the guy, the shooter, had an extremely low IQ, mentally disabled. His story is wild. He had one friend, a wealthy lady. She died in a car wreck that injured him but she left him a ton of money. Then his dad killed himself and left him more money. He always acted weird and dressed weird so everybody avoided him and laughed at him. He got so lonely he would travel on planes just so he could talk to people, cause on a plane they couldn't avoid him. He paid to fight his loneliness for a few hours. Then, after the shooting, the news doctored pictures of him to make him look more evil. And those pictures are still used today."

The darker clouds began to cover more of the area west of us, nearing Harris Hall. "Yeah. That almost doesn't surprise me," I said. "People go to great lengths to not be alone. That's one thing I've learned. You see adults do weird things because of that. But boy, those clouds, I hope it doesn't rain."

CHAPTER TWELVE

Tyler Takes a Break

I didn't see Tyler again until classes started back up in January. I hadn't even thought about texting him over winter break. I had other things on my mind, like visiting Katie's family and having Katie meet mine at Christmas parties. In a weird twist it turned out that Katie helped us meet up again. Back in the fall, she convinced me to sign up for the Human Sexuality course with her in the spring, a low-tier psychology class with a reputation for being easy and interesting. Most of the grade was based on online quizzes and the professor took a more engaged approach to lecturing. She started the first class like this:

"Pleasure is good. Sex is good. They are nothing to be ashamed of. They are an important part of life. If you don't pick up anything else from this course, at least remember that." Then she introduced herself and worked through the nuts and bolts of the syllabus, which included a grade for participating in surveys she conducted on our sexual lives.

Sometime during that first course I mentioned in passing to Katie how my schedule kept me from seeing Tyler. Katie still hadn't met him at that point and kept asking to meet him. She said I could invite him to come to some of these lectures with us. She had heard of other students who came to the class to see the professor do things like bring in sex toys or demonstrate safe rope-bondage techniques, or have male students who were waiting until marriage explain their decision to wait. Nobody in the old 200-seat lecture hall would notice that Tyler didn't belong. And the professor didn't take attendance. It sounded like a good idea. I got to catch up with Tyler and have him meet Katie, so I texted him and he said he would.

The next week I walked into the lecture hall and spotted Tyler half-way down the stairs searching for me, legs together, body stiff and slouched. Katie was already there but he didn't know what she looked like. I got his attention and introduced him to Katie right before the lecture started.

The professor brought out one of her friends, a tall, middle-aged man, who was willing to answer any questions about his sex life. The first question was how many sexual partners he had.

"Fourteen."

The whole class erupted in an awestruck "wow" that filled the lecture hall. Some of the students even clapped.

"No, no, that's not how—" The professor waved her hands to try to stop the class as a lot of chatter started. She settled things down and there were a lot more questions for the man. One of the questions was how he had managed to get such a high number.

"Oh, friends with benefits," he said.

"Raise your hands, class," the professor said. "Who here has ever had a friend with benefits?"

About eighty percent of the class raised their hands. The number kind of shocked me, and it seemed to startle Katie too. Neither Tyler, Katie, nor I raised our hands—either we were missing out on something or a lot students were only raising their hands to make it look like they weren't missing out.

"And this is why I believe sex is so important," the professor continued. "It's so common. It happens all the time. It's an integral part of our lives, but it's something we don't like to talk about openly."

A student raised her hand.

"Yes?"

"I don't think it's just important, I think it's more like a necessity. It's crucial for development. There's physical intimacy and passion and heartbreak. We need to experience that when we're young so we know how to handle it in the real world."

"Some people do say that, that sex is part of adult life, a life skill."

"And there are a lot of health benefits too," the student added.

"There are. Sex can make you healthier both physically and mentally in ways that masturbation can't."

The rest of the lecture continued like this, with students adding questions and comments that made the class much more conversational in nature. The professor's friend was open and brutally honest, something I had never seen anyone do when it came to their sex life. The three of us listened, but didn't speak up. Tyler fiddled with his thin hands and spent more time looking down than watching the professor. I had a notebook open, though it was more for show than actual note-taking. Katie clung to every word uttered and jotted down every point the professor emphasized.

When the lecture ended Katie unleashed a series of questions on Tyler, covering topics from his major to his job to his relationship status. I guess he had been a bit of a mysterious figure to her, someone she had heard about for months and yet had never seen, and she sought to dispel Tyler Eberle in one rapid-fire interview. I watched it with a half-smile. Tyler struggled to answer the questions, and only offered short replies, glancing at me a lot for help. I gave Katie a few minutes to quench her curiosity before rescuing him.

"Okay, that's enough prying, Katie. Give the poor guy a break. Do you want to give him a polygraph next?"

"I'm curious. I'd like to know who your friends are."

Tyler eyed me, biting his lip.

"He needs to go. He's got important things to do."

He stood up and moved into the aisle, looked back at us and then, without speaking, turned, eyes down, and climbed the stairs to the exit. His footsteps creaked on each stair and receded over a nearby negotiation for buying fake IDs with a growing group of students, some of them coming back into the hall as word spread of how cheap they were. Katie watched Tyler retreat with a mixture of worry and astonishment.

"Have you ever—" she started.

"Hmm?"

"Have you ever wondered about him?"

"What do you mean?"

"Have you ever met someone that quiet? You've said he barely talks, except to you. Gosh, I thought you were exaggerating. When I was asking him all those questions it seemed like he was having trouble talking, not like he had lost his voice but like something in him was stuck. He didn't even ask me anything back."

"Maybe he doesn't like being bombarded with questions. I think it takes him a long time to feel comfortable around other people."

"He could be gay."

I jerked back in my seat. "Why do you think that?"

"Cause he's so…timid"

I couldn't help but roll my eyes and shake my head.

"If it's not that then what's wrong with him?"

"Why does there have to be something wrong with him?"

"He has to be hiding something."

"And so what if he's gay?"

"Come on, you know I would have nothing against him if he was gay."

"Then why is it such a big deal?"

"You're right it shouldn't be a big deal. But he could be suffering, too afraid to come out. You said his family's Catholic. They don't like gay people. You should really ask him if he is. You guys sound like you're close enough that he would tell you the truth. He might need help."

"Look, I don't think he's gay. And I don't want to ask, because if I ask, then he would think that I'd thought he was gay."

"You don't know that. And what makes you think he's not gay?"

"Just some things he's said."

"Like what?"

I took a moment. "We talked about losing our virginity and becoming men."

"Aww." She placed her hand on my arm. "You guys are close."

"I know it's probably prejudiced but I don't think a gay guy would bring that up, and he did."

"Alright. But keep an eye on him. You know LGBT youth are at higher risk for suicide and self-harm."

"Yes. I hear it all the time."

"Actually, back in the summer, when we were talking at the store, and you hadn't asked me out, I was starting to think that you were gay."

"Really?"

Katie nodded.

It took some time for me to process how Katie had reacted to meeting Tyler. He kept showing up to Human Sexuality, about once a week, and the three of us would get to speak before and after class, but as Katie learned more about Tyler, she kept confiding in me that she had serious concerns about him. She said he was too stilted and reserved and looked too uncomfortable having normal conversations. She built on her theory that he was gay or hiding something deeper. Her concerns reminded me of Mrs. Eberle questioning Christopher McCandless and his decision to uproot his life. I grew more and more annoyed at her. I didn't think it was fair to him and lacked open-mindedness. After a lecture about losing your virginity, where many of the students snickered or openly laughed at the thought of still being a virgin in college, which upset me enough, I waited for Tyler to leave and then unloaded a stern warning to Katie to lay off him. I said he was fine. The fact that he was a little different didn't mean he was gay or had a terrible home life or some secret eating him from the inside.

He didn't speak up. So what? I didn't speak up much myself and yet she was dating me.

Katie listened and admitted she had gotten a little too carried away with Tyler. She knew he was a close friend of mine and wanted to make sure I had healthy friendships and happy friends. From then on, she eased up on him. She accepted that sometimes when she asked him a question and he didn't respond it was because he didn't want to answer the question. He wasn't being rude or afraid that some secret he had would come out; he wasn't eager to open up yet, and he was too shy to tell her to knock it off with all the questions.

Once I had issued the warning to Katie, the spring semester rolled by in blurry routine. I had so much on my plate with classes, homework, dating, and my job that Tyler and I never met outside of the Human Sexuality class. I hardly noticed when he started showing up less and less. Well, I did kind of notice, more than a little; I just didn't do anything about it. Katie guessed his homework was mounting as the semester drew closer to exams. We didn't see any change in his mood. I thought he was burying himself in his classwork, putting in the hours to smooth out his GPA from the hit it took the previous semester. By March, he stopped showing up altogether. I didn't think it was an issue.

———

At the end of March, over a week after spring break had ended, I received a text from someone not on my contacts list. It was an ordinary breakfast. I was sitting at the small kitchen table in my apartment, alone, eating cereal with my laptop open. An annoying crow kept cawing nearby. My phone, also on the table, buzzed against the wood. In cold letters the message read: *This is Tyler's mom. I am sending this because Tyler had an emergency and is at a hospital. Please call me.*

I stood up so fast I knocked the chair into the fridge behind me. A part of me wanted to deny it, like maybe the text was some terrible prank. But I knew better. My high school friends might've done something like that, but Tyler and his family were out of the question. I tried to clean up my breakfast, fumbling with the bowl and the phone. I didn't want to hear the news that he was in a bad car wreck and injured or maimed or had some freak medical issue that put him into a coma. I tossed my bowl into the sink, splashing milk everywhere, and jammed my fingers on the phone to call Mrs. Eberle. It rang twice before she answered. I braced against the countertop.

"Hello?"

"Hello I got your message what's going on with Tyler?" I asked in one breath.

"Oh, Dylan." Static on the line obscured her tone. "Tyler is okay now. He's still at the hospital."

"Where?"

Mrs. Eberle gave the name of the hospital and Tyler's room number. She did mention the psychiatric ward, but I only memorized the words and didn't register their meaning.

"When can I visit him? Are there rules for that?"

"You can visit him now. Later on he has an appointment. I'm sure you have classes so you can come tonight, he won't mind."

"Fuck those classes I'm going right now." Never in a million years did I think I would let the f-bomb slip to the Catholic mother of one of my friends, but I blurted that out in a heartbeat.

"Don't rush. There's no need to break any traffic laws."

"Sure. Yeah. Uh, are you there with him?"

"Not at the moment. I went to get something to eat but I'll be back there."

"Alright."

I didn't run any red lights to the hospital, which stood between the campus and Tyler's house. I checked in at the psych ward desk and Mrs. Eberle met me there. She looked tired, too tired to express anything else except a longwinded weariness. Her sunken eyes locked onto mine.

"Hi Dylan."

"Hey."

She led the way to a corner of the waiting room where the giant windows bleached the area with the morning's sun.

"I've been up all night, haven't slept at all." Mrs. Eberle rubbed down on her cheeks.

I wanted to help her so badly but I didn't know what to do or what to say. I had never been in a situation like this in my life. I couldn't even remember the last time I had been in a hospital.

She continued, "They had to pump his stomach. I found him last night, on the bathroom floor. He had taken pills. Way too many." She glanced at the packed waiting room and breathed deeply. She seemed even taller than usual. Her hair hung disheveled over her shoulders. "He's been depressed. He had been feeling down for a while and was afraid it wouldn't go away. That was over a month ago when he told me. I—I never expected anything like this to happen. I thought it was temporary, part of the stress."

"I want to help, Mrs. Eberle. Whatever I can do."

"If I could—ask you a few questions?"

"Sure."

"Has he ever said anything about this, or mentioned it?"

"No, never."

"When was the last time you saw him?"

"Probably close to a month ago. I've texted him since, but it was boring what-are-you-doing kind of things."

"And nothing about harming himself or wishing that he was dead?"

"No. Yeah, I never heard anything like that from him. When I got your text I didn't even think of that." I kept shaking my head. My nerves had flipped from wired to numb. The waiting room and the news still felt unreal.

"Were there any other warning signs? Something you might've missed?"

"I don't know. Like what?"

"Talking about death, saying goodbye, giving away valuable possessions. That's what the doctors said. They—" Her voice cracked and she took another breath. "They asked if he had cleaned up his room at all. I said, well, his room is always clean. It's almost immaculate. He just needed to dust." Mrs. Eberle let out a gasp of hurt laughter and in an incredible act of willpower I'll never forget, she turned the hurt into a genuine smile. "But he made it. He pulled through. His dad and Chloe already saw him over the night. They're at work and school now but they'll be back later."

"Does Chloe need a ride? I can take her."

"No. And I'm sorry, I shouldn't ask you any more questions. I shouldn't have asked you any questions. I'm keeping you."

"No, it's alright."

"Go ahead and see him. He's still a little groggy."

I hesitated.

"Go ahead, please."

———

I eased my way into Tyler's room. His eyes were locked to the ceiling, out of focus. His hair was short. The blinds were open and sunlight poured into the white room, illuminating and softening every edge in a garish, celestial effect. His eyes drifted down toward me.

We made eye contact and didn't say anything. I stepped closer. Bedsheets covered his body up to his neck. A small tube ran out from his right arm. He looked young and boyish still, and thinner than normal, but his movement and voice reminded me of my great-grandpa before he passed from cancer.

"Hey," I said.

"Hey," he groaned. "So, you know?"

I nodded. I held my hands together—fingers interlaced, like I was praying—and rested them against my thigh. I hadn't prepared myself for what to say to him. The whole time rushing there and talking with his mom I had only wanted to see for myself that he was alive. I swallowed and spoke with as much honesty as I could muster. "I'm not sure what to say. I want to ask you if you're alright, but that sounds like such a stupid question."

"They had to knock me out to do the pumping in the ER. Whatever they gave me has bad aftereffects. They said it's like a hangover, but I didn't know what hangovers were like. I guess I do now."

I smiled. "Remember midterms last year for Chem 101, we were studying at your dorm when Jake popped in, started a party? Then we went to my dorm and didn't even study?"

"That was great. Party nights don't make the best time for studying."

My phone buzzed. "Crap." I couldn't believe anybody would bother me at this moment. The text was from Katie asking me why I hadn't shown up to class.

"If you have to respond you can go ahead," Tyler said.

"No no no. No, it's fine." I turned it on silent and slipped it back into my pocket. "This is way more important." I turned and checked the hallway. Empty. I closed the door to his room.

"Listen, Tyler, I won't tell anyone about this or what happened, at all, in any way."

"Thanks. My family's already made the agreement to keep it secret. And you're the only one other than them who's visited me. My mom will probably ask you to keep quiet about it before you leave."

"Okay."

I wanted to ask him more things but I forced myself to hold off on any questions until he had said what he wanted. If he chose to share then he would share, and if he didn't, I wasn't going to push anything. He felt comfortable with me. He might even say something he wouldn't tell his parents or his doctors. Though I wasn't sure how to respond to any confessions. I had no training for this—I was a college sophomore with no serious crisis in my past to draw from.

"Did you know I was depressed?" he asked.

"No. Not until your mom told me before I walked in here."

"It's been happening for some time. I want to say I'm sorry because that's been why I haven't hung out with you."

"Don't worry about that."

"I didn't want to tell you."

"I get it. It can change how people view you."

Tyler readjusted on the bed, pushing his body up so his back was on his pillow and his head was on the wall in a slouched position. His head tilted to the side like it was too heavy to hold up. He took in long breaths and spoke slowly.

"It started, well, I don't know when it started. I think it's been with me all my life. I've always been very quiet, introverted. Just the way I was. But it all became a big problem at that party we went to, freshman year, with your friends, remember that?"

"Yeah. You had to leave."

"I didn't realize it at the time, but I had a full-fledged anxiety attack. I never would've believed that just going to a party could cause that. My heart was pounding in my chest, but pounding at weird intervals, sometimes rushing fast, with little beats, then stopping for several seconds before a really big beat. I thought I was having a heart attack. I was afraid I was going to pass out. Then my mind would blank out completely and I'd stare into space. I think my brain was overwhelmed by it all and shut down everything, like a computer overheating. But I was staring, and I knew people were noticing me and you were wondering, too. I wanted to stop, but I couldn't. No amount of willpower changed it. And, once I stopped blanking out, the anxiety rushed back. I didn't understand what was going on. I'd never felt that way before.

"After I went back to the dorm, I guessed I wasn't used to parties. The last one I'd gone to was when Joe pulled down my shorts. Maybe

I had built up a fear of them. I had heard of this thing that people can do to conquer their fears called exposure therapy, where you ease yourself into the fear. So, I tried that. I tried hanging out with a few engineering guys, even went to some of their parties. But it backfired. Every time I went it got worse. I was so stubborn and so convinced that I should be able to go out and do normal things that normal kids do all the time that I kept trying, and then the anxiety attacks started happening even when I wasn't at a party. They started happening at random times: in class, getting ready for school, at home watching TV. I'd wake up in the middle of the night shaking uncontrollably. I had to sleep with all my clothes on to stop it. And I didn't tell anybody. I didn't want to surrender. I had already lost so many battles in my life I didn't want to lose another one. So, I made a compromise and slowed down trying to make friends, but I was too late. I had set off something in me that took over from the anxiety that made it all—"

"The depression?"

"It prevented me from doing a lot of things. It drained all of my energy. I started skipping classes in January here and there, and I've never skipped classes in my whole life. I couldn't will myself to go. I got so lazy. Everything I did became joyless too. Video games, searching for interesting things online, listening to any kind of music—it seemed useless, like I was wasting my time. Anything I could think of doing felt like a waste of my time. My mind blanked over and over and I couldn't do homework because I couldn't focus on any problems. I saw the words and numbers but they blurred together in my mind. I stopped worrying that I might have heart problems and thought about brain cancer. Then in February I would wake up on some mornings already deep in that fog. I couldn't make myself even get out of bed. I'd lay there for hours staring at the ceiling. It's the worst I've ever felt. It's an altered state of mind. I couldn't even imagine what normal felt like.

"I had to keep calling in sick to work. I couldn't even do chores at home and my mom had to do them for me. I had to quit my job before they fired me. My muscles ached and so did my joints. My knees hurt the worst. But it goes deeper than that. There's loss of appetite. I stopped feeling hunger, stopped eating. When I did eat it all tasted like mush. Snacks, chocolate, steak, all the same. I'm like twenty pounds underweight now." He paused to catch his breath. His body looked skeletal under the sheets. I had to glance away from him. "The best I could manage was watching TV on some days. And I couldn't make sense of what I was watching. A basketball game would be on and I couldn't tell what the score was, or who had the ball. I didn't get bored either. No thoughts popped into my head, that's what was so scary. I had no thoughts to distract me. And it's not that you don't feel anything. You feel a pain of burden and dread. You get that distinction? It's worse than feeling like your life is passing you by. It's active suffering. It's misery in the purest form I know."

"I think so."

"There were some days I'd put on all of my winter clothes and coat and gloves and a hat and go outside on my patio even if it was freezing and dark. And I'd just stare into my backyard. I froze out there, but I wanted to. It dulled what I felt, so I sat on one of the patio chairs and forced the coldness and the shivering on myself. Sometimes, when I was doing that, it would ease up and loosen its grip to something tolerable. And Dylan, those moments were surreal. I wished that I could stay there forever like that, in a neutral state, free from that weight, and nothing about the situation would change either. I was willing to give up a lot so I could experience a calm." Tyler paused for more breath.

"When I was a kid I was always scared I'd fail at something, scared of Joe beating me at some game he made up, which he did all the time. I was terrified around him and I was terrified at school and at church. And I hated him, too. He was right about everything. I hated him so bad. But during puberty I think I learned to shove everything into a void. I couldn't express what I couldn't feel. At least, it was my strategy. That's when people started saying how quiet and calm I was. That's also when I started thinking about doing what I tried to do last night. I wrote notes in case I did do something. So I guess it's been in the back of my mind for a long time, around the last years that Joe tormented me. Maybe it was natural though, bottling it all up, something that was in my blood to begin with, there since the beginning. Either way it's my fault. I should've learned how to handle all of it better. Other people can and do move on from worse stuff."

"I wouldn't blame yourself for dulling your emotions. It's self-defense. It's a logical step to take. What other options did you have? Admit weakness to Joe and hope he backed off? What you did was what you thought was best. You can fight it but it's futile. No person can will themselves out of a mess like that. If you ask me, Joe put you in this hospital."

Tyler shook his head and yawned a slow and mouth-gaping yawn that sent a wave of tensing and stretching through his whole body.

"I don't want to keep bothering you here. You need some rest."

"No. Don't leave. I haven't even told my parents everything that I've told you. I just told them I was sorry."

"Are you on any medicine?"

"I started with something a few weeks ago but it takes over a month to have the full effect. The chemicals have to build up in my brain."

"Have you been seeing a psychiatrist?"

"No, well, it's a bit confusing. I saw a psychiatrist here after they pumped my stomach, but before this I visited a therapist—not a psychiatrist, they're different. The therapist I've been seeing can't diagnose me or prescribe medicine, and I can only see her a limited number of times under my mom's insurance. The therapist told me to go to my regular doctor, that's where I got the anti-depressants from. Told her I've been feeling down and empty and she handed me a prescription. They're SSRIs. She also took a blood sample to test for thyroid issues; they affect mood, but they came back negative."

"Are you going to see a psychiatrist when you get out?"

"My mom's health insurance doesn't cover it and they denied our claim for any more help. I still could, but I'd have to be put on a waiting list that'll take months. Once I get through that it'll cost at least a hundred for each hour, and the psychiatrist can choose not to take my case, you know, as a regular patient. And then it'll take a bunch of sessions to get an official diagnosis. My mom is barely getting by with money, even with dad helping. The housing crisis back in '08 hit them both hard—they're still recovering. It's out of the question for right now. I can stay here until tomorrow morning. The hospital has a three-day waiting list for the psych ward. Emergencies like mine get priority and can make the waiting even longer. I guess there are a lot of people like me out there."

"MU has a student wellness center. Did you try that?"

"Oh no. Remember Melody's class? Everyone knew that one girl had gone there because she was so overloaded with stress. If anybody goes there half the campus knows about it in a week."

Tyler was right. I had heard about plenty of students who had gone there. It was the center of gossip on campus. "How bad is it, right now?"

"Not bad." Tyler scoffed and smiled. "People don't kill themselves in the throes of deep depression. They don't have enough willpower to take their own lives because they're too depressed. It's a weird paradox. They only try when it's more moderate and bearable."

"Wow. What about your classes?"

"I think those are a lost cause. I missed midterms. And because I'm an engineering major, every class has to be taken in a certain order, so this could delay my graduation by a year. And withdrawing from all of those classes will go on my permanent record. I'm not worried about my record now. The delay is going to cost me a lot more in debt. I didn't know depression could be so expensive. But right now, I'm worried about the side effects for the pills. They said it neutralizes your mood. Turns you into a kind of zombie. Makes you restless, trouble sleeping, they might even fail to work, and they'll have to try a different dosage or a different brand."

"Damn."

Silence stole the room for a few moments. I looked around, noting the clock, the dormant machines next to his bed and a lone potted plant in the corner. Tyler watched the floor.

"There are over seven billion people living," he said. "I read it's estimated that if you add up all the humans that've ever lived, it's about one-hundred billion people. So for every living person on earth, there's about thirteen dead people."

"That's a lot of ghosts." I cleared my throat. "Have you ever heard why we say someone commits suicide? Like why we use the verb 'commit'?"

"Why?"

"Suicide used to be illegal, and we say crimes are 'committed.' Which makes me think: How did they punish suicide-committers back in the day? Did they throw the body in a jail cell?"

"Dylan?"

"Yeah?"

"Could you stay very positive for my mom? She was the one who found me in the bathroom. Don't tell her any of the bad stuff I told you."

"Okay. I can do that. How is your family doing?"

"They're more happy than anything. Happy that I survived."

"That's good. Is Chloe having a tough time with it?"

"I was pretty out of it when she visited. Good news was she didn't find me last night. She was out on a date with her boyfriend. He's like twenty-one, older than us."

"Does he go to MU?"

"I don't think so, but she won't tell us much about him." His eyelids then fell like shutters. He raised them and then they fell again.

"I'll go man. I'll see you. Don't worry about texting me. Take your time healing."

"I'll have to study up on healing first. I haven't had that class before," he said, eyes unfocused.

"The book costs about five-hundred dollars but you won't even need it."

"Until next time," Tyler nodded.

———————

Mrs. Eberle sat on a bench further down the hall. She got up and we walked toward each other. I stopped a few feet short, but she came right up to me and wrapped her arms around me, embracing me in this powerful hug. She had a tight grip and I could only move my arms enough to place my hands on her back. She rested her chin on my shoulder.

"Mrs. Eberle."

"I'm sorry but I'm not allowed to hold him yet." She sighed in tremendous relief. Her breathing eased against mine. "You're a lot like him."

"Yes."

"What matters is the people you grow close to. The world shrinks down to them. You're a good friend."

She released me from the hug and took a big sigh.

"I know Tyler's been lonely. You're the only person he talks about from MU. He doesn't spend much time with anybody else around his age. He's always been very shy."

She asked me to keep this private and I said I would. We gave brief goodbyes and I headed out of the hospital. Sitting in my car in the hospital parking lot, the urge to cry crept up on me. But I never did. I couldn't. Other cars searched for parking spots around me. I couldn't remember the last time I had cried from anything emotional. Physical pain, yeah, I could think of times when I cried from that. The urge passed. I saw an Audi and thought of Joe in his driveway. Then a pop can tilting off a rotted board. Joe had sent him to a hospital twice now. I drove back to my apartment, growing happier by the moment when I focused on the simple fact that Tyler had survived.

———————

Back at my apartment I checked my phone and discovered more text messages from Katie that began with curiosity and progressed into worry. I told her I had slept in and skipped the class. She had no problem with me skipping the class; she just wanted me to let her know. My open cereal box still rested on the kitchen table. Puddles of milk had dried to stains. None of my roommates were in at the time but there was a good chance one of them had stopped back to sneak in a nap or load up on protein powder. I cleaned up the mess. I packed my backpack and went to my next class. I focused on the lesson. But school didn't distract me for long. What happened that morning plagued my mind for weeks. Should I have seen it coming? There were signs, weren't there? He had vanished from Human Sexuality, and I hadn't paid much attention. Was that even a red flag? Tyler didn't act like any other college student I knew. He never gave any obvious signs—maybe I would've noticed them if he had. He had skipped classes because of his depression, but I didn't know that until the hospital visit. Nobody I ever knew had taken their own life, or, to my knowledge, attempted to. I had no other example to compare his behavior to. I ended up over-analyzing every second, questioning every word and gesture I had made toward Tyler and even his mom, as if there were right and wrong actions, like some sort of suicide-attempt exam.

My parents stayed in the dark about this. I never told them that Tyler had tried to take his own life. They found out after he was dead. I didn't think they suspected anything. They went on assuming Tyler and I were coming out of our shells, making brash decisions and learning from them. I had no trouble hiding it from my family.

I kept my promise to Tyler to keep his suicide attempt a secret, though I did know that a lot of people in my situation would have confided in others for support. I understood secrets have a way of eating the soul from the inside, but I hid it away, and so did Tyler's family. It became a point of debate in the aftermath of the shooting and I'll offer my reasoning: Letting his problems out would've made matters much worse. If people knew he had depression or had attempted suicide they would've moved further from him. Most would've seen him as responsible for his depression, avoided him like he was contagious, viewed him as a weakling for trying to take the coward's way out, and ostracized him. Secrets spread fast. And even faster with the internet. A black mark would've been scribed into everyone's mental profile on him. Like a scar it would've faded with time but never would have disappeared.

CHAPTER THIRTEEN

The Interlude

I kept up with Tyler through texting. They were short exchanges. Tyler never texted first, so I measured out how often I checked up on him. He struggled. His depression raged again as he recovered at home from his stomach-pumping. He was bed-ridden and virtually catatonic for hours, sometimes days, at a time. His doctor upped the dosage of his anti-depressants and they finally kicked in. Only then, once his mood had buoyed to a normal and stable level, did Tyler invite me over. He seemed distant and unengaged, incapable of smiling. He didn't find any of my jokes funny at all. But he could do chores, make his own meals, help his sister with homework, and keep himself busy. Mrs. Eberle was thrilled in a subdued, hold-your-breath excitement. Tyler said he was glad. They had figured out how to combat his depression. Getting more sunlight and exercise was his next step, as advised by his doctor. The visit lasted less than an hour and had me hopeful when I left. Tyler had fallen, but he could get back up.

I aced my spring finals without trouble and then reconnected with my high school friends around June. We had kept up on each other's whereabouts through text. Spending time with them for a little nostalgia grew appealing after Tyler's ordeal, so I messaged them. We agreed to meet on MU's campus in the student union, the same place we had met for supper with Tyler back in our freshman year.

Though we met in the middle of a weekday, no more than a dozen people milled around. The summer had again turned the campus into a ghost town. We ordered our food with no line. After handing us our food, the cafeteria workers went back to their phones in the air-conditioned stillness. We talked for over two hours, reminiscing on old times, giving updates on what had happened to old classmates, and giving each other crap, as usual, acting like it didn't bother us that we had gone a full year without meeting up. It was what I needed.

"When are you and Miranda getting engaged?" I asked Charlie.

"We're engaged to be engaged. Or that's how she puts it." His face had begun to fill out and he had a thick goatee, the first time I had ever seen him with facial hair. "Something's much more problematic than that."

"What?" Mark asked.

"She wants to have a threesome. And I'm being serious, no sarcasm."

"Great. How is that problematic?" Mark asked.

"It's the bad kind of threesome. Two dudes and her. She won't say it but I think it's her way of making up for me cheating on her."

Mark made guttural sounds of disgust. "I couldn't do that. No way, even if the girl was a supermodel."

"That's easy," Derek said, "Charlie, just say 'no homo' right before you start. Then if you touch tips it won't count as gay."

"So does she want one guy in the back and one in front, double penetration, what's the plan?" Mark asked.

Charlie shook his head. "I don't even want to think about it."

Mark chuckled. He held his hands up, fingers splayed apart. "Okay. So where is everybody at with their number?"

"Huh?"

"It's been two years of college, that's halfway. We should be at two by now, at least. I've had four. My frat's helped with that. I think we said five was our target number?"

"I'm working my way up, Mark, don't worry," Derek said, "but my number is staying secret. We've still got two more years."

"Sounds like somebody's falling behind," Charlie said.

"You're stuck with Miranda, how are you going to get any higher?"

"We also said doing weird, out-of-the-ordinary things counts, too. Miranda and I are close enough to do those things. A relationship has its advantages."

"Like threesomes?"

We all laughed—even I couldn't help myself. I missed their stupid brand of humor. Two months of joyless updates from Tyler had me desperate for something light-hearted. I laughed a lot more than I had expected to as we covered the same old topics that we had always covered, with a little catching up on all of the changes. And a lot had changed. They asked me about Katie and the Human Sexuality class and my job. But they didn't ask about Tyler, and I didn't say anything about him. I figured they had forgotten all about that quiet kid I had brought along to meet them, who went with us to our first party.

The conversation shifted from our lives to our other classmates from high school. Some were maturing, some weren't, some were dropping out, and some were getting DUIs. We talked about the creeps and the losers, and whether they were still creeps and losers. We talked about which girls had gotten hot and which guys had come out of the closet and which ones we thought were still in the closet. I learned that several of the straight-edge, straight-A students were now complete party animals. We had all changed a lot more in two years of college than in four years of high school.

Slowly we ran low on things to talk about. Derek had to go back home and I had a shift at the supermarket. We parted in a slow, almost imperceptible walk away from each other, like treading water in a split current, our jokes hiding our reluctance. That was the last time I saw any of them face-to-face. Another mini-reunion never materialized. They didn't meet me after what happened.

On my way out, I pushed through the double glass doors stained with dirt and shaded my eyes from the wrath of the sun. Someone called out to me.

"Dylan, is that you? Dylan Evans?"

"Yeah?" I said, without looking up. Whoever was speaking had a deep voice.

"Hey, it's Jeremy, remember me, your old RA?"

I forced my eyes up and saw Jeremy sporting a pitch-black pair of sunglasses. "What are you doing here in the summer?"

"I could ask you the same thing. I had a little too much fun in the spring and now I've got to make up some classes. Real boring shit. The second time around sucks."

"Are you still an RA?"

"Nope. I did it this past year but now I say screw it. Back in January a kid who wasn't even on my floor came back so drunk he head-butted one of our water fountains over, broke the water line, and flooded the hall and some of the rooms. I didn't get in trouble for it but man I am sick of babysitting. These kids coming in don't know two shits about having a good time. So how have you been? Getting panties to drop or what?"

Jeremy slapped me on my upper arm and knocked me off-balance. His tanned arms looked larger than they had at Harris Hall.

"I do have a girlfriend and I started an internship. Information technology."

"There you go. There you go. Success on two fronts."

"Thanks."

"Are you twenty-one yet?"

"I've got almost a whole year to go."

"Mm, well when you do try some of the bars around here, the good ones, I'll run into you. We can hang out then. I'd love to hear your story over a cold one."

"Sure, yeah, that sounds good."

"What else are you doing? You know? For fun?"

"Catching up with old friends, but other than that, I've got work soon."

"How about your friend? Tyler?"

"He's alright. Doing about the same things I am."

"But what about fun? You can't be stuck in textbooks or work. You'll have plenty of time to work later. You've got to get your fun in now. If you live your life too cautiously it's like you haven't even lived. Name one thing you've done to live it up."

He looked eager to be supportive—a smiling mouth under a dark band of sunglasses. A happy face without eyes. I didn't want to be rude.

"I went to a couple of parties."

"Man, what you guys need, I've seen this before, you need to be social. Get yourself and him to some parties, I mean real parties. Have Tyler meet your girlfriend's friends. Get wasted. Get super-fucked-up. Seen this happen with some of my students before and they need to get out. They were pent up from studying, classes, jobs, and they just needed to burn off some stress and let loose. Dude, this is college. It's time for everyone to come out of their shells. You end up regretting the things that you don't do a lot more than the things you try out. That's what I say. Friends don't let friends become losers. Alcohol. Dancing. Getting laid." His eyebrows rose over his shades. "Never failed to cheer anyone up—especially getting laid. I'm telling you, that's the answer."

I didn't think that was the answer at all. I had already heard it too many times at MU. Maybe everything wasn't about racking up experiences. I was losing faith in the concept of chasing what's considered fun and then treating everything else like it wasn't living. Tyler had tried to do what Jeremy prescribed and it had made him worse for it. Tyler wasn't built for that. Maybe it worked for some people, but not him. "I don't know, but thanks. I'll take it into consideration."

"I know I'm not your RA anymore but I'm always here for advice. I've got four years here and two of them as an RA. I've seen and dealt with it all, trust me bro."

"Alright."

"Business class is calling now, so I'll have to see you later."

"We could run into each other in the fall. The campus isn't that big."

"The more time you spend here the smaller it gets. See ya." Jeremy jogged toward one of the business buildings in the sticky heat. I headed back to my car on Lyndon Avenue.

What surprised me about the time from Tyler's suicide attempt in the spring all the way up to the blizzard a year later was that almost nobody asked me about him. Though Tyler did start classes again during our third year at MU, he didn't do much else, and I expected more people to ask how he was doing or where he was. People like roommates or friends or even Professor Melody, or Tyler's engineering classmates, or other professors or counselors. He had disappeared during our sophomore year and not even my roommates asked about Tyler even though they had seen him studying with me in the apartment multiple times. I guessed that he had said so little that they never paid attention to him and he never made an impression. I invented a whole story about stress to explain why he had to skip and then drop his classes in the spring but I never had to use it. I wasn't sure if everybody suspected something was wrong and they wanted to respect his privacy or forgot about him or didn't care. College was supposed to be an exciting time.

Maybe everyone wanted to filter out the negative. I certainly tried to distract myself in the months following his stay at the hospital.

One person who did ask and did persist was Katie. She noticed I had stopped talking about Tyler. She never saw him on campus anymore. To her, Tyler had dropped off the radar. I held off on telling her about him until our junior year was about to begin, when she grew impatient with my dodges and half-assed answers to her questions on where Tyler had gone. I did tell her he was struggling and had to take some time off. I played dumb and said I didn't have any specifics, other than he still wasn't gay. She reacted not with shock or sympathy but with clinical precision, analyzing the situation and trying to explain to me the immense strain some students were under, like I didn't know. Her line of questioning then narrowed to his grades, expectations, and a social safety net. I told her about his engineering project disaster.

"So, grades are that important to him?"

"I've been telling you: I don't know. When you're friends with someone you don't draw up a list of your priorities and exchange them. He worked hard on that project. I can tell you that. He single-handedly built that robot. He made a habit of studying hard and I'm sure he felt proud of his grades. Did he place the value of his life on them? I don't think so." We were at Katie's apartment. I had been helping her move some of her stuff in before fall classes began. I plopped down on her couch, facing a TV stand with no TV.

"Well, a strong circle of friends and a close community are vital for someone who's struggling to get back on their feet."

"What community? He's from the same kind of suburbia we're from and you know what that's like. I've been to his street. No one leaves their house unless it's in a car to go somewhere. There are no block parties. No grill-outs. Their next-door neighbors moved in six years ago and they've never met them. They're all stuck inside staring at screens. We all are. And his circle of friends? The neighborhood kids picked on him. He was their laughingstock. Well, it was one older boy. He always set up these games rigged to make Tyler lose. I'm glad he doesn't hang out with that bully anymore. He was a huge blow to his confidence."

"What about his family, are they there for him? Everyone around him needs to pitch in and stay supportive, including you."

"You sound like a textbook, Katie."

"Okay but you know what friends are supposed to do."

"Make insulting jokes?"

"Come on, what's gotten into you? I'm trying to help."

"No, I'm sick of—never mind."

"Sick of what?" Katie asked.

"We're all sick of things."

"Anything that we're not sick of?"

"I think that what we're told is the best for people isn't always the best for every single person. We think that joining a group will always help people even if we have to change who we are to do it. Isn't that conforming? I thought that was supposed to be a bad thing. Tyler's been spending most of his time alone in his house and he's doing much better. Trying to party, trying to fit in, drinking, having a good time, doing what everybody else is doing—that's what was hurting him. People are wired differently. One solution isn't going to work for them all."

"I can see that. It's frustrating. But you can't sit and sulk."

"That sounds like a good plan."

———

Tyler returned to a normal load of classes in the fall. He held off on finding a new job. Through texts, he told me he was taking the full schedule well. The medicine kept his mood in check and if he wasn't at school or at work he stayed home. I started hanging out with other students from my new internship and only visited Tyler a couple of times. We texted each other here and there, replying hours or even a day after one of us had sent something, which made simple conversations take weeks. But that had become the norm for us. Tyler would call if he wanted me to come over and if my schedule allowed it, I would. All we did then was talk. We didn't touch video games or use the internet to look up disturbing videos. The conversations were peaceful and slow and came with long silences. His mom sometimes spoke with us, always calm and gentle. No one was pressed for information. Chloe asked politely if Tyler could help her with homework. He always did. The allotted sessions with his therapist had run out by then, and the SSRIs were the last remaining tangible defense against his depression and anxiety. I could tell Mrs. Eberle monitored his mood and made every effort to reduce his stress level. We never went shooting again. The subject of his dad's guns never surfaced after his suicide attempt. I assumed they had become off-limits.

Katie and I broke up around October. Despite the media reports, our break-up had nothing to do with Tyler. She had gotten busier like I had and the relationship faded fast, so we made the decision together. Tyler had no reaction to the news except to give his dry sympathy—the medicine sucked all inflection out of his voice. He never got to know Katie. I wish he had.

CHAPTER FOURTEEN

One Last Time

The last time I saw Tyler was in November, three months before that terrible event. I drove over to his house on a Sunday afternoon when I was off from work. He answered the door and I took off my shoes. The stairs creaked under the weight of our bodies. In his room we held a long, drawn-out talk, much longer than our earlier conversations that fall. The topics jumped in different directions like a rock kicked across pavement. We brought up a lot of facts. Our fact-finding and sharing had resurfaced with new and old topics. His body had a little meat on it, up from the anorexic look of his hospital stay. On the other hand, his acne had returned with a vengeance, mixing a blotchy red with the pale tone of his face. His eyes had a polished tint. His room was spotless, save for the dust on his shelves, trophies, and medals.

"Did you know there are strong financial ties between the American Psychiatric Association and pharmaceutical companies?" Tyler asked me.

"Yeah, I knew that one."

"And the DSM-5, which is like the bible of psychology, was written by people who had ties to the pharmaceutical industry?"

"I bet you didn't learn that at MU."

"No. I had to find it online."

I sat at his desk. Tyler had let me use his laptop to show him some things on Facebook. "Where's Chloe and your mom?"

"Chloe left to go bowling with her boyfriend. My mom's lounging outside on the patio, reading a book."

"At least the weather's still nice." The window was wide open and a fresh flow of comfortably cool air streamed in. Tyler stood near it, sometimes staring out at the unchanging view. Joe's car was parked in the driveway across the street. Did Joe still have the paintball gun he used to shoot Tyler and send him to the hospital? He probably kept it as a trophy, collecting dust somewhere like the plastic trophies on Tyler's shelves.

I watched Tyler's gaze. His eyes held onto nothingness beyond the window.

I scrolled through my Facebook feed. Sometimes I showed him my social media accounts. He didn't have any. He knew all about Facebook and social media—but he had no interest in making any accounts. A solid block of text appeared on the screen and I stopped to read. Any status longer than a few sentences caught my attention. This one was an essay defending a baseball team's trades written by Derek. I skimmed through it.

"Tyler?"

"Huh? Sorry, I blanked out."

"Is that the medicine? You were staring for a while."

"Sometimes it feels like I lose the ability to think. My body still works fine, but my mind seems to shut down all the higher functions. I can't get a train of thought going."

"That sounds like the depression."

"No. There's none of that sinking awfulness. Blanking out is actually kind of good because it counters this urge I get to move all the time. Restlessness is one of the main side effects."

"Here, let me show you this."

Tyler read part of Derek's post and we talked about how some students could struggle so much in class and yet do great critical thinking when it came to their own interests. We moved from Derek's post to several pictures of my friends and their friends partying and drinking. Most of them were still under twenty-one. I said how the pictures worked more like presenting proof of having an enviable life than any sort of actual sharing. Tyler agreed.

"When I was at the hospital the doctors told me I needed to stop drinking alcohol," Tyler said. "If I wasn't miserable, I would've laughed then. They didn't believe me when I said I didn't drink. They asked me a bunch of times if I did, and said they wouldn't get me in trouble because I was under twenty-one."

"Alcohol makes what you have worse?"

"Yeah. It can contribute to it. That's what my mom was worried about, back in March, before I went to the hospital."

"She thought you were drinking?"

"When I started having all the anxiety, and later the bad depression, I didn't tell anybody, not you, not my mom. I wanted to get through it myself. But back in the spring it got so severe I couldn't hide it anymore. I was acting weird. I wasn't eating. My mom told me she thought I was binge drinking or on drugs. I almost lied to her and said she was right. Telling her what I had really been going through felt like admitting defeat, that I couldn't even handle a problem that I had created. I should've told her sooner. It had gotten bad. I was having trouble telling what I was experiencing, like if it was real or not. I became paranoid that everybody knew that I was losing it. My therapist asked me if I was hearing voices. She was asking me if I was coming down with schizophrenia. I'm at the prime age for when you get it—late-teens and early-twenties."

Tyler took a step back and sat down on his bed. I had to turn away from his laptop to face him.

"That's when you—"

"I saw the therapist first. That was too little, too late." Tyler took a quick breath. "I had already fantasized about ending it a bunch of times. Imagining myself jumping off a high cliff was relaxing. It was reassuring. It brought me peace. Like I had to remind myself there was a way out and I wasn't trapped. I didn't like taking all those pills in the bathroom. I didn't think it was an honorable way to go, but I had to change something. Then I failed at that."

Tyler, still on his bed, arched his back, his legs inline, the bony protrusions of his knees touching each other. "The psychiatrist at the hospital said just talking about what was going on with me could help. She asked me a lot of personal questions. She asked me if I had a recent break-up. Nope. I was probably watching her too closely but she looked like she didn't believe it. All those questions reminded me of something else. In high school my mom had this big talk with me about sex and sexuality. I wasn't going out or doing anything then, just playing video games. And I liked that, no one was picking on me. But she told me that sex was about love, you know, and even though we're Catholic she didn't see it as wrong to have sex before you get married, and to not feel guilty about pleasure. And then she said there was nothing wrong with homosexuality either, despite what my school or my priest said. And having feelings for the same sex was okay and she would love me no matter who I was. I hadn't been on any dates yet or asked out a girl. I had been afraid she was going to say something like that. Before this year she would try to push me to go out or try to set me up with girls. And I did go a few times. But now, since the hospital, she doesn't anymore."

"Neither of my parents had any talk with me like that. Only the standard birds-and-the-bees breakdown. The rest I learned from the internet."

"My dad never talked to me about it. Those things were off-limits with him. Both the right and wrong of it and how I should approach it. They were topics I knew just didn't get brought up when he was around."

We paused. I glanced down at the carpet. The wind pumped fresh air into the bedroom. Not even a tinge of awkwardness marked the quiet moment. We soaked in the silence.

———————

"That's part of why I kept going to parties," Tyler said.

"Hmm?"

"I wanted—I wanted friends. I wanted people to hang out with. That's what everybody does in college. I wanted to have relationships with people my age. I thought somebody might ask me to hang out with them, like not at parties, but that hasn't worked, other than you. I'm too much of a coward to start a friendship myself. I thought parties could help me become part of a group, and that would give me better chances of finding friends. That, and I could actually have a life."

"Hard partying isn't for everybody."

"Isn't that what college is about? You don't remember the classes; you're supposed to have the wild and fun times and remember them."

"You know I don't party that much."

"But everybody does some. And you could if you wanted to. I'm not looking to pack a lifetime into four years of weekends. I see a lot of people trying to do that. But if I could have a little fun. Those parties with my engineering classmates are like trials. I can't make friends unless I go to them. And I lock up when I do go. It's like I can't let loose and never will be able to. It's embedded in my personality or something."

"What we're capable of can change over time. Our limits aren't set in stone."

"It's not only the big parties. Normal stuff is a problem for me, when it comes to groups or strangers. I can't even talk sometimes. I can't even bring myself to say anything. I've always thought having a very small social life was wrong. So I've always felt I've been living life the wrong way. And my therapist and my parents said I need to socialize more. Their message was that too much loneliness will make me crazy."

"Yeah." I stood up and stretched my back and arms. Outside, there were only empty yards. Nobody was out.

"Why do I have so much trouble doing something that everybody else can do?"

"I don't know. I feel like I'm not the most qualified person to answer that question. You seem to do better when it's a one-on-one setting, like here, just us two."

"But everything's done in groups. We have groups in my classes, crammed parties, even at my job we worked in teams. I know if I try to adjust myself to it the anxiety and depression will come back. Worse than before."

I was at a loss here for Tyler. I didn't want to comfort him with empty words or sayings. We were both too smart to think motivational phrases or changing our attitudes was going to do anything. Tyler didn't take medication to change his outlook on life. He took it to fight a disease.

"I'm afraid I'm going to have to play it safe to stay healthy," he said. "Couldn't that backfire too? I don't know how to deal with this. I'm trying to grab onto whatever I can. I'm scared."

I bent my head down. "You're being too hard on yourself. Yeah, risk is a part of life. It's almost like you have to do self-destructive things to grow as a person. I hear a lot of adults say 'I'm glad I got all of the partying and drugs out of my system when I was young' like it's a healthy rite of passage, but I'm not so sure. It sounds wrong to me. Is everybody supposed to pass through certain hoops? And once they've done those things, that's when people can say that they lived a full life?"

Tyler put his hands on his head.

"How're you feeling now?" I asked.

"It's mild. It's at a standstill. I've heard of something called anhedonia. You can't feel good about anything. No pleasure, no excitement—you don't enjoy things you like. But I can get out of bed in the mornings and go to school. It's a bizarre feeling. I've spent so long completely out of it that coming close to a normal state of mind doesn't seem natural. I got so used to being on the cusp of an anxiety attack or in the abyss of depression that this calm is weird. I don't think I'll take a moment of peace for granted anymore."

"What can you do now?"

"A part of me wants to make more friends and basically try again with a social life. But right now I can't stop looking back on bad things that have happened in my life. I have to stop running those movies in my head over and over. Some of them bother me a lot. I don't know how to forget them."

"Like being at the hospital?"

"That will never go away. I was thinking of smaller stuff. Like in the summer, I think in May, one night I was wandering around in my house—I wandered around a lot back then. I needed something to distract myself, keep my mind busy. I went to the spare bedroom to look for some old *Hardy Boys* books to read, and I walked in on Chloe and her boyfriend, in bed. I closed the door and we've pretended like it didn't happen. I don't want to think about it. It was so embarrassing, but it keeps resurfacing. I'm only telling you about it because I hope that telling other people will help this stuff go away."

"I once walked in on one of my roommates with his girlfriend. The idiot forgot to lock the door. We didn't look at each other for a week. But why was your sister in the spare bedroom?"

"I don't know. They would've gotten all the privacy they wanted in her bedroom. I never went in there if the door was closed."

"Did they forget to lock the door too?"

"The door to that room doesn't lock. The frame doesn't align. It's a problem with this whole house. A couple of other doors won't lock either. It was poorly built and all the wood warps with the changing weather."

"Then why would they use a room that doesn't lock?"

"I'm not sure."

"Maybe they wanted to change things up. Sorry, shouldn't speculate."

"No, that's alright."

"Is it hard to forget what Joe did to you because of the scar on your head? Does it ever hurt?"

"My hair keeps the scar out of sight. But the pain flared up a lot back when it was healing. Then I got small shocks of it in high school. Nowadays I don't think there's anything wrong with it, but it feels uncomfortable at times, like it didn't heal quite right. Or some sort of phantom pain because I know how much damage was done there."

I changed the subject back to some of our fact-finding. He grew more disconnected as we talked through his personal memories. His eyes kept wandering and sinking to the floor or to his knees. I didn't want to end our conversation on such a low note for him. Some of the facts were about drone strikes, MK Ultra, the Bath School massacre, COINTELPRO, and Olga Hepnarova. Despite the morbid subject matters, they cheered him up. They were a great distraction.

I left Tyler's house before he had to help prep for supper. I didn't look back at his house as I strolled to my car, parked along the curb in front of Joe's house. We never bothered to wave or watch each other leave our streets. I expected to see him in a month or more, depending on finals. I turned my key and started my engine. Tyler had Mass with his family that night, Sunday night, a Mass known for having more young people. They sang faster and more upbeat hymns and the gospel and homily focused on how to gain confidence and form your identity. Tyler had told me about it. As I drove down the barren street, I hoped he'd enjoy his meal and the Mass.

I never saw him alive after that November day, not even on campus. I kept expecting to catch him in the crowds filing through the halls or the walkways or the old tunnels, his head hanging down. I planned on jogging up to him and asking what class he was headed to, maybe ask if we could restart our study sessions. But the opportunity never presented itself.

The area in and around the city and MU saw snowfall in the winter, typically from mid-December to early March. That winter, the winter of our junior year, stayed mild with almost no heavy snowfall. A thin coating turned the campus white through January, but the snow and cold never went beyond a minor inconvenience. The surprising lack of bad weather came up a lot around campus. Everyone viewed it as a lucky break.

My roommates took advantage of the toothless winter. They went to tons of parties that raged off campus. Sometimes I tagged along. Drawn-out, bitter winters dampened the wild nights, but during that winter the rampant drinking and unfettered celebration electrified the mesh of side streets around campus. It made me think of a dystopia where the government required nighttime festivities for its citizens to distract them from their lack of freedom. Usually I'd lay in bed in my apartment, trying to sleep, trying to block out shrieks of joy, the constant chatter, glass bottles tumbling down salted sidewalks. I had a lot of time to think then, to wonder why all of it was going on. There did seem to be a special vibe in the atmosphere. Even in the daytime there was some cheer in the students moving through their schedules, and at night, buzzing under clear starry skies, there was ecstasy.

During the same months, after a December of almost no communication, Tyler and I started to text again when Christmas break ended. He let me know that the side effects of his medicine had taken a turn for the worse, so he had stopped taking them. Not that long after, his texts began to worry me. At first they seemed disconnected from what I texted back to him, like he wasn't receiving my texts, or ignoring them. Then they grew from reasonable fears about his medication, grades, and mood to much more unreasonable paranoia, often mentioning Joe and other past bullies coming back to hurt him further, along with a fear that some students at MU were plotting and conspiring against him, seeking to humiliate him and get him kicked out of MU. My texts reassuring him that this had no chance of happening and that the students were far more concerned about their own partying and problems did nothing to keep his thoughts in check. He didn't text me a bunch about this, only here and there, but it was a major shift from any past conversation we had had. He sounded regretful about not defending himself from Joe years earlier, and started to sound like a conspiracy theorist on campus activities and parties. One time police had to break up a rowdy party that had spilled onto the streets off-campus. Tyler latched onto this. Something sinister was brewing in and around campus, but he couldn't quite figure it out. He asked me a lot of questions about what I could see from my classes and apartment, like he was recruiting me for surveillance.

I had never seen him so blind to any sense of reason before. He seemed unable to question his own beliefs even when I pointed out their problems. Though it did take me too long, I tried to help Tyler by going around him. Maybe I did cut him too much slack, but I had nobody to consult on this. He hadn't threatened anyone and I assumed his medication would be changed again and he would drop his delusions. In February I reached Mrs. Eberle by finding her number on my phone from when Tyler had been hospitalized. She said the whole family and his doctor knew about his shift—he had been skipping classes—and he had started a new medication. She thanked me for my concern, and added that I should see him when he got better. A week later Tyler's slow but steady trickle of texts stopped, without warning. Every day that followed brought silence from Tyler, and relief from me. I didn't hear anything from him again.

CHAPTER FIFTEEN

The Blizzard

On Wednesday, February 18th, forecasts began warning of heavy snowfall incoming, sometime around Friday. Nobody on campus took much notice. I remember that clearly, how no one reacted. Several inches of snow falling in one night or one day was not abnormal. We were all kind of expecting it to happen sooner or later. But on Thursday, the 19th, the forecast worsened, and the timetable was bumped up to Friday morning. A winter storm was approaching, preparing to unleash up to half a foot of snow, surging icy winds, and a sharp drop in temperatures. Advisories and warnings were sent out and MU cancelled all classes for Friday. At this point I was in a technology course. When the news broke of cancelled classes, everyone cheered and clapped, even the professor. No mention of the word blizzard had shown up in the weather reports. Everyone took it as a blessing, not a danger. To celebrate the three-day weekend, students planned or moved parties up from Friday night to Thursday night to get ahead of the weather.

I had one more class on Thursday afternoon in economic theory. By that time in the semester maybe half of the students showed up for class given good weather. On that day a quarter of the class decided to show up. The professor waited past the start time for more students to arrive late, as they usually did, but no more entered through the fireproof steel doors. It felt like the last day of classes before Christmas break in grade school, where every student couldn't wait to head home for presents. Instead of bored disengagement, we were restless, fidgeting and squirming like children. The professor, at first hesitant, gave a shortened but fervent lecture on Friedrich Hayek and then dismissed us. She offered more personalized help to any student who wanted to stay. I was the only one who did. We spoke for a short while, clarifying differences in terms until she dropped a clue about what would be on the exam. She said she was impressed by my questions in class and asked why I didn't think of making economics a minor. I said I already had a pretty good grasp of how it worked.

I hurried across the campus and headed for my apartment before it began snowing. The fragile sun struggled to warm the roads and walkways. I watched my breath linger in front of me as I waited to cross Lyndon Avenue. My apartment wasn't far from campus. I looked back at Harris Hall, towering over the street and the off-campus housing beyond. The massive brick building appeared as ancient and brutal as when Tyler and I lived there our freshman year. I counted the windows and found my old dorm on the twelfth floor. The window was open, which meant the boiler was running. I missed it. I missed the cramped halls and Henry's empty bed. I imagined my younger self staring out the window, watching the parties across Lyndon, Tyler joining me as we took in the planned chaos below, our faces darkened by the steel netting. The crosswalk symbol changed and Harris Hall continued to draw my attention, forcing me to look back as I crossed. The cold exhaust from the mass of traffic soon obscured the view. I returned to my apartment and finished some homework. By the time I went to bed only one roommate was there with me—the other two had left for parties. I fell asleep with nothing on my mind.

A blizzard was a surprise to everyone that night. Weather forecasters knew it was serious, but they had underestimated the speed and strength of the incoming storm. MU sent email warnings out to students, advising them to take caution over Thursday night and Friday morning. No one paid any attention. As the parties began to ramp up near midnight, so did the storm, dumping heavy snow in erratic, gusting winds with freezing temperatures that rendered road salt useless. States of emergency were declared and the roads gradually emptied as the snow built up, erasing lanes and then entire streets, piling up at record speed, with accumulation totals reaching over a foot-and-a-half to two-feet by morning. The blizzard broke multiple snowfall and temperature records for February, but no one hit by the storm would care too much about it.

Tyler attended his two morning classes that Thursday as usual. Advanced calculus and an engineering course he had to drop out of the year before because of his suicide attempt. He showed no signs that anything was out of the ordinary. He then left campus and stopped at a fast-food place for lunch. From there he drove straight to his new job at a local business, where he did part-time data entry for minimum wage. Tyler never told me about that job—I found that out later. His co-workers and boss said he was quiet that day, same as he had been in his two weeks there. He didn't bother anybody and no one bothered him. When the shift ended, he got back home at around six and reheated leftovers for supper. He ate alone in his house. Chloe was at her boyfriend's house and would be trapped there in the blizzard. Mrs. Eberle had left to run some overdue errands and pick up salt for the coming snow. On the way back she stopped at an electronics store. They were having a sale. While browsing she ran into an old friend and talked for over an hour about their current lives and their old ones. She made it back to the house at eleven, and by then Tyler had gone. This left a roughly five-hour gap in Tyler's last day in which nobody knew what he did. He had no activity on his phone for that time. The last text Tyler sent was to his mom, on Wednesday, letting her know about his shift on Thursday. Mrs. Eberle didn't worry over his absence when she got back. She was glad he had left, and thought he had gone to do something with me. She had made a point to stay out of his personal life in hopes of encouraging his independence. Though his depression was still there, it didn't weigh too heavily on him. The paranoia had ebbed and risen like a pendulum, but held within manageable levels. She thought the worst was over, and so did I.

Rumors on what he did with this free time never reached a consensus. Some said he used this time to watch the weather reports and formulate his plot to attack a party during the storm. Others said his depression would've prevented any kind of clear planning, and he most likely did something harmless like watch TV in a stupor until something in his mind broke.

Either way, he had to make a choice at some time because he left the house and drove to his dad's, where neighbors noticed his car pulling in the garage at around eleven-thirty. At the time his dad was two weeks into a three-week business trip to Oregon. The neighbors who saw his car thought nothing of it. They did note that he stayed in his dad's house for over twenty minutes, which meant Tyler didn't go straight for the guns. No one can know what he did there, if he hesitated, changed plans, or had some terrible epiphany. It is plausible that Tyler drove to his dad's house to check on it. He gave no definitive signs of setting in motion a plan until he left his dad's house with the guns. Tyler still knew where the key to his dad's gun safe was. After his suicide attempt his parents had told him he couldn't use the guns unless he had permission from both of them first. They never took the key away. All his life he had been an obedient son to them. He had never acted up or broken the rules. Telling him he shouldn't do something had been sufficient. His sister was the problem child, always doing things she wasn't supposed to. She went over to her boyfriend's when she wasn't allowed to a ton of times. The previous summer they had taken away her car keys for two weeks when she drove home from a friend's house drunk.

Tyler took his dad's .22 lever-action rifle, the same one we had fired in the field, a .40 caliber semi-automatic handgun, which we never used in the field, and a box of ammunition for the rifle. He loaded them in his dad's pick-up. It was four-wheel drive. Snow was building in the roads by then and Tyler's car was front-wheel drive. He would've never made it to campus if he had driven his car. Security cameras at the North Garage caught Tyler scanning in his parking pass about forty-five minutes after leaving his dad's house. The police calculated that given the snowy conditions he drove straight to campus. Plow trucks were failing to keep up with the snowfall. If he had left his dad's house a half an hour later the blizzard would've made driving impossible for him, four-wheel drive or not.

A dozen outdoor security cameras captured him moving through the campus as the intensity of the blizzard grew. He wore several layers of clothing, a winter beanie, his warehouse work boots, and his backpack, still holding books and homework. He carried the rifle in his backpack and the handgun in one of the large pockets of his winter coat. He couldn't zip up the backpack all the way because of the rifle's length, so the stock jutted out of the backpack by almost a foot. He probably left the stock exposed so it would've been easy to pull the gun out when the time came. Given the weather conditions it's reasonable that no one would've noticed it. To stay out of the cold Tyler went into empty classroom buildings, walking in one side and coming out the other, hopping from shelter to shelter like students did between classes. The cameras were not monitored, but even if they were, a student on campus at night during a storm wouldn't have raised any alarms.

A few other students did the same thing that night. The camera footage released to the public shows more than one dark outline moving through the thick white pouring in. Tyler almost crossed paths with one of them. Some of these students have since come forward and explained they were travelling to or from parties. This doesn't surprise me—thousands of students dorm at MU and I knew plenty who were nocturnal. I had sometimes walked around campus at 3 a.m. with Katie for the hell of it.

———

Tyler vanished from the last security camera at 12:55 a.m. The last camera caught him as he crossed Lyndon Avenue at about the same spot I had crossed that afternoon, hours earlier. Technically he crossed Lyndon a day later, since it was Friday morning. From Lyndon, Tyler went off the radar again, venturing into the maze of off-campus housing that stretched for miles beyond campus. Harris Hall stood tall over his back as he made his way into the corridors, though he could've barely seen it through the snow.

Not much is known about Tyler's actions from here as no cameras or witnesses spotted him. With raging weather and nighttime creating a dense darkness, he probably got lost and wandered aimlessly for about half an hour in the deepening snow. He could've used a porch or one of the massive trees for shelter. The temperature didn't fall steeply enough to harm him. His body had no signs of frostbite. He then could've heard music or have seen lights coming from the house and trudged through the snow to reach it. The house was a century old, red brick, much smaller, but similar to, the house where Tyler and I had gone for our first real party two years earlier with my high school friends. Inside, about thirty students were enjoying a low-intensity three-day-weekend celebration. Originally slated for Friday, they had moved the date up because of the cancelled classes. Six students lived there—three were present and acted as hosts. Everyone inside knew about the storm. They either didn't care or considered it too late to do anything about the blizzard and continued like nothing was wrong. The hosts had even shut all of the blinds to block the view of the white torrents and growing snowbanks burying cars and bushes outside. By the time Tyler opened the front door the snowfall total had surpassed a foot in some neighborhoods west of the city. The MU area, then cresting eight inches, with snowbanks doubling that height, would end up with the highest snow accumulation in the region.

The hosts left the front door unlocked because that was their habit during parties. They wanted large parties and didn't care who showed up. The hosts didn't know half of their guests that night. Tyler opened the door and entered the house unnoticed, thanks to the music and wind. He took off his beanie. He took off his backpack and set it down. He most likely took a moment to warm up his hands and fingers. Right inside the door a flight of stairs ran up to the second floor, a hallway next to it ran to the kitchen, and a dining room veered off to the left, used as a storage room for old furniture. The nearest people to Tyler were two students: twenty-two-year-old Erin Seig and twenty-year-old Luke Baker. They stood halfway down the hall chatting. Others nearby recalled in interviews that Erin and Luke were talking about what their proms were like.

Tyler removed the rifle from the backpack. He raised it to his left shoulder and aimed down the hall, still unnoticed. The first shot hit Luke in the right side of the chest, fracturing a rib and ricocheting through his abdomen. He stumbled in shock and grabbed his side. His beer bottle fell first, bouncing on the hardwood floor but not breaking. Luke grimaced and stumbled some, and then collapsed onto the floor. Erin watched Luke fall as Tyler pulled the lever and fired again, striking her on the left side, puncturing her stomach. She doubled over from the sudden and extreme pain, groaning uncontrollably. Students further down the hallway said that was the most pained sound they had ever heard a human make. She then passed out, landed on Luke, and rolled off him. Blood and stomach fluids crept over her teal shirt. Neither of them died right away. It was a gruesome, ugly spectacle. The bullets made a mockery of their bodies.

After Erin lost consciousness, students nearby realized something had gone wrong. The thick plaster walls and confined spaces of the house had efficiently funneled the ring of the gunshots to every floor and every room, but those further away couldn't tell what caused the sound. Someone turned off the music. There are differing accounts of how the party first reacted. Some witnesses say everyone ran amok in a volley of shrieks and curses and a mad rush to the backdoor in the kitchen, and others claim there was confusion and a slow, partial evacuation. It's assumed that Tyler had difficulty cycling to the next round because he did not fire as students fled across his line of sight to the kitchen. There was a side hallway that split off from the main one which led to the bathroom and two rooms with more students. They had to cross the main hallway, where Tyler had his line of sight, to get to the kitchen. As word spread deeper into the house that those loud noises were gunshots and not the house buckling in the storm, more and more students wanted to escape. Some didn't want to risk crossing the hallway so they broke windows with chairs and other furniture and hurdled out into the rampaging blizzard. The old, single-pane glass gave way easily to blunt force. A few of the guys stayed near the windows to assist the students piling out. Several cut their arms and legs on broken glass. These gashes and scrapes would account for most of the injuries sustained in the shooting.

Tyler must've fixed the rifle within a short time because he advanced down the hallway as students continued to flee. His boots made heavy thuds on the hardwood. Snow melted and dripped from them. He would've had to step over the still-breathing bodies of Erin and Luke. He didn't shoot either of them a second time. Maybe he didn't inspect them closely enough to tell if they were dead, or maybe he didn't care.

Past them he reached the end of the main hallway. He checked the now-deserted kitchen to the left, its backdoor wide open and askew, the hinges partially ripped from the frame. Amidst the confusion a few students had chosen to hide in closets or behind couches instead of escaping. Some saw Tyler and later became important witnesses. They said he moved slowly and deliberately, his face blank, his head hanging like weights had been attached to his skull. He said nothing the entire time and wore a dull-orange winter coat, the handgun still in its pocket. He turned right into the side hallway, glancing around. With the music off only his footsteps and the whistling wind could be heard. The open window frames let in flurries and freezing air. Students hiding from him covered their mouths and noses so he couldn't see their breath. When Tyler turned into one of the rooms off the hallway almost all of the students had either hidden or escaped; however, a drunken student who said there was nothing to be afraid of stood in the open. Curtiss Staudigel, a tall, muscular grad student, who was known for drinking too much, stood in the center of the room facing Tyler, bottle in hand. Tyler raised his rifle and fired at him. The shot struck Curtiss in the chest, severing his abdominal aorta. He was unconscious before he hit the floor and dead within a minute. The blood leaking out of his wound coagulated in the cold room. He was twenty-three.

Tyler stood and watched Curtiss's motionless body for some seconds. Curtiss was the third to be shot and the first to die. Even though Tyler had more potential targets in that room he turned around and went to check on the other room. Everyone there had found a hiding spot or left. One girl had even hopped out the window and ducked below it to hide. She would later re-enter the house and help others get out. Tyler did not make any effort to search the room—he scanned it and then paused again, facing the open windows. It's not known why. Some have theorized that this was where he started to understand the gravity of what he had done.

He then turned and plodded back down the hallway, boots hitting the floor in hollow stomps. As he walked past a closed bathroom door, a cellphone began to ring behind it. A sophomore, Cory Gentry, had locked himself in the bathroom right after the first shots went off and crouched in the shower for protection. He had a girlfriend who was also at the party, but she had made it out. Desperate to know if her boyfriend was alright, she called Cory's phone once she found shelter in a nearby house. He had forgotten to turn it off or put it on silent. The flimsy wooden door did nothing to muffle the ringtone on full volume. Tyler faced the door and pulled the lever on his rifle—because he had forgotten to do it after he shot Curtiss. Without even trying to open the door he fired through it, aiming high because the rifle was too long to hold level across the tight hallway. Though a small and slow bullet, the .22 managed to penetrate the door and embed itself in the tile above Cory, spraying wooden splinters and tile chunks like shrapnel. A few of the splinters struck him in the arm and back, causing superficial wounds. Tyler did not try to call out to him or force his way in. He did not fire into the bathroom again. He turned toward the kitchen.

Trevor Darrington did not attend the party. When Tyler fired his first shot, he was at a different party in a nearby house, in the upstairs bedroom. The racing wind stole the sound of the gunshots away, but the snow could not blot out his view of students escaping through the doors and windows. With no other information to go on, he assumed there was a fire, a danger that was very common in off-campus houses, especially during the winter. He ran downstairs and alerted others to the possibility of a fire in the nearby house. Injured and frantic survivors streamed into Trevor's party, spreading their panic and confusion. Conflicting information spread fast. Some of the survivors believed it was a fire. Trevor probably couldn't stomach the thought of doing nothing about students trapped and injured in the house, in desperate need of help. He donned a winter coat and boots. No one noticed him leaving. He made the short distance through the deep snow, retracing the steps the fleeing students had made, entering the kitchen past the broken backdoor. It didn't take him long to figure out there was no fire. Nobody was in the kitchen and there was no smoke. He might've smelled the burnt cordite from the rifle. It's an acrid smell. Tyler shot him in the torso from the hallway. The bullet struck one of his ribs and shattered it, sending shards of bone deeper into his body, puncturing his lungs. He tried to remain standing and swiped for the countertop, knocking several bottles of liquor, beer, and shot glasses onto the linoleum below. They exploded into a puddle of refracted light. He finally found grip, leaning on the countertop for support, trying to make his way toward the door. But his blood loss, both internal and external, took its toll. His heart raced in vain to regain pressure. He heaved to gain his breath, over and over. Air filled his chest cavity. He lost consciousness and passed out near the door. The impact with the floor broke his jaw and knocked out several of his teeth. The spilled alcohol diluted his smeared trail of blood. A great deal of forensic analysis during the investigation revealed every step of his last moments. Anybody can find it in Whitman County's reports of the shooting. It is not known whether Tyler stayed to watch or moved on. Trevor Darrington was nineteen.

Tyler retraced his path and lumbered back down the main hallway, again moving past Erin and Luke and their growing pools of blood. One or both of them could've been conscious at this point. Nothing too vital in either of them had been hit. But no one was around to witness this encounter. All the way up the hallway to the front door Tyler walked, back to where it started. He set down his rifle. He pulled the handgun out of his pocket. He kneeled down and, with his left hand, put the gun to the side of his head, not at the temple, but further back behind his ear, and fired. It was 1:43 a.m. The shooting had lasted no more than ten minutes. Tyler was twenty-one.

Those still alive in the house believed that gunshot to be someone continuing to kill more students or finishing off those he had wounded. There were still several students on the second floor of the house. At the sound of the louder handgun firing next to the foot of the stairs, two students broke out a window and jumped from the second story. The thick snow cushioned their falls. But most students hiding in the house when the shooting stopped remained in their places until police rescued them. One couple was found naked in the upstairs bathroom of the master bedroom. Cory Gentry stayed hunched down in the shower for more than an hour. An officer broke through the bathroom door when he saw the bullet hole. He discovered Cory still in the same position, splinters sticking out of his body.

Calls to the police and campus security poured in as students who escaped reached the safety of neighboring houses. Units were dispatched immediately and the SWAT team was alerted. Texts and social media posts spread varied accounts of what was happening. Previous false reports of shootings and bombs around MU made many skeptical of the early updates. Rumors of a fire spread faster than the reports of a shooting. The wave of panicked calls, questions, and doubts over what had happened created widespread confusion that plagued 911 operators and emergency personnel in their response to the attack.

The initial calls reported a shooting of an unspecified nature. These callers were told to hang up to clear the lines for students with more information. A few calls referred to an active shooting where victims were chosen randomly, but more stated it was a targeted shooting. They thought a relationship dispute had turned violent because Tyler had shot a man and a woman right away, and did not fire again until most of the partygoers had escaped. They expected a rapid succession of gunshots in an active shooting and they had heard only two. Luke and Erin weren't in a relationship, but the students at the party were a mixed group of separate cliques—most didn't know Luke and Erin. Reports of a hostage situation surfaced, which added to the already murky picture. Students hiding in the house could only listen for clues about what was happening.

But the largest problem was the most obvious: the blizzard. Cop cars had tremendous difficulty powering through the snow and many got stuck or wrecked on the way to the house, deep in the maze of side streets. Some campus police officers abandoned their cars and waded through the snow. Police stations nearby sent out four-wheel-drive trucks and contacted municipal departments to redirect plow trucks to the main roads feeding into MU.

The first officers to arrive on the scene were campus security officers driving a patrol SUV. They slid to a stop at 2:10 a.m. in front of the house. Under active shooter response procedures, in which they were trained, they would've stormed the house and hunted down the gunman or gunmen with weapons drawn, ignoring the wounded until the threat was neutralized. However, given the mixed reports and lack of instructions, they decided to help the wounded and wait for clarification on what to do. More units showed up, some on foot, some following plow trucks in patrol cars down Lyndon Avenue. Officers spread out, evacuating nearby houses and surrounding the one with its shades drawn and its heavy front door shut. EMTs treated students who had escaped the house for gashes and bruises. A few were put in ambulances and driven to hospitals, suspected of hypothermia.

At 2:26 a.m. a female student jumped out of a broken window and told police she hadn't heard shots in the house for close to forty-five minutes. The decision was then made to go in. The SWAT team still hadn't arrived at this point. Their vehicle had slid off the road and they had to wait for another one. Officers entered through the back door into the kitchen. They discovered the four victims—Erin and Luke were by then both dead. They found Tyler at the front entrance. They still proceeded with caution to the other floors, wary of more possible threats. Nobody was found in the basement. All of the survivors were then escorted out. The front door was kept shut and locked to prevent contamination of the crime scene by the blizzard. The wind was said to be so strong that its force on the front door bent the frame inward.

———

News vans showed up much later. Footage of reporters half-buried in snow and screaming about broken records over the wind was replaced by the crime scene. The police had already secured the house when the first van careened to a stop at a roadblock the authorities had set up. Their initial on-site broadcasts offered scant details and blurry images of flashing cop cars and parked plow trucks. The police used some plow trucks as barriers. Small groups of students gathered to gawk at the scene. Some were interviewed, but they yielded nothing, only more questions. The police then enlisted news teams and students to help push stuck police vehicles and clear paths in the street. At 5:00 a.m. a police captain came forward and gathered the reporters for a preliminary press conference. Standing beside a plow truck for shelter, the cameras and mics huddled around him, he confirmed that a shooting had taken place and that there were fatalities. He declined to give more specifics but warned everyone watching to stay inside and lock their doors. Local news stations aired it live, but they kept the bulk of their coverage on the storm. The general feeling was that a fight at a party had escalated to a gunfight. National news would later air the blizzard-conference often, noting how little everyone knew, the reporters and the captain shivering and bracing against the cold.

Campus was put on lockdown, which meant nothing at that stage. There was no need to guard empty classrooms. When the dim sun rose that morning, the campus would be swarming with maintenance workers and security, but few students. Those living in the upper floors of Harris Hall had a fantastic view of the crime scene and the snowy devastation. Pictures taken from Harris dorms would spread online and become the face of the shooting. Rows of off-campus houses jutting out from the white trees set a uniform pattern against the snow-scape, except one spot, lined with police cars, vehicles, barriers, police tape, and plow trucks, encircling one of the larger houses, an island precisely isolated, like a cancerous sore prepped for removal.

———

My roommate shook me awake around eleven in the morning. He had seen the breaking news on TV. By then the snowfall had stopped, and everything was calm and sunny and white. Our power had gone out during the night—the oven and microwave clocks flashed nonsense. We watched the local news. A shooting at a party during a blizzard of historic proportions. The media had little information. They couldn't even say how many were killed or how many shooters there were or what caused it. Speculation ran wild. The police were warning everyone in the vicinity of the shooting to stay inside. Even they weren't sure how many people were involved. Reports streamed in from all over the MU area of possible gunshots or sketchy characters walking in the deep snow. My roommate and I figured it had been an argument that escalated to violence. Drunken fistfights and threats of violence weren't uncommon in the larger, more chaotic parties. It wouldn't have surprised us if someone had left a party after a disagreement and went to their car for a gun.

After absorbing the initial news reports, we grabbed our phones. We couldn't wait to tell our roommates and friends what had happened in the night. But our calls and texts wouldn't go through. The combination of the blizzard and the shooting made thousands of panicked MU parents attempt to reach their children to find out if they were alright. Everyone then reverted to social media for communication. I let my parents know I was fine with a quick Facebook message to one of my sisters, who was staying with my parents. She asked for more information but at that point I couldn't give anything reliable. Nobody knew what was going on, not even the news.

The rest of the day dragged on once the initial scramble calmed. The updates trickled in, reported at hourly intervals. The national news picked up the story too, focused on the blizzard and how it had virtually shut down the city. Our other roommates returned and students walked through the new winter wonderland outside. Some ignored the warnings and went out to build igloos and snowmen. But a lot were still asleep, still in the same house they had partied at the night before, and they wouldn't wake until late in the day. The news coverage would shift its attention to the shooting later, on Friday evening, when a press conference by the Whitman County Sheriff's Office revealed it was an active shooting, the victims were chosen at random, and the shooter had committed suicide. At least four were dead. Names would not be released until the families had been notified.

———

Even as the double news story of a shooting during a blizzard gained traction, and even as the second news conference made it clear there was an active shooting, I never thought of Tyler. He was far from my mind. When Friday drew to a close, I was playing video games deep into the night to pass the time. I had no idea Tyler was the one who lay dead against the front door of that big house, the one at the center of all the news broadcasts.

CHAPTER SIXTEEN

Flowers

The next morning, plow trucks, warming temperatures, and salt had cleared roads to drivable levels. Traffic choked all roads leading into, out of, and around MU for the entire day. Everyone wanted to evacuate. Parents came to pick up students. My parents demanded that I come home. It took me two hours to do so, a route that usually took thirty minutes. They wanted to hug me when I returned but I refused. They had a thousand questions. I asked for peace and quiet. The silence of my bedroom helped. The furnace kicked on and heat seeped from the vent. I checked social media. It had blown up. Everyone was asking questions and searching for answers. People were missing. I turned off my phone and shut my laptop. I tried to take a nap but couldn't fall asleep.

On Saturday afternoon the names of the four victims were released. I scanned them to see if I knew them. I didn't. I didn't read the rest of the article on what the news had gathered about their lives and I didn't watch for updates either. My parents told me MU had cancelled classes on Monday out of respect for the deceased and, less importantly, to let the rest of the snow melt and to repair damage from the blizzard. My parents wanted to have a talk. They said they knew I was in shock and talking it out would help. I asked if they had said who the killer was. The name hadn't been released. Not all next of kin were notified as of yet. We found out later that the authorities had trouble contacting Mr. Eberle, who was still on his business trip.

My parents reasserted the need for me to open up and break the shock. The thing was—I wasn't in shock. I told them I honestly wasn't surprised that an active shooting had taken place. MU was fertile ground for enriching the lives of those who fit in, but those who didn't fit in were left behind to rot. I had seen my fair share of outsiders and rejects—and I didn't mean the LARPers or campus cosplayers, who had their niche—I meant the ones scattered like ashes across campus, the ones who hadn't been collected into any group. I saw them alone at food courts or sitting alone in lecture halls, watching other students in groups. They were going to have to pull through college and probably adulthood alone. Some internal rage and a mental issue were all that it might take. My parents wouldn't have any of it. People choose to be alone, they said. I told them to hold this off until Sunday or Monday. They agreed with muted smiles. That day, my two sisters, both home for the weekend, shoveled the driveway with me. We dug out their cars and cleared what we could. Afterwards we played in the wet snow, tackling each other and throwing snowballs like when we were kids. It was the last time I felt like one.

———

I can still see the TV screen from that Sunday morning. One of the national news shows, a female anchor in a bright newsroom. She announced who the killer was, saying it over and over, mispronouncing his name. Tyler Eberle, it said on the screen. They put up a picture, his senior-year photo from high school, the most recent one they could find of Tyler. His smile exposed blue braces covering small teeth. He had strong acne and looked like a freshman in high school, not a senior. You might remember that image. That's how most people came to know him. There aren't many photos of him from college. There is the security camera footage, but a dark blur on a grainy screen doesn't say anything about who he was. His senior-year picture, plastered on the widescreen TV in my house, glaring at me, was taken eight months before I had met him. That picture was used as filler because the news anchors could only say how much they didn't know about him.

I don't remember how I felt when I saw Tyler and his name on the screen. That's a vagueness I don't want to visit, like re-experiencing a nightmare that made you wet the bed when you were a child. It shouldn't be as frightening with all the time that has passed, but it scares you more now because of the effect it had on your younger self.

The next thing I knew my mom raced down the stairs and found me on the couch.

"Is that him? Is that Tyler? Is that your friend?"

—————————

My parents grilled me on Tyler, asking me a slew of questions to force me to spill everything about him. I told them the truth, but a limited truth. They had seen him over here and knew that I hung out with him, but they largely kept out of my social life. I had to give them a shortened rundown of our entire friendship and then go over our most recent meetings in detail. I told them I hadn't seen him in months and hadn't texted him in weeks. I had nothing to do with the shooting, I assured them. I had no idea. I was in as much shock as they were. My parents, gray-haired and nearing sixty, worried more than I had ever seen them worry. They had dealt with one of my sisters running away in her teenage years and a bad car crash that injured my other sister, but this scared them far more. They grabbed their temples and paced through the living room and dining room. They cursed me for making friends with a lunatic. They called my sisters and had them come home immediately. They closed the blinds, locked the doors, and banned any of us from leaving the house or contacting anybody about the shooting. We paid close attention to the news, looking for any signs of me. My parents hoped the frenzy would die down and we could quietly slip by undetected with no known connections to the shooter.

I closed down all of my social media accounts, getting one last look at my friends' online profiles amidst the firestorm erupting over Tyler. People were asking a lot of questions. I expected texts from friends who knew I hung out with Tyler, but I received none. Later on, they told me they were afraid the police would be monitoring my phone and didn't want to be caught up in any investigation.

I never left my house all Sunday. No press swarmed our house and no police officers knocked on our door. The agitated fear grating my parents faded. My sisters went back to their apartments and their boyfriends. We thought we had made it under the radar. It was no comfort to me, though, because I started to grab a hold of what Tyler had done.

———————◆———————

I emerged from the stupor of shock and fought against the idea of Tyler as a killer. That battle did no good. He had taken innocent life. The greatest sin. The Fifth Commandment. A crime worthy of the death penalty. For no obvious reason. It was the worst of all possible acts he could've committed. Everything about it was bad. There was no silver lining. And he was dead. My friend was dead. He had taken the coward's way out—as my dad called it. A one-way ticket to hell. My dad had always said people committed suicide because they were too afraid to face the consequences of their actions. I had never told him that Tyler had attempted to do just that a year earlier. Or that I had visited him in the hospital. But that was exactly why I didn't tell him, because he wouldn't have understood. Same with my mom. Or any of my friends or any teacher or any student who could've talked to him. Because they never tried to understand. They made efforts to stay away from the shy, awkward kid, to give quick smiles to him and then turn around and make fun of him, or be too afraid of the social cost to reach out. They went out of their way to harm him, or they played it safe and didn't help. I got angry. Way too angry. That was my reaction—pure rage. I was in my room, watching the news coverage. Students were creating and visiting makeshift memorials near the house and on campus. Flowers and pictures and messages piled up, not only for the victims, but for Tyler as well. *Oh, now you give a shit. Now you care.* On-site reporters interviewed students, some crying, some in plain shock, but no one seemed to have known anything about Tyler. They wanted to know more. *Now you want to learn.* They asked as many questions as the reporters did. They had no idea there could be so much unhappiness at MU. *It only took five dead bodies for you to open your eyes.* One girl brought a huge bouquet of flowers and a hand-written note. She had no connection to anyone in the attack. *Too little, too late.* Other than myself and Tyler's family and maybe Katie, who the hell cared about him? I tried. I fucking tried. And I cared. Now everyone wanted to be thoughtful and compassionate. Where was that when Tyler was quiet and shy at the welcoming party? Where was that when he was coping with depression? I slammed my fists into my mattress and choked back tears. My throat had gone dry. I was so pissed I couldn't see straight. I had to stay in my room a long time for that feeling to fade.

With little else happening in the news cycle, the shooting and blizzard took center stage. Headlines burst onto screens and webpages: Party Massacre. Blood Fest. Beer Pong and Blood. They sounded like second-rate slasher films. Footage of MU, off-campus housing, and the house where everything had happened were sent all over the world. The collective reaction was swift: not another one. And this time at a party. The shooting's sustained infamy is from the novelty of where and when it took place. Everyone expects the gunshots and bodies to come from the classrooms, but these were kids who were making the most of their time and enjoying their lives. Innocent and unsuspecting. Though not the first—a 2006 shooting in Seattle cost six people their lives when a man opened fire at a rave after-party he had been invited to, which was referenced in the news coverage—the existential threat it posed to the culture of college partying scared students and parents across the country. It started a popular but short-lived discussion about security and safety at parties near campuses.

The news honed in on Tyler. It didn't take long for them to announce that he had attempted suicide a year earlier. That's how my dad found out. He was not happy I had kept it a secret. No details were given though, because the news didn't have any. The networks made sure to air video of Tyler's dad's truck cordoned off in the North garage, surrounded by security, cameras, microphones, and onlookers. Nothing out of the ordinary was found inside. But the real show was at Tyler's house. News vans, cop cars, and curious onlookers clogged the street. Tyler's large house, with its cracked siding and off-level garage door, stood like a meager and battered fortress under heavy siege. That was by far the most activity that street had ever seen. The police had served a search warrant of his house, photographed Tyler's room, and seized a great deal of the Eberles' possessions. A Whitman County Sheriff spokeswoman explained their first goal was ruling out terrorism and any accomplices. Mrs. Eberle and Chloe were brought in for questioning. They would be held for almost the entire day, which delayed Chloe in shutting down her social media accounts. Shaky and distant footage of the two being escorted to unmarked cars was broadcast. The news had to rely on pictures taken from the internet to show the gorgeous mother and beautiful sister of the deranged killer. Mr. Eberle was questioned in Oregon without the fanfare. His house was also served a search warrant under much quieter conditions. The media frenzy on Tyler's street got so bad that reporters knocked on doors up and down the subdivision, asking and sometimes offering money for any information on Tyler.

Police received numerous calls of reporters trespassing and even harassing some of the neighbors, including children.

As for the house across from Tyler's, where Joe lived, nobody spoke to reporters. His Audi was nowhere to be found. Joe was never mentioned in any of the broadcasts or articles about Tyler. He has since earned his Master's in Business Administration and moved to Atlanta with his fiancé.

———————

I entered the public ring of the fallout on Monday morning. My parents' plan of keeping me isolated had succeeded for roughly a day. A Whitman County detective and a police officer knocked on the front door. I was alone in the house and thought it best to answer the door and not make them wait or return later. The stoic men said an examination of Tyler's phone records showed I had exchanged texts with him over the past two and a half years, and Mrs. Eberle had confirmed that I was his friend for that period. They said I wasn't under arrest or in any trouble. They asked me how I was doing, if I was under heavy emotional distress. I was hanging in there, surviving. They wanted me to come down to the station to be interviewed about Tyler. I agreed. I texted my parents and grabbed a light coat. By then the snow had all melted and the temperatures had climbed into the fifties. The ride in the backseat of the detective's car was so silent I thought I had gone deaf. The houses flicked by like in old silent, black-and-white movies.

The interview room at the Whitman County Police Headquarters sported a two-way mirror, a table, chairs, unforgiving lights, and pretty much nothing else. Two detectives came in, introduced themselves and offered me chips and pop, which I declined. They said this was the first in a series of interviews. If I needed to take a break or didn't feel comfortable answering I could stop at any time. I asked if this was all going to be recorded and they said yes. I didn't have anything to hide but I still trembled. Something about the atmosphere, like a spiteful job interview, or really, an exit interview for a job I failed. I had made up my mind to tell them the whole truth. I wanted to be sure that they got the full picture. I wanted them to understand Tyler, to know what he was like and what he had gone through. The media had already done a good job of manipulating the perception of Tyler, but these guys would pay attention to every detail. They'd listen to me. I had the invaluable personal experiences with him. And, as a non-family member, they'd view me as less biased and emotionally clouded.

The first two detectives started with basic questions about our friendship and about Tyler. They asked if I had anything to do with it or knew anything about it before it happened. I said no. They then moved to questions about terrorism, asking if Tyler had any terrorist ties or followed or adhered to any terrorist groups, or had any strong political beliefs. I repeated the same answer in several different ways: no. They said they couldn't find any social media accounts he ran but wanted to know if he kept any secret ones. To my knowledge, he didn't. I asked if they would be able to find this out from his laptop or ISP. They said they couldn't comment—the investigation was only beginning. The next line of questions addressed the victims and whether or not Tyler knew them. He didn't. I was sure of it. And neither did I, not even the injured listed on the news. MU had an enrollment in the tens of thousands. It functioned like its own small city and it would be hard to know even a fraction of the student body. I asked some questions of my own, like if they believed the party was targeted. They gave me little information. I sometimes spoke about Tyler in the present tense, as if he was still alive, and the detectives didn't correct me. I half-expected them to blame me for not being there enough for Tyler as I talked about our irregular friendship, with its gaps of inactivity, even as Tyler dealt with depression. I wanted to reassure them that we were close, and explained that we weren't the type of friends who constantly needed to meet up. But the detectives didn't seem to care either way. They remained neutral as I floundered through my memories.

They ended the interview and a man and a woman entered the room. The woman wore a black jacket with an FBI logo on it and the man had on a tan sport coat and no tie. They waited for the detectives to leave and then sat at the table across from me. They brought out thick binders and their phones. They calmly introduced themselves. One was a criminal psychologist and one was a forensic psychologist. They offered me a break and water, but I declined. The woman began, making eye contact with me the entire time she spoke.

"We heard the interview you had with the detectives, Dylan. We're not going to ask the same questions here. But first we're going to explain something."

She then told me the difference between active shootings and mass shootings. Ambiguity between the two terms created a lot of confusion, and they wanted me to be clear. Tyler would be labeled a lot of things in the media, but they were treating him as an active shooter—he had chosen his victims at random. The victims and Tyler had no connections. They had nothing in common except for attending MU, and were all white. They differed even in political views, majors, and socioeconomic status. Then she asked if I was ready for deeper questions.

"Okay with me."

"We want you to know that what you have to say here, about Tyler, is important."

"I know."

"Alright. Now, what do you want to tell us? Is there something you think we should know?"

"Absolutely. His concussion. Do you know about that?"

"Yes. We know Tyler was hospitalized years ago as a child for a concussion and hairline fracture."

"But do you know why?"

They shuffled through their notes. "Yes. He got into a dispute with another boy."

"That's not right." I explained to them what Tyler had told me on that August night. "You should get Joe to come down here. Ask him a few questions. He bullied Tyler for years."

They asked me to elaborate on that and I did. They showed no shock at what Joe had done.

"Have you checked on possible brain damage from that? On what that might've done?"

"Due to the manner in which Tyler took his life that is going to make it difficult. We are performing an extended autopsy. But this will delay the funeral."

I hadn't thought about that. "Tyler's mom wants a funeral?"

"Yes, there usually is a funeral of some kind."

"Huh. What about the depression? You guys know he had that?"

"Yes, we do know. We were wondering if you could tell us about his depression and paranoia. How did it affect him?"

I recounted what Tyler had told me about the depression, when it affected him and how I rarely saw him when he was most depressed. They asked if he saw any therapists and what medication he took. I didn't know the specifics and could only offer general timelines. I asked if he was still on anti-depressants when it happened and they said they were waiting for lab results. I pried a little further, asking them what they knew about the relationship between depression, paranoia, previous suicide attempts, and sudden violence. There was no clear answer, they said—that was one of the reasons why they were interviewing me, to try to find out.

The next question they had for me was much more difficult: "What was Tyler like when he wasn't depressed? What was his natural personality?"

I had to take some time to explain this one. "He's quiet—was quiet. I guess that was his most obvious trait. But it wasn't like he was quiet all the time. When it was me and him, and no one else, like when we were studying or playing video games, he could be pretty talkative. Or when we were at his house he could talk with his mom or his sister just fine. If he was interacting with people he didn't know or we were in some crowded place on campus, he'd be very quiet."

"What did you talk about when it was you and him?"

"Classes, grades, our video games, the campus."

"Did you talk about your plans? What you wanted to do after graduation?"

"Not really. Neither of us had any fleshed-out plans."

"Did you ever talk about active shootings or any kind of terrorist attacks?"

"Well, we talked a lot about these facts, about these horrible things like genocide, war, suicide, atrocities, or terrible things that famous people did. Disturbing tidbits—big and small. We both liked looking them up on the internet and sharing them. And some of them were school shootings and mass killings. And terrorism too."

"Did either of you have an obsession with these?"

"I wouldn't call it an obsession. I mean, in my high school on every April 20th we'd all go around saying 'Happy Columbine Day' to each other. And I know none of us were obsessed with Columbine. I doubt any of us could've even named the killers."

"Then why did you talk about these disturbing things? You're two young men in college. You must've had other things going on."

"No. What else was there for us to talk about? Classes were boring. We could only say so much about those. And we weren't that into the partying or the drinking and it was hard to join a group. Finding that stuff online and memorizing it was cool to us. We liked knowing all this horrible stuff had happened. We never learned any of it in our history classes. That stuff was like a really good history class."

"Tyler didn't attend any parties or try to adapt to MU's culture?"

I brought up the party we went to our freshman year. The investigators hadn't heard of it so I had to recount the entire night.

They whispered a few things to each other. "Dylan, at MU, how important are academics compared to a social life?"

"I'll put it this way: Partying is mandatory. Classes are optional."

"Isn't it possible to socialize without partying?"

I shrugged. "To an extent. Whenever I started to become friends with somebody there would always be a point when they invited me to some kind of party. It was like a rite of passage to becoming a good friend with somebody. Tyler ran into this too. You could make acquaintances in classes and dorms, but that was usually as far as it went without a shared party experience."

"And this left him isolated?"

"Very." I told them about his roommate Jake and the parties he had held in their dorm. How Tyler would avoid these by going to the library or over to my room. They nodded their heads. I had never seen a therapist before but I figured this was what it must be like. I couldn't shock or surprise them or provoke any response above a measured one.

"Was he ever violent, or did he ever threaten to commit violence?"

"He was shy, never violent. He didn't even like to make threats, not even as a joke. He didn't even make fun of other people. I think he had been at the receiving end too much. To me he was the least likely person to be violent." I went on, describing his behavior as best I could. The psychologists pressed further, posing an array of questions covering different aspects of Tyler and his life: his intelligence, his analytical skills and his creativity, his interests in movies, music, TV shows, and books, anything he collected or any objects he valued. Then his mom, his sister, and his dad. I had never met his dad, so I could only say what I had heard about him. They asked me what his home life was like during his college years and when he was younger. I gave my best guesses. It wasn't like I went over to his house all the time. I had only slices of his family interactions. The largest of which was that night in August when we saw Joe. I told them about the Christopher McCandless discussion and Chloe's habit of relying on Tyler for homework help. Again and again they nodded.

Near the end of the interview, after hours of talking about Tyler and his life, they asked something I hadn't expected. They asked about his sex life.

"What do you mean?"

"We mean, did he have sex with anybody?"

"Not that I know of. We wouldn't tell each other much about that."

"Did he ever have a boyfriend or girlfriend?"

"No. If you want to know, I think he was straight. He didn't constantly signal that he was straight by bragging about getting laid like all the other guys. I think he gave up on that competition back when Joe was hurting him. But he did talk about manhood and ask me about sex once."

"So you think he was at least interested in it?"

I thought it over. "Yes."

"One last question: Do you think he held a grievance against Joe, or all of society? Did he ever express a need for revenge?"

"I think he felt wronged. By Joe, that's for sure. He never said he wanted revenge, not even against Joe. I don't think he saw life as something to be 'evened out.' He seemed defeated about how unfair life was."

Not much later the two psychologists concluded their interview with me. They thanked me for my time and offered their condolences. They asked if I had seen a counselor over my loss and shock. I hadn't. They gave me a few cards with contact info and told me about grief counselors deployed at MU that students could see for free. They said that some survivors of a 1989 active shooting in Canada had committed suicide over feelings of guilt. They said I had no reason to feel responsible. They left with their binders tucked under their arms, warning me to stay in the county for follow-up interviews.

By the time one of the detectives dropped me off at my house, my name and face were on the TV screen. The news outlets had my first and last name up there in large letters with a cropped picture of me that a friend had put online. I was the poster boy as Tyler had been on Sunday. They touted my name and my relation to Tyler as his only known friend. However, with three days separating me from the shooting, a great deal of the media firestorm had died down. The news networks were still running regular segments on the shooting and the effects of the blizzard, but the panic had fallen, and so had the urgent desperation for more updates. My parents drove me to a relative's house. They had seen the circus on Tyler's street and did not want me to be there for a possible round-two on our street. My sisters drove by our house and saw a few reporters camping out on the street, but no parade of news crews had steamrolled into the neighborhood. I hunkered down at my relative's house and watched the news for any information they had about me, which luckily was next to nothing. My parents extended our plan of isolation for the rest of the week. Updates trickled in as the fervor died down even more. On Saturday we moved back into our house. There were no more journalists around, as best we could tell. The bigger event on Saturday came from a phone call from Mrs. Eberle. She asked me if I wanted to come to Tyler's funeral the next morning. Her voice sounded small and far away. Everything had to be kept secret. She said funerals like this were conducted in private and announced after the burial so as to not attract any attention. Without thinking, I agreed. I told my parents. They were not happy.

Speculation still lingers over why the funeral took place more than a week after the shooting. Usually killers are put underground or cremated as quickly and quietly as possible, but there were two reasons for the delay. First, the autopsy of Tyler's body required more time and skill. The investigators wanted to know what damage the concussion had caused to his brain before he shot himself, so specialists had to be flown in and Tyler's brain was examined, dissected, and preserved as best it could to glean as much as possible about how it functioned or malfunctioned. The second was that the priest in charge of the Eberles' parish refused to conduct the funeral. He cited Tyler's suicide as the reason. In Catholicism, suicide is a mortal sin, and Tyler had no chance for forgiveness. Historically, suicide cases had no Catholic burial rites, though it's unheard of in recent times—except in Tyler's case. So when the funeral was scheduled on Saturday the Eberles had to delay it a day longer to arrange for a priest from a different parish to give the funeral Mass, absolution, and blessing of the grave.

My parents dropped me off at the funeral home a little late, promising to wait in the car for me at the cemetery. They didn't want their car to be seen following the hearse. They told me I had to carpool with someone at the funeral. My mom had sunken eyes. She had cried the day before. Cried and cried. My dad consoled her as pundits on TV explained what they knew about my role as Tyler's friend in college.

The layout was closed-casket. The casket's charcoal steel almost glowed in the soft light. I had never been to a closed-casket layout before. And never for anybody under seventy. I didn't know if the body was inside or not. Very few people were there. The room was so silent it felt like a large sound booth. No one spoke above a whisper. Two bouquets of white flowers flanked the casket, one on each side. They were some kind of lily. Mrs. Eberle and Chloe stood to one side of the casket in black dresses. They looked beautiful. I remember that like a picture. Two women, both trying to smile, next to something too big and awful to explain.

A man stood on the other side, middle-aged, tall, and broad-shouldered: Mr. Eberle. He didn't look like Tyler. No acne scars and a mature face with sharp features. He wasn't trying to smile and he looked a lot less burdened than the women. I didn't recognize anybody else at the funeral. I guessed they were all relatives.

The only people I really spoke to were Chloe and Mrs. Eberle. I approached them first, walking with my back straight and my shoulders square. I had no idea how things worked for a funeral like this. We had one chance to try and celebrate the parts of his life that meant something good. This was the time to ease the pain. I came to Chloe first. Her boyfriend had broken up with her. She had dropped out of MU. She would have to restart college elsewhere. She saw me as I neared her and she recognized me right away. That sweet face. I hugged her first thing and told her that it was alright. She tried to utter a full sentence but couldn't. She held my shoulders for support and trembled. She didn't have any tears left. What we then said to each other will remain private. We embraced again and held each other tight. I had a feeling that everyone at the funeral was watching, picking up on our expressions and what we might have said to each other. They all knew who I was. Mrs. Eberle stepped closer. Chloe gave up her hug, her hands sliding down and away from me, her head bowed.

"Hi Dylan," Mrs. Eberle said. Her hair wasn't in a ponytail this time; instead, it curved behind her ears and rested on her shoulders. She looked calm and composed.

"Hi." Then I waited for her to speak. She took a few breaths before she began.

"You know, Tyler always admitted when he did something wrong. He broke an old lamp in our basement once when he was in the third grade. He did it purely by accident. When I asked him how the lamp had broken, he started crying. I couldn't figure out why he felt so guilty. As a parent I didn't expect my son to behave that way. It confused me so much. I had to learn to raise him so he wouldn't see everything he did as wrong. He would try to hide things from me that he had no reason to hide. And last year, when I found him in the bathroom—I thought that was the end. He had hidden too much. Stored it all away."

I nodded. I glanced down.

"I'm sorry, Mrs. Eberle. I'm sorry for all of this. And I don't know what else to say. I know it's been a week but it feels like I found out ten seconds ago."

"You were a good friend, Dylan."

"I could've been there more for him."

"Don't worry now."

"I have no more chances to help him."

There was a brief pause. I noticed Chloe clenching her mom's hand.

"Dylan," Mrs. Eberle began, "there are only going to be a few people who will hold onto him. Please be one of them. Please be one. Our lives are not over. It's possible to keep Tyler in your heart despite what he did. Despite what he did."

———

Chloe, Mrs. Eberle, and I did talk some more. When we finished, I turned to the casket, touched the cold steel, had some thoughts I'm not keen to share. Some of them were ugly and there's been enough ugly surrounding this bloodshed. I faced Tyler's father, Mr. Eberle. He didn't budge, so I stuck out my hand and he shook it and I nodded to him and he nodded back to me. We didn't have any more communication. After the funeral Mr. Eberle moved far away from the city.

The other part of the funeral that I will mention were the pictures of Tyler taped to a small board off to the side. They looked like the same pictures from the Eberles' fridge, mostly of Tyler when he was younger and on vacation. I took my time to look over these. I guessed I wouldn't be seeing them again. The priest gathered us together to give the time and location of the funeral Mass. I asked for a ride and one of the relatives offered to drive me there.

The Mass was shortened to less than thirty minutes. They had one singer and one organist there. They performed Schubert's "Ave Maria." There were no flowers placed on the casket and nothing but the bare bones of the Catholic Mass were given to speed things up. I didn't know the pallbearers—maybe relatives or funeral workers who rode in the hearse—but the casket was unceremoniously carried out of the church. A few of the women had teary eyes. No one openly wept. There was no funeral procession or police escort to the cemetery. No little flags on our cars. At the gravesite the priest said a prayer as it started to drizzle. When it was over people said their goodbyes and dispersed. Relatives escorted Mrs. Eberle and Chloe back to the cars and I didn't get a chance to say anything more to them. Tyler's funeral was the last time I saw any of his family members.

I found my parents waiting in their car for me. On the ride back to our house I had doubts over whether the funeral had happened. I felt like I didn't have the chance to give him a proper goodbye, somehow robbed of it. But maybe Tyler had forfeited that chance.

The funeral was announced a day later. Tyler's simple gravestone was both defaced with graffiti and adorned with flowers.

CHAPTER SEVENTEEN

Aftermath

From right after the shooting all the way until now, over three years later, there have been rumors and theories about Tyler and his motives. The news painted a rough portrait of him as a recluse who had few friends and avoided interaction with the outside world. This bothered me to no end, but there's been a ton of speculation about his personality and what might've been wrong with him. He was, and still is, treated as a riddle to be solved.

So, I'm going to address these things. I have to. Some of them are blatantly false and borderline defamatory, and need to be dispelled, but others are rooted in the truth and give me a lot to consider. With these theories, no one is trying to excuse Tyler's actions. They are for understanding, for figuring out what happened.

———

I'm not sure where to start so I'll pick the biggest issue to begin. Tyler's depression became a major point in the aftermath. News of his suicide attempt the previous year, sessions with a therapist, and his SSRI medication made heavy ripples in the discussion of his state of mind. It's not known exactly how Tyler behaved or how much depression he was experiencing before the shooting because the authorities haven't released an in-depth report—and may never. Their interviews of Chloe, Mrs. Eberle, Mr. Eberle, and me have remained private. However, some information has been released to the public in the meantime. Much has been made of Tyler's decision to stop taking his meds. Stopping anti-depressants without a doctor's oversight can pose grave dangers to someone's mental health. I think Tyler did this because he thought he could handle his problems on his own. After his suicide attempt, he socially withdrew, which went against the advice of pretty much everyone, but it helped him. He might've tried that tactic again for his meds when their side effects worsened. Either way, his paranoia bloomed right afterwards into powerful delusion. He skipped classes, behaved oddly, and suspected a lot of the student body was plotting against him. Due to the severity of his depression and his behavior, many psychologists have brought up psychotic depression, a type of depressive episode that comes with delusions and a break with reality. Or this could've been the beginning of paranoid schizophrenia. Either way, his mom and his sister worked with his doctor to get him started on a new SSRI, this time at a higher dose. The Coroner's Office did confirm that he was on that new SSRI at the time of his death. But it's not likely that the new meds brought about the shooting; they take weeks to accumulate to a meaningful level in the brain.

There's no doubt in my mind that his depression and paranoia played a role in what he did. They had a huge effect on what he thought and how he acted. From the viewpoint of his delusions, the shooting makes sense as a preemptive strike on those trying to harm him.

Other ideas about Tyler's depression have come up as well. One is seasonal affective disorder, an illness that causes depression in the winter. Tyler both attempted suicide and committed the shooting in late-winter/early-spring after a period of severe depression. The dark, cold days with little sunlight could've sunk his mood to extreme levels. That said, the winter of the shooting was very mild up until the blizzard.

Another issue has been his weight. Investigators have noted his body was very skinny and underweight, to the point of malnutrition. It's believed this was a side effect of the depression, which decreased his appetite and eliminated any pleasure he got from tasting food. Though he was always skinny, the depression made the problem much worse, limiting how much he ate and decreasing his already low energy levels. Depression has many physical side effects apart from the low mood, and these may have fed into a downward spiral, further deteriorating his mental state.

Another theory to bloom is that Tyler had undiagnosed Asperger's or some form of autism. I'm sure this came from reports of his extreme shyness and his inability to adapt to the social climate of MU, and a variant of autism, criminal autistic psychopathy, has been attributed to many rampage killers. But autism is more than having trouble talking to people. There are repetitive behaviors and limited interests, and it's not clear to me if he had them. Some psychologists and experts have speculated that he may have been on the spectrum, which led to his other issues, but there is no consensus on this.

Something that has gained less traction but is probably more accurate is that Tyler had what is called selective mutism. It's a disorder in which a person can only speak to certain people—people they know and are comfortable with—but can't talk to others, like strangers or authority figures. Investigators have noted this condition in Tyler's case even though he was never diagnosed or treated for it. This would explain why he could speak to his mom, sister, and me but kept close to silent with other students or in groups. That also means I must've done a good job of making him feel comfortable around me—I had a high tolerance for his quiet demeanor. It's been noted that Seung-Hui Cho, the Virginia Tech gunman, had selective mutism too. This doesn't prove anything, though Cho did have therapy and treatment for the disorder before he went to college, and then laws prevented Virginia Tech from knowing his condition. I don't think Tyler or anyone around him knew what selective mutism was or that it was a real disorder. I didn't. People who knew him when he was younger also said he was very quiet, but everyone expected him to outgrow it and come out of his shell as he matured.

Allegations that Tyler's severe concussion influenced his behavior have been around since the concussion was first reported. All of the studies and testing on Tyler's remains have been inconclusive. Sections of his brain are still preserved at a special lab and may be subject to future examination, but for now, any long-lasting damage he had will remain unknown. This has drawn a lot of comparisons to Charles Whitman, the 1966 University of Texas shooter. In his suicide note he predicted that he had something wrong with his brain. He requested an autopsy of his body and also asked that his life insurance policy be donated to a mental health foundation. He murdered eighteen people and was killed by police. An autopsy confirmed his suspicion and found a brain tumor. To this day it is debated whether the tumor had an effect on his actions. I think Tyler's concussion will persist in the same way.

The most outrageous claim, which became widespread when my role in Tyler's life was revealed, centered on Tyler's sexuality. Accusations that he and I were secret lovers and some kind of fallout between us sent him into a rage originated on MU's campus and were publicized by reporters keeping their ears close to the student body. An offshoot of this theory, also from MU, was that Tyler was infatuated with me, and my relationship with Katie created an unbearable amount of jealousy in Tyler. After Katie and I broke up he made advances toward me and I rebuffed them, so he lashed out at parties, where I would go to supposedly hookup with girls. Though this kind of drama made great stories for news outlets it's downright sickening and has no basis in fact. The previous chapters have proven this.

One big question about the shooting continues to be asked: Did Tyler plan the attack ahead of time? He might be one of the rare few "heat of the moment" active shooters. Most spend months, or even years, planning, gathering weapons, and scoping out locations for their attack. Eric Harris, one of the Columbine shooters, timed down to the minute when the cafeteria had the most students to maximize the damage his bombs would make. If his bombs had exploded, hundreds of students would've been killed.

Tyler's actions seem to suggest he did no extensive preparation. First, he never bought any weapons or ammo himself. He was twenty-one, old enough to buy a whole arsenal, and he could've passed the most stringent background checks without a problem. Yet he never attempted to buy a gun or ammo. He never once told me about buying a gun and never said he had plans to get one. Another reason was the timing and the blizzard. It may look like he chose the night of the blizzard so the police response would be delayed to buy him more time to kill, but there are major problems with that. Weather forecasters never predicted the blizzard early and didn't realize its severity until the same day it arrived. If he planned out the shooting ahead of time, either it was an extreme coincidence that he picked the same date as the blizzard, or he quickly changed his plans and moved up the date, which would have rendered his preparations useless. And Tyler was somebody who did not like spontaneity. If you ask me, he was sticking to the plan all throughout February: dealing with his depression. But I think he lost and something in him did break. Maybe from the paranoia. Maybe from the concussion. The maliciousness required for cold-blooded murder does not seem compatible with the Tyler I knew.

A brief report of his internet history was recently released. Nothing suggested he was planning for an attack, nor did he have extreme political views or any links to terrorist groups. He liked a variety of music, including classical and metal, did hefty research for his homework, and looked up guides for video games. He also had a habit of searching for very dark things, including wars, atrocities, genocides, harmful science experiments, technology gone wrong, or any tidbit from the dark side of history, including rampage killings like mass stabbings and active shootings, bombings, suicides, and a great deal about depression, researching his own illness.

Another complicating factor was Tyler's odd choices for the shooting. Active shooters are known for killing until the police show up and then ending themselves, or dying in a gunfight with the police. Tyler didn't do this. He was dead well before he could've seen red and blue lights. Also, Tyler had chances to check if Erin and Luke were dead and could've shot them multiple times to make sure, but he didn't. If it wasn't for the blizzard, paramedics may have been able to save them and halve the number of lives he took. He also used a small-caliber lever-action rifle to kill when he could've used the faster-firing handgun in his pocket, or another gun in his father's safe. It's like he wanted to save the handgun for himself. Tyler made an odd choice for the target of his rampage. The old house he entered had many exits and plenty of rooms and closets and bathrooms to hide in or barricade. He had no idea how many people were in the house. On the other hand, most classrooms on campus have one exit and very little to hide behind. They would've made excellent targets for maximizing his kill count. The old house also had single-pane windows, which some students broke without any difficulty to escape the frenzy. All of the classrooms on MU's campus have energy-efficient double-pane windows that are resistant to force. And all windows above the second story on campus have suicide-prevention screens, even classrooms and offices. At the house, he had to search for students. MU had active shooter drills and test lockdowns on a regular basis, which he had experienced, so he would have known where students would be. Revenge is often cited as a motive for rampage killers—revenge against society for having wronged them—and they seek ideal conditions for their revenge. Tyler didn't bother to look for ideal conditions. That doesn't rule revenge out. That motive could've mixed with a disorganized mind, one that distorted reality or created an intense, irresistible violent desire, fueling and fueled by his internet research. But if these questions are answered, ultimately, it won't matter. The damage has been done. Premeditated or not, if there is a hell, Tyler is down there burning.

I've gone over every major point I wanted to. I feel exhausted. This took more out of me than I thought it would. There's a little bit more that I want to cover, about what happened afterwards, if you're willing to see this story through to the end.

For the next month or so after the shooting, very few parties were held in and around MU. Calls from the police, FBI, the MU president, and other school officials to cease partying in order to prevent copycat attacks, coupled with the intense fear that there might be more shootings, essentially shut down weekends.

The detectives who had interviewed me warned me that in cases like this, where the shooter is dead, the public can't focus its anger against the attacker and will redirect it to family members and friends and that I should take steps to stay out of the spotlight. After taking Mrs. Eberle and Chloe down to the station for their initial interviews, the police gave them car rides back to a relative's house and were given that same advice. They hid with various relatives for a much longer time than

I did to avoid the press—and because of the storm of death threats. Mrs. Eberle later quit her job and the bank foreclosed on her house. I returned to MU the day after the funeral. My parents did not want me to drop my classes and cost myself an extra semester of tuition and marks on my permanent record. They drove me to campus and dropped me off before they went to my apartment to move my stuff back to the house. They told my roommates that I wouldn't be returning. By then the news had died down to a fading simmer, with only the local news still dedicating time to the shooting. The national news had lost most of its interest and an insider-trading scandal had grabbed its attention. Of course, MU hadn't forgotten. And I hadn't been there since I left my apartment over a week earlier. Some things had changed. Everything was calmer. I could hear birds chirping in the young trees. The last piles of snow hid in the shade. Spring was dawning and some students were already wearing shorts and T-shirts. Despite the uptick in weather, the prevailing mood was one of mourning. A collective grief. A deep sense of loss and a whispered solemnity I had never witnessed before on campus. I felt a lot of sorrow on the paths and in the halls. There was a lot of disappointment in hushed voices, disappointment in the student body, the school administration, campus police, parents, and even some directed at the lack of parties. I overheard more than a few sarcastic comments wishing that Tyler had shot up a classroom instead of a house party. But I also heard bitterness, anger, and a desire for revenge. Some students were pissed at Tyler and ranted against him in the tunnels and courtyards. They wished for horrible things to happen to him and his family, for his name to be forever associated with hideous evil or to be erased from this world. They were furious. Some took it a step further. They wanted his body mutilated and desecrated and left out for the vultures to feast on, for his soul never to find peace, to burn for eternity in the special circle of hell reserved for killers of his kind, damned by God and all the angels in heaven.

I wore sunglasses everywhere except in my classes, wore the most generic clothing I could, kept my head down, grew a beard, and let my hair grow long—the opposite of the clean-cut look in my picture that the news had posted everywhere. Outside of my classes few people recognized me on campus, and if they did, they didn't say anything to me, only to their friends, who stole glances at me as I tried to pretend that I didn't notice them. In my smaller classes everyone had to know who I was, including the professor. I could fake my appearance, but I couldn't fake my name. Tyler Eberle had the most publicity but Dylan Evans had its share of time on-screen too, and anyone who went to MU paid some attention to it. The professors did a good job of ignoring the fact of who I was and setting an example for my classmates to follow. I got a few questions from some asking if I was that Dylan and if I was his friend. I shrugged them off in a well-practiced show of grumpiness that said I didn't want to be prodded about Tyler. I never had anyone confront me about it or press me for answers. I think an aura of mystery grew around me on campus that no one wanted to touch or be associated with, like someone who had something extremely embarrassing posted about them online. They are quarantined indefinitely. All of my friends, both new and old, steered clear of me and I didn't try to contact them. I didn't want to bring anyone else into my mess. The one person who didn't avoid me was Jeremy, and he felt comfortable enough to talk to me right outside the student Rec Center.

I hadn't spoken to him since the last summer. He seemed as down as the rest of the campus. His shoulders sagged and he glanced at the ground and at passing students more than he looked at me.

I broke the silence first. "Shouldn't you have graduated last year?"

"I'm taking a victory lap. I don't think I'll return here for a graduate degree. I want to go somewhere else, see a new place, maybe on the east coast."

"Still a business major?"

"Yeah, I hope to get on the analysis side of things. Are you holding up okay?"

"I'm more weirded out than anything right now. The campus feels different. Holding up doesn't sound right when there's nothing to hold up."

"I don't know what you've been through, dude. I can't know your situation. But I remember you guys were pretty close." He paused and scraped his shoes against the ground. "You say there's nothing to hold up. I think there is. I just don't know how to explain it."

"I feel defeated, it's like all of us have been beaten and are suffering, but I have to do it alone, hiding in a corner, away from it all."

"Have you been to any of the memorial sites? They've got loads of flowers and messages. I've seen some stuff for Tyler. And they're good things. It's compassion man, people are wishing they knew him before this. People are wishing they were in your position. I know, it's weird, but they want to know more about him, what he was like. You've got those experiences. They're one-of-a-kind. No one else knew him like you did. You're not on the outside."

"Do you hear people talking around here? When they post online or write something for a memorial it's all nice and focused on the victims, but in private their message is different. I've heard a lot of bad things said about this, Jeremy, and I don't want to go into them. He's a pariah, as he should be. And my friendship with him is only valuable because of what he did. Before that they couldn't care less." I shook my head and looked down. "Tyler could never fit in. You wanted us to go out and party when we were at Harris. People keep bringing up these plans about how we can all deal with this tragedy but don't want to look too hard at how things might've built up in the first place. I'm having trouble thinking—thinking this through."

Jeremy stood and listened. This was the first time I saw him at a loss for words.

"You know Tyler did go to a party. I was there. He couldn't join in. He couldn't become part of it. That wasn't his nature. And I failed to help. I don't know. I do know I'm tired of all this. The candles and wreaths—I guess they're heartfelt. But this all figures into the college experience. Everyone here gets to say they were at MU the same time as the shooting."

Jeremy looked full of guilt. "I'm sorry. I'm being an idiot. I talk too much and get myself into trouble."

"All of my friends are keeping a safe distance and you come and talk to me, and ask me how I'm doing. I should be thanking you."

"Really, I want to thank you. Now we sound like we're jerking each other off. Heh. It may be weird to say this but I think you were a good friend to Tyler. People have been saying you were a bad influence on him or made his problems worse, but you were nothing but helpful to him. I remember you guys at Harris, you seemed so close and you weren't backstabbing assholes to each other like the other guys. They should've been taking notes on the way you guys were friends."

"Yeah, there's way too many rumors floating around about us."

"Dylan, I'd love to talk more but I've got two classes back-to-back coming up. My attendance slumped last semester and I've got to hit the books. I'll have to catch up with you sometime, okay? You're cool. I don't care if people see me talking to you."

"Sure. Sounds good."

"See ya later."

Jeremy jogged off down a crowded concrete path and blended into the shuffle of backpacks and young faces. We never saw each other again. He graduated that May and I guess continued his education elsewhere.

———

Jeremy's remark about the makeshift memorials did sink in. I had passed them by many times but I never gave myself the chance to stop and look. They scared me. I ended up visiting a couple of them before they were taken down a month after the tragedy. By then the petals on most of the flowers had wilted and shrunk to flimsy tissue paper, tarnished brown along the edges like they were slowly burning in the spring air. Cards and notebook paper with messages scrawled on them were tucked into bundles of flowers or stood on their own. I saw pictures of the victims and the victims' families. Erin, Luke, Curtiss, and Trevor. A lot of messages said goodbye to them, said they would be remembered, that although their lives were cut short, they had done so much good. More personal messages promised to meet them in heaven when the time came. There were some photos of Tyler cut out from news articles. They were small. I had to peer through gaps in flower stalks and leaves to get a glimpse of his face. I saw him a few times resting against candles. The melted wax had dripped on him and cooled again, bonding him to the candle itself. I found cards that addressed Tyler. What they had to say varied. I saw some sympathy and some disgust, confusion, and utter terror. I read one that felt sorry for him. They took pity on him. Others forgave and others swore never to forgive. One called him a piece of shit and another nearby called him a bitter loser. Many of the notes could not comprehend the act. They wanted to understand but couldn't begin to. So many wanted to know why.

I stood and stared at the memorials for a long time. I didn't want to leave them. I somehow felt at peace taking in their colors and words. They were reassuring. At night students would light the candles. When I had an evening class, I'd visit for a time to stare at the flames. They cast a flickering glow over the pictures and flowers. When MU took them down, I felt another loss.

I did see a grief counselor in the aftermath of the shooting. Not one of the counselors offered for free by the university, but a private one that my parents found. They worried that I was taking things very hard. They noticed I seemed disconnected and the shock hadn't worn off long after the funeral.

The counselor told me that my reaction was normal. With everything I had gone through I had no reason to fear my complex, debilitating grief. She made me open up about what I was feeling. The guilt was the hardest part to admit. I held myself partially responsible.

I imagined him thinking of me while he was taking life. Did he curse me when he took his own? Did he feel abandoned by me? Was I the last dead-end to him? We had to hold some intense talks. I don't want to go into them. I will say that guilt can really mess with the grieving process. It felt immoral to be sad that he was gone, as if missing him was a sin. She suggested picking out something that reminded me of Tyler and keeping it close. I rummaged around my house and found the clay angel we bought before we went shooting. The ashen figure rested at the bottom of one of my desk drawers. I hadn't seen it in over a year. I put it on my windowsill. She told me that I had to learn to live with it, to get used to seeing it. Over time I did. It took months with the grief counselor, but I coped. I began to have entire days where I wouldn't think of Tyler or what he had done. I stopped noticing the angel on my windowsill; it became part of the windowsill, part of my room. On some days I'd open up the window and let fresh air blow over it, clearing the dust that had gathered. I asked the counselor if it was okay to wonder what Tyler might be experiencing in the afterlife. She said that was fine. After a year, the guilt and grief eased away. Like dew on a cloudless morning. Once it faded, I couldn't remember what the worst of it had felt like, even when it crept back. We agreed to stop meeting. That counselor was the only person I spoke to at length about Tyler.

When classes restarted at MU after spring break the partying was back in full swing and the pain of the tragedy eroded as finals approached. A small, permanent monument was built on campus to replace the numerous temporary memorials. I finished my time at MU commuting from home, parking in the North Garage, the same one that Tyler had used. I gave more interviews to the FBI and refused interviews with journalists and reporters who stalked me on campus. MU officials did sit me down once to have a talk about my reputation as Tyler's friend and the reporters following me. I graduated cum laude on a rainy day. Since then I've entered what everybody in college called "real life," and worked part-time jobs for a year before I found a full-time job. I had no plans to tell my side of this story and give the whole world access to it, but my thoughts on telling this story have changed, and, honestly, I haven't been able to find a decent-paying stable job. It's not a noble reason, but I have student loans that my current job can't put a dent in. I wish I could tell you this was all from the bottom of my heart, but it's not, and that's the truth, and I didn't want to write the whole story telling the truth and then deviate from it at the end.

I hope you've gotten something out of this. I've certainly put a lot into it. Diving into the deep end is not fun. These are memories I've ultimately failed to put behind me. Over the past few years, I've studied the times I spent with Tyler again and again and again, searching for where I went wrong, or where I could've changed what we did to avoid this all. The party—I could've done something when he left that party—or when he brought up his bullying and concussion in the summer, or after his suicide attempt. I could've done more. I had plenty of chances to be a better friend. Tyler was waiting for the right person to come along and make him feel not alone. I could've been that person and I should've been. But that's sealed shut, irreversible, like death itself. Four innocent lives and Tyler's life are gone. We could've been lifelong friends. He was a lonely boy at a dorm party when we first spoke. At the edge of college, and the prime of our lives. He's now a gravestone at a small cemetery that I haven't visited since the funeral. And a tiny clay figure on my windowsill. I was the one good friend he had. I'm afraid I never got to know him.

THE END

About the Author

This is Brian Rader's old bully. That was pretty intense. I can't believe he dedicated this book to his bullies. Love it or hate it, you can thank me for this novel. He put some of the things I did to him in this story. Man, I really messed him up. Made him cry a lot. And I never said I was sorry. If you want to know more about Brian, don't worry, you're not missing out on anything. He went to college, got a degree, struggled financially. He's left-handed like Tyler was. Can drive a stick shift too. This is his first book. There's no way he'll write another one cause I'm sure this won't get any reviews. Whatever you do, don't write a review of this and post it on Amazon or Goodreads. I don't want more people to read his book.

Twitter:
www.twitter.com/BRaderAuthor

Instagram:
www.instagram.com/brianraderauthor